18095

M
Shannon

THE RINGER

THE RINGER

by Dell Shannon

William Morrow and Company, Inc.

New York

Threefold the stride of Time, from first to last!
Loitering slow, the Future creepeth—
Arrow-swift the Present sweepeth—
And motionless forever stands the Past.
                —Schiller, *Sentences of Confucius*

What seest thou else
In the dark backward and abysm of time?
                —*The Tempest*, Act I, sc. 2

THE RINGER

1

MENDOZA CAME BACK from lunch at one-thirty, and in the lobby of the big Police Facilities Building ran into Lieutenant Goldberg waiting for the elevator.

"They keeping you busy, Saul?" he asked idly.

"So-so," said Goldberg, bringing out the inevitable Kleenex. "As if I hadn't enough on hand, Auto Theft coming asking cooperation. So we overlap some, let them do their own damn routine." The elevator landed and they got in; Mendoza punched the button for Goldberg's floor. "They've been after this hot-car ring for months, and the Feds sniffing around too on account of the interstate bit. That Van Allen." Goldberg snorted. "We've all got our own troubles."

"*De veras*," agreed Mendoza absently as Goldberg left the elevator. He punched the next button and stepped out upstairs. In the Homicide office, Sergeant Lake was gloomily contemplating a paperback book titled *How To Stay Slim*. "Anything new in?" asked Mendoza.

"Well, Jase just picked up that Sam Chase. He and John are leaning on him—don't know if they're getting anywhere."

"Him," said Mendoza. It didn't much matter whether they got Sam Chase to open up and sing a pretty song; his prints had been all over the handbag rifled of about eleven bucks, last Friday night, after a mugger had jumped the old lady from behind on her way home from the market. The old lady had been knocked down hard enough to brain herself on the sidewalk, which was why Homicide instead of Robbery had been looking for Chase. Chase had a record back to age fourteen.

Mendoza dropped the black Homburg on his desk and went down the hall to look into the interrogation room where Jason Grace and John Palliser were leaning on Chase. They were both looking pleased;

they left Chase huddled in the chair looking miserable and came over to Mendoza.

"At least he's got just enough sense to realize we've got him nailed for it by those prints," said Grace. "He came apart when we broke that to him."

"And this time he may get a real sentence," said Mendoza, "if it'll be a charge of involuntary manslaughter—all we can hang on him."

"On that I'll take no bets," said Palliser sardonically. Grace only brushed his narrow moustache, as dapper as Mendoza's, and his chocolate-colored face wore a cynical, sad expression.

Chase sat up a little and said, "Can I have a cigarette?" Palliser gave him one, lit it. Chase was a thin, unhealthy-looking fellow, not very big, with a pasty complexion and china-blue eyes under nonexistent eyebrows. He was twenty-nine, and he'd done little stretches here and there, as a j.d. and afterwards: six months, nine months, a year on probation. He looked at the three plainclothes detectives and said, "I been thinking. It's kind of an accident you got me for that—and there's that damn guy livin' high on that job he pulled last week. Things ain't fair, you know?" He looked aggrieved. "Jesus knows he'd be the first one open his jaw about me, shoe on the other foot. I guess I'll tell you."

"That'd be nice, Sam," said Grace gently. "What job? What's your pal's name?"

"Guy. I said. Guy Godfrey. I never did but one job with him, we aren't exactly pals. He did this job up in Hollywood—busted in a dame's apartment. I ran into him inna bar and he was telling me, see."

"And what was the job you pulled together, Sam?"

"Well," said Chase nervously, "it was his idea. And it was him did it. I mean the— Well, Jesus, the old lady'd seen both of us when we busted in, she'd reckanize us, see? And that was Guy's idea too. I said so all right, it's his idea, he does it. He says, we're in it together. So," said Chase lugubriously, "we ended up playin' a hand of blackjack, loser do the old dame, see."

"Well, I will be damned!" said Grace. They looked at each other.

"You never know," said Mendoza, "when the rabbit's going to jump out in front of you. *Caray*, I thought that one was dead."

"Mrs. Reiner," said Palliser. "That thing over on Constance Street, back in April. Be damned."

"I never heard the name," said Chase sadly. "I guess that was her. But it was Guy—"

That one they hadn't had any leads on at all, and it had got shoved in Pending nearly six weeks back.

"That hand of blackjack laid out on the kitchen table always did bother me some," said Grace now. "I had a little hunch it was something like that. So the loser took on the job of strangling Mrs. Reiner, was that it, Sam?"

"Well, it didn't matter how— And Guy lost the hand," said Chase hurriedly. "I didn't know nothing else about it—"

Mendoza laughed. "What odds do either of you give that Guy'll say the same thing?"

"That long a gamble I don't take," said Palliser. "I've got house payments to make these days." He went out to start the machinery for a warrant on Chase, and Grace took Chase off. When he'd deposited him at the jail he'd have a look in Records for Godfrey.

Mendoza wandered back to his office, called Wilcox Street precinct and asked Sergeant Barth if they had had an apartment break-in last week, in that territory. Barth said, with a vengeance, thirtyish divorcée living alone had surprised the burglar, got beaten up, and was still in a coma with a skull-fracture. "You don't say," said Mendoza, reflecting that it might have been Godfrey who accounted for Mrs. Reiner at that; he seemed to be disposed to violence. This count of violence on Chase was the only one that showed. "We've probably just found out for you who did it. An erstwhile pal came apart. I'll let you know the details when we get any ourselves."

"And not to sound ungrateful," said Barth, "but we've got a thing up here we're thinking about handing over to you. We've been going round and round on it, no smell of a lead at all, just a big fat mystery. Maybe you bloodhounds down at headquarters are smarter."

"Well—June," said Mendoza amiably. "Things a little slow at the moment. The nice weather. I don't mind taking a look at it for you. What is it?"

"A mystery," repeated Barth. "Which we do so seldom see. I think I'll pass it on in person. We're kind of busy up here with this gang of kite-flyers going around town." The precinct stations weren't neatly divided up into the different bureaus; those detectives took whatever cases came their way. "I'll see you sometime," said Barth, sounding harried. "G'bye."

Mendoza put the phone down, lit a cigarette, and ruminated on the cases Homicide had on hand to work.

Chase had cleared up the mugging for them; and they'd now haul all the material on Mrs. Reiner out of Pending and try to nail this Godfrey on that, along with Chase. The blackjack game had bothered Mendoza too; it was nice to have that explained; but just how much evidence there might be— The confession, of course, according to any smart lawyer Chase and/or Godfrey got, would be a nasty invention on the part of the brutal cops. However.

There were other cases in Pending too, all of which would probably stay there.

Somebody, last Thursday night about midnight, had held up Mr. Roy Manfred as he was closing his small liquor store on Third Street, and either because Manfred had put up a fight, or for no reason discernible, had shot Manfred dead. They had picked up some nice latent prints on the front door which belonged to a small-time pro named Lester Gumm, and of course that was frustrating. Gumm was off parole from his last sentence, and there was no reason he shouldn't walk into a liquor store and buy a six-pack of beer; he lived in a room just around the corner on Hartford Avenue. And of course that was just what he said he'd done: gone in and bought some beer, and that was how come his prints were on the door. It could be true: there was a fifty-fifty chance. If he'd shot Manfred, he'd got rid of the gun; they'd never tie that to him.

Then there was Carolyn Katz. She'd been a waitress at a small café, and had an apartment in an old place on Westlake Avenue. Last Tuesday night, a week ago today, she had come home from a movie about eleven o'clock. Other tenants on the first floor had heard screams and come out to investigate; but too late to save Carolyn's life. She hadn't been raped, she hadn't been robbed, but she'd been beaten severely enough to die of a skull-fracture next day. And that X might have been any mugger or, take your choice, any rapist, in Records—or not in Records.

Or it just possibly might have been someone who knew her who had a reason to want her dead.

There was the usual unidentified body found on Skid Row. Nothing much for Homicide to work.

There was the rather ambiguous case of Rose Plaidy, retired schoolteacher, Negro, widow without family, found dead in her own little house on Twenty-third Street, thus far of unknown causes. Wait for the autopsy report.

There was a flyer out from the FBI on one of their Ten Most Wanted men, Lloyd Arthur Jenkins, a long record of violence, thought to be in California.

There was a rather funny little thing that probably wasn't anything for Homicide, but it was a sudden death and they had to look. An usherette—in fact the sole usherette—at a little movie-house on Main that ran exclusively Mexican movies. She had apparently fallen from the balcony and broken her neck. She hadn't any reason for visiting the balcony, so the manager said, and so they were taking a second look. Hackett and Higgins were out on that.

Glasser was asking questions around the apartment on Westlake; Landers and Piggott were asking Carolyn Katz's friends about discarded boy-friends and so on. That could have been a private kill; it wasn't very likely.

Mendoza yawned and lit another cigarette. Without much doubt, as these things died on them, or got solved and tied up, there'd be other cases coming along. But the pace was a little slower than usual, which figured—the first week of a nice warm (but not too warm) June. And, thank God, the heavy cold which Higgins had brought back from his unwilling sojourn in the mountains last April had run its course through the office and nobody was out on sick leave.

Praise heaven for small favors, he thought. . . . That was funny, Chase coming out with the answer to the Reiner murder, just like that. . . . The other curious case shoved in Pending, last month, William Moberly with a knife in his chest and fifty bucks in his pocket, in the rest room of the Greyhound Bus station, probably they'd never have the answer on that one.

The inside phone buzzed and he picked it up. "Seventy-seventh Street think they've got that Jenkins spotted in a bar," said Sergeant Lake tersely.

"So let them go pick him up," said Mendoza. "Do they want us to come hold their hands or what?"

"Do I pay attention?" asked Mr. Carlos Hernandez, shrugging violently. "Me, I'm a married man, I got my family, I don't go noticing girls I hire here. Only two girls. At a time. To take the money, show people inside the theater. These girls, *Dios*. They're lazy little good-for-nothings mostly. This one, I don't know nothing about her. Named Luisa Fantini, is all. Italian. She only worked here two weeks, about."

The two big men stood looking at him: the twin bulks of Sergeants Hackett and Higgins, the two senior sergeants at Homicide. They'd worked together a long time, and they didn't have to use words to com-

13

municate. They were silently agreeing that Mr. Hernandez was probably an honest man telling them all he knew.

"How did you happen to hire her?" asked Hackett.

Hernandez shrugged more. "Other girl walks off job, I put ad in the paper. The Fantini girl answers it. It's part-time, you unnastand, we open at six—six to two A.M. but the usherette's here only till nine, I pay her five bucks for three hours, and it's not worth it. I guess I don't bother with another girl. Listen, are the customers that dumb they can't find seats for themselves? Do we get that many customers?"

"Do you know if she had another job somewhere?" asked Higgins.

"No. Maybe the ticket-girl would know. I guess they'd talk sometimes, maybe inna ladies' room after work. Yes, I got her address. Ticket-girl is pretty good girl, worked here nearly a year, Annie Sanchez. It's Antonio Avenue—I got it wrote down somewheres."

They were using Hackett's screaming-red Barracuda; they left the theater and got into it where it was parked in the yellow zone in front. "Why the hell," asked Higgins, "are we jumping the gun on this, Art? It looked as if this Fantini girl just fell over the balcony. All by herself. We haven't seen the autopsy report yet."

"So we're making work for ourselves," said Hackett. "Luis just said it looked funny, because she wasn't supposed to be up in the balcony at all. No, he didn't say he exactly had a hunch about it, but—it does look a little funny, George."

"Funny hell," said Higgins roundly. "She was off work at nine. She met a boy-friend in the lobby and they went up to the balcony to neck."

"And the boy-friend pushed her over the rail?"

"They could have been drinking," said Higgins. "They could have been high on Mary Jane or H. You know these run-down old houses, Art. The place wouldn't be crowded, not by a long shot. There probably weren't a dozen people in the place—and half of those drunk, sleeping it off, and the rest neckers. And she fell over and he panicked and ran."

"Well," said Hackett. "I don't know. It looks as if she went over after the place was closed, because she wasn't found till next morning when Hernandez came in."

"You know these places, Art! Maybe nobody noticed her land. I say, wait for the autopsy report."

"Which makes sense," agreed Hackett. He sat back and lit a cigarette with no move to start the engine. He didn't ask Higgins how the family was because he knew. Higgins the confirmed bachelor, humbly falling for Bert Dwyer's widow, had finally got her to marry him and acquired the secondhand family; and these days they were all looking forward to the firsthand family due in October, and maybe the Dwyer kids Steve and Laura even more thrilled about it than Higgins.

"The one we ought to be working," said Higgins suddenly, "is that Katz thing."

"Not a smell of a lead," said Hackett through a yawn. "We probably never will have."

"You sound like Matt."

"I tell you what it is, Tom," said Piggott as they waited for Mrs. Ruth Sneed to open her door, "it's just one of those things we'll work our legs off on, and never turn up a smell. The devil going up and down inciting to mischief."

"There's a lot of that going on all right," said Landers, and automatically reached for his badge as the door opened. "Mrs. Sneed?"

"Why, yes—you're *police*? Oh, about *Carolyn!* Oh, dear me. Come in, come in. I don't know how I can help you at all, but anything I can do—"

It was just a chance that Carolyn Katz had been killed deliberately, or accidentally, by somebody she knew; that was the only reason they were asking questions of people she'd known. They hadn't got anything at all to bear out that idea, and they didn't get anything new from Mrs. Sneed.

The picture that emerged, reinforced by the photographs taken of the corpse, was of a not-very-pretty, not-very-interesting young woman: a rather dowdy young woman who didn't have any steady boy-friends, or date much at all. She'd attended a Reform temple on Hill Street, but hadn't mixed socially with any of the other regular attendants. She'd been a reliable employee, said the manager of the small café where she'd been a waitress. The other two women working there said she never talked much about herself, had been a little standoffish—or perhaps shy. Reserved.

Everybody Landers and Piggott had talked to had said, Wasn't it terrible what had happened, these awful muggers and sex-fiends—and had asked discreetly, Had she been raped?

She hadn't been. And there had been thirty-four dollars in her handbag, dropped beside her. And that might be because he'd been scared off, by the other apartment people coming out, hearing her screams: he might have meant to rifle the handbag, and not had time. Or he might have meant to kill Carolyn for some private reason.

Landers was beginning to doubt that. When they'd wasted nearly an hour hearing much the same things from Mrs. Sneed they'd heard from everybody else who'd known Carolyn, he said so to Piggott. And Mrs. Sneed had known Carolyn somewhat better than anyone else they'd seen: she had worked at the café with her before she got married, five years back, and they had "kept up." Mrs. Sneed struck both Piggott and Landers as another one like the Carolyn they'd heard about: a plain, uninteresting woman with not much to offer.

It didn't seem very likely that anyone had felt strongly enough about Carolyn Katz to care whether she lived or died.

"Just the mugger after her bag," said Piggott as they got into Landers' Corvair. "Or, take your choice, the rapist. Most of 'em don't care what the girl looks like—just so it's female."

"'S right," said Landers. "And it might have been any of a thousand guys around town."

"No lead," agreed Piggott.

But they both knew where they went from here, on Katz. Look in Records for the similar M.O.'s—and on a thing like this there'd be literally hundreds of possible choices—and start the routine on it. The boring legwork.

They sat thinking about that, dispiritedly. Landers sighed and said, "I think I've still got a little spring fever, Matt. I just don't feel like doing the damn legwork. Who's going to miss Carolyn Katz?"

"Now that's no way to look at it," said Piggott seriously. Piggott was an earnest fundamentalist Free Methodist, if he was also the perennial pessimist. "Equal in God's sight, you know."

"Oh, sure, sure," said Landers hastily. "I just hope the lieutenant isn't feeling all eager on any of this piddling stuff we've got to work, to put us doing the overtime."

"Well, tomorrow's my day off anyway," said Piggott. "Lucky to get Wednesday for a change, choir practice and all. You have a date?"

"Tomorrow night," said Landers. He started the engine. "Might as well go back and do a report on this—handful of nothing." He laughed suddenly, shook his head at Piggott's inquiring look. He was thinking about his date.

Landers had taken out quite a few girls in his time. Of course, he had a little problem there: for whatever genetic reason, he had one of those faces that would look about twenty-one until he was a grandfather, and he was nearly resigned by now to having witnesses tell him he didn't look old enough to be a cop. Mrs. Sneed just now hadn't said it, but he'd seen the words, as it were, trembling on her lips.

Still, he'd known quite a few girls, and he was scarcely the innocent he looked. And some of the nice girls he'd known had been impressed because he was a plainclothes detective, and attached to Homicide at that. They just didn't know, he thought ruefully, how utterly unglamorous, how drearily undramatic, the job could be. The thankless and frequently boring job.

At least, he thought—looking forward, with an eagerness he'd never thought he might feel for a girl, to tomorrow night—at least this girl would never make that fundamental mistake. . . .

He'd been out with her three times in three weeks, the three weeks since they'd met.

He'd gone down to Records to check out a pedigree with the computer there, and he'd run into her quite literally, coming round a row of file-cases with a pile of manila envelopes in her hands. Papers scattered, and Landers apologized, bent to help her gather them.

"Never mind, they're all out of order now," she said philosophically. "There are still quite a lot of things computers can't do, that's what they keep us around for."

"You're new here," said Landers, looking at her. Sergeant O'Brien came up behind him and clucked at the mass of untidy papers.

"These damn bloodhounds," he said. "They don't understand paper work." And Landers was so bemused he didn't even try for a retort on that. "She's new all right. Miss O'Neill. Detective Landers, Homicide."

She wasn't anything like any of the female officers Landers had ever noticed before. She didn't, even in her neat navy uniform, look like a policewoman at all.

"I've been at Hollenbeck," she said briskly, giving him a friendly nod. And Landers never remembered afterward whether he'd said a polite Hello or How-do-you-do.

She must be over twenty-one, but he couldn't guess how much. She was only about five-three, and slim; and she had very thick, very curly, very flax-blonde hair in a neat short feathery cut, and, astonishingly, navy-blue eyes. He didn't discover that until the third time he looked at her. He'd never known anybody could have navy-blue eyes.

He'd taken her out to dinner three days later. They got along, they were the same kind of people. They laughed at the same things; and they both felt the same way about being on the force. He told her how he'd got fed up, still in uniform, only four years in then, and how that good cop Bert Dwyer had talked him into trying for rank. And how Dwyer had, later, died under the bank-robber's bullets.

She said, "You must have made rank early."

"Damn it, I'm older than I—well, I was five years in. I was twenty-six." And that was damn young to make Detective, as she knew; she just nodded.

She told him about herself, a little humorously. "Of course Mother couldn't know I'd grow up to join the force—I was named for her best friend, she was killed in an accident just before I was born—but honestly, what a name for a lady cop! Phillipa Rosemary—I'm Phil to all my friends." Her parents lived in San Diego, where her father was a pharmacist; she had a married sister in San Francisco.

Landers guessed you couldn't exactly call Phil O'Neill pretty; she had a nose that turned up, and a sprinkling of freckles on her white skin, and her mouth was really too big; but she was, well, Phil. A direct sort of girl, and you'd always know where you stood with Phil. She wasn't like any other girl he'd ever known at all.

It was really too soon to start thinking it could be anything serious—Landers guessed it was too soon. But, anyway, he was looking forward to seeing her again tomorrow night. To picking her up at her apartment on Kingsley Drive in Hollywood, Phil not in uniform but neat as ever in a pretty light-colored dress, high heels only bringing her blonde head up to his chest, and some perfume that smelled like lilies. And going out to Frascati's or that Hofbrau place on Sunset, for a drink and a leisurely dinner.

It was, he thought, an important sort of thing—that they laughed at the same kind of jokes.

Right now, go back to the office and get this damned report typed up. The handful of nothing on Carolyn Katz.

It was half-past four. Let the night men prowl around Records pulling the pedigrees on similar M.O.'s.

At about the same moment, Lieutenant Goldberg was feeling annoyed. "Look," he said, "it's your business, not mine. All right, I see the point, but we've got cases to work too, you know."

Captain Martin Van Allen of Auto Theft just scowled at him. He was a big stocky man going bald, with an incipient paunch and a very rudimentary sense of humor. "So it was this Sergeant Betts who picked

Horace up before. I've seen Horace's pedigree, naturally. I want to hear what Betts can tell me about him. When'll Betts be back?"

"How the hell should I know?" said Goldberg. "He's out on this hotel burglary. He'll be back in his own good time. What can he tell you but what's in the record?"

"He's talked to him—I haven't. Horace has been picked up once before, after you laid a charge on him—as a dauber."

Goldberg sighed. He wasn't much interested in Auto Theft, or even the grand-scale ring which, so Van Allen said, was stealing cars wholesale and ferrying them back east in disguise, to be sold to the honest dealers. Jack Horace was a small-time thief; so he had a prior record as a dauber—a fellow hired to repaint stolen cars—Goldberg couldn't have cared less.

"We've got a hot tip he's in with this ring," said Van Allen. "The Feds are on it too, you know."

"So I'll let you know when Betts shows up," said Goldberg. He sneezed and reached for Kleenex.

Mendoza wasn't, if the truth was told, much interested in any of the very routine things Homicide had on hand. He agreed with Landers and Piggott that Carolyn Katz had probably been a very random kill. They'd see what showed on the autopsy reports on the Fantini girl and Mrs. Plaidy. He didn't have any hunches about those at all.

And he had entirely forgotten Goldberg's mention of that hot-car ring. Nothing to do with Homicide, anyway.

He went home early, to the house on Rayo Grande Avenue in the Hollywood hills, and as he garaged the long black Ferrari beside Alison's Facel-Vega, he found both redhaired Alison and Mrs. MacTaggart in the back yard. All four cats, he discovered, were huddled on the back porch watchfully. The shaggy dog Cedric sat at the foot of the back steps.

"Oh, Luis," said Alison. "You're early."

"You'll be wanting a dram to whet your appetite," said Máiri Mac-Taggart automatically, turning for the house.

"¿Qué ocurre?" asked Mendoza, kissing Alison. "You all look as if you're waiting for the bomb to drop."

"¡Qué disparate!" said Alison. "It's only—well, in this climate—"

There was a sudden gray-white flash and flurry in the alder tree, and Cedric barked. A too-well-known voice whistled shrilly, *Yankee Doodle came to town—coroo, coroo—AWK!*

"*¡Porvida!*" said Mendoza. "Don't tell me that obnoxious mockingbird is back again—"

"In this climate, *amado*," said Alison resignedly, "they nest three times a year, you know. He's building another nest. And dive-bombing the cats."

And the twins erupted from the back door. "Daddy, Daddy, *el pájaro* comes back! *El pájaro* he bites Bast on *la grupa*—" Johnny.

"Daddy, *el pájaro* making *la casa* all pretty for his *esposa!* Mamacita say, *la esposa* have little *niños* pretty soon—" Teresa.

"*¡Dios!*" said Mendoza. "Why I ever got embroiled in all these domesticities—"

"You know," said Alison despairingly, "they'll be three in August. They've got to get Spanish and English sorted out before they start school—"

"*¡Vaya!*" said Mendoza. "I think I need that drink."

Hackett went home to his Angel, and Higgins to Mary and Bert Dwyer's good kids, only now beginning to feel they were all truly his. Palliser went home to the house on Hillside Avenue, and he still didn't altogether approve of Roberta going back to teaching for a year to help on the payments, but they could delay starting a family that long. Jason Grace went home to his Virginia in the house in Leimert Park. They were hoping against hope, still, to start a family some day. Tomorrow, Piggott would be off, and take his nice girl Prudence Russell out to dinner before they both went to choir practice.

And if Policewoman Phil O'Neill was looking forward to tomorrow night and her fourth date with Tom Landers, nobody but herself knew about it.

But as time moved forward inexorably, the trap set by Fate was waiting to snap shut.

2

ON WEDNESDAY MORNING the autopsy reports on both Luisa Fantini and Rose Plaidy were waiting on Mendoza's desk. By the time he'd glanced at both of them Hackett and Higgins had drifted in.

"So now we know," said Mendoza. "Who else is in? You'd all better hear about this." Hackett brought Landers and Palliser into the office; Piggott and Glasser were off, and Grace hadn't showed up yet.

Mrs. Plaidy had died, quietly, of an embolism. That inquest was scheduled for tomorrow, and the verdict now foregone. But Luisa Fantini hadn't died so easy.

Dr. Bainbridge estimated the corpse's age as between twenty and twenty-four. Not *virgo intacta* but had never had a child. No indication of any chronic disease or addiction. Cause of death, a broken neck, apparently brought about by the fall. There were visible dark manual bruises—he had clipped photographs to the report—on the tops of both shoulders and the neck.

"So somebody shoved her over," said Higgins.

"Or," said Hackett, "she was struggling with him and fell over backwards."

"Either way it adds to violent death," said Mendoza. "Bainbridge says she was twelve to fourteen hours dead when he first saw her—that was ten A.M. on Monday or thereabouts."

"And," said Landers thoughtfully, "this is Wednesday. Haven't any relatives shown up?"

"We don't even know where she lived," said Hackett. "She'd only worked at that theater a couple of weeks."

"Well, you know the routine—motions to go through." Mendoza lit a

21

new cigarette. "Somebody must know something about her. She wasn't living on that five bucks a day, either."

There was also the routine on Carolyn Katz. But as they all got up to start the day's work, in various directions, the office door opened and stocky Sergeant Barth of Wilcox Street came in. He clutched a bulky manila envelope to his chest.

"Morning, Mendoza. Said we'd be turning this one over to you."

"Your mystery," said Mendoza. "O.K., Tom, you and John go sniff round Fantini, see what you can turn up. I'll brief you on this later on. Sit down, Barth. You know Art Hackett—George Higgins. What's your mystery?"

"It's a funny one," said Barth. "When you come to look at it close." He opened the manila envelope. "About all we've got for a week's work on it is the photographs and a lot of statements that add up to nothing. Or, I should say, the mystery." Mendoza picked up one of the 8 x 10 glossy photographs and looked at it: a very candid shot of a corpse. The corpse was a woman, lying on her back on a carpet in front of an upholstered couch. A dark-haired woman, quite impossible to say whether she'd been good-looking or not, the face dark with blood and features battered. She wore a dark dress twisted and pulled up above her knees as she'd fallen. There was blood on the carpet: the one eye visible in this photograph was wide with surprise. "Harriet Hatfield," said Barth. "Age forty-seven, and as far back as we looked, absolutely nothing showing on her but the picture of the respectable upright matron." He picked out another photograph. "This is what was used, the lab thinks." Close-up of a wrought-iron poker, a miniature shovel from a matching set of fireplace tools. "Blood and brain tissue on both. And the handles too rough to take any prints at all." He sat down.

"So, the mystery," said Mendoza.

"Short and sweet," said Barth. "It's just—funny, Mendoza. What do I want to say, no shape to it. Here's Harriet Hatfield. There's plenty of money, not millions but substantial. Her husband Howard is the head chemist for Hollywood Girl Cosmetics—big firm, you know it. Owns stock in the company. Doing fine, but by the house, all we've turned up, they weren't throwing it around—just living well, you know. It's a big house, not new, up on Castaic Drive in Nichols Canyon. Class, you know, but not ostentatious. Harriet belongs to a bridge club, she goes shopping, she gives little dinner parties—sometimes she and the husband go to a show together. Quiet old-fashioned kind of family. Three kids. John, the boy, is eighteen. In his first year at Pepperdine

22

College, lives on campus, comes home some weekends. Linda, twenty-one, is in her first job as steno in a big lawyers' office in Hollywood —she lives at home. The oldest girl, Catherine, is twenty-four. She works at an exclusive dress shop in Beverly Hills, and I do mean exclusive. Shop owned by an old friend of her mother's, a Wilma Tanner. She's a designer, if that's the word—trademark Tanya Creations. Sold only in this shop. You get the picture?"

"Vaguely. ¡Adelante!"

"So, Catherine comes home about six-thirty a week ago Monday night and finds that." Barth gestured at the first photograph. "And we come running to start the routine. I'll just give you a general breakdown on what showed—or didn't. The statements are all in there. First, nobody had been home all day but Harriet. Catherine left at eight o'clock that morning, Linda at eight-thirty, her father about the same time. Now, there was quite a lot of valuable stuff in the house. Mrs. Hatfield had jewelry valued at around ten grand, and Hatfield has a cash-box in his desk with a wad in it all the time—about two thousand, he said. And nothing was missing. The house hadn't been ransacked—all shipshape. Nothing even out of place except in the living room." He nodded at the photograph. "Second, when we got the autopsy report the time of death was estimated at between one and three P.M., but the neighbors hadn't heard any disturbance at all, no screams or bangs. Thirdly—"

"Private motive?" said Hackett, jumping to conclusions. "If it was a break-in for loot and she surprised him, he wasn't scared off by the screams to bring neighbors. Neighbors close?"

"Well, those are big lots, but the nearest house isn't more than sixty feet away from the living-room windows of the Hatfield house—some of which were open. And it's a quiet neighborhood. Mrs. Brownlee next door was home all day. She didn't hear a thing, she says, and the dog didn't bark once. She says the dog always barks at strangers anywhere around."

"And," said Higgins, "dogs having better ears than we do, the dog would have heard any screams or struggle."

"I suppose," agreed Barth. "Anyway, we can write off the casual burglar just on that. He'd have known he had time to go through the house. So we started to look at everybody the Hatfields knew. The way she got it—the doctor said, at least a dozen blows—looked as if somebody didn't like Harriet much. But there was just damn all." He put out his cigarette. "She was a nice woman, everything we got. Family all broken up. A nice family, seems like. Perfectly harmless, kind-hearted woman. We talked to all the women she knew best. She wasn't a gossip. She wasn't a snob. She was, by everything we heard, a nice kind generous woman without an enemy in the world. And then we dug a little deeper and came up with Howard Hatfield's girl-friend. Ex, that is."

"Ah," said Mendoza interestedly.

"And it fizzled out like—like stale champagne," said Barth mournfully. "He's fifty, not bad-looking. He was embarrassed we'd found out about it. It was two years ago. Girl on the make, receptionist in the company office. He said he'd been a damn fool, she'd flattered him was all, but he'd come to his senses after a couple of months and ended it. His wife hadn't known about it at all. And it couldn't have anything to do with this. And it couldn't, that I can see."

"Girl wanting him back? His money, that is?" said Higgins. "Or putting the bite on him?"

"Why?" asked Barth. "He'd have seen his wife didn't know. We looked the girl up. One Bobby Sarsfield. She's got a good job as receptionist for an actors' agent on the Strip, and he's keeping her on the side. Very well, if you want to know—apartment on Sunset. Why the hell should she hark back to a brief affair two years old with fifty-year-old Howard? He says he hadn't seen her since. I believe him."

"Well, I don't suppose you stopped looking there," said Mendoza.

"Where else is there to look? They know the neighbors—the Brownlees one side, the Rockhams the other—but not very well. Say hello when they notice each other, that's it. The neighbors say they're nice people, no noisy parties, the young people polite. Brownlee's an attorney —they've got two married daughters and grandchildren. Rockham's a stockbroker, big firm in L.A.—he's sixty-four, she's sixty-two, and he's got a heart condition and she's got high blood pressure. Not that there was any reason, we *looked,*" said Barth. "Both Brownlee and Rockham at their offices as usual all day. The Hatfield kids—" he sighed. "Nice polite people, all broken up over Mother getting killed. John is a bright boy—studying engineering. We looked back to when he started first grade and there's not a hint of anything against him. Ditto for the girls. Bright, nice girls."

"Boy-friends?" asked Mendoza, leaning back with his eyes shut.

"Sure," said Barth. "Linda's got a couple of fairly steady ones. Peter Webster, Fred Hoiles. Both from much the same kind of family. Both upright respectable young fellows in good jobs, no black marks. The Hatfields liked them both. Catherine's going steady with Owen Hartigan, and the Hatfields liked him too. He's interning at Hollywood Community, a clean record."

Mendoza's long nose twitched. As usual, he was fastidiously dapper in silver-gray dacron, with snowy shirt and discreet silk tie. He straightened the tie absently and fiddled with his gold cuff links. "This is a little mystery, *de veras*. Of course, say it was a casual break-in, she surprised him, and he grabbed up what was handy to knock her out—"

"And battered her face in with a dozen blows? Nobody could have thought the house was empty—she'd been out to the market earlier and her car was left in the drive."

"Oh, really? Well, what I was going to say," said Mendoza doubtfully, "was that if it happened like that, she could have screamed at least once and if he thought anybody had heard—"

"You've got no out there," said Barth. "We went all round on this too. We thought, say it was a nervous j.d. pulling his first job—even so, it's a very outside chance. That's an old house, and there are a lot of bushes and trees all round it. The natural thing for the casual burglar to have done, if it had happened like that, would've been to dodge into a bedroom, the back porch, even outside behind the bushes, to see if anybody had heard anything. And nobody had—which thirty seconds' wait would have told him. I don't think she had time to make a sound at all, Mendoza. And anyway, the casual burglar—*or* the nervous j.d. —wouldn't have been such a fool as to try the daylight burglary with her car there in plain sight in the drive."

"And a pretty little puzzle that is, all right," said Mendoza. "I don't see—"

"You're welcome to it," said Barth. "I'll lay a bet you'll be hiding it away in Pending after you think it over."

"Any ideas?" Mendoza asked when Barth had gone.

"I'd like to see those statements," said Hackett slowly, rubbing a thoughtful hand over his jaw. "There's got to be a loophole, Luis—you know as well as I do murders get done for damn little reason sometimes—"

"That was what I thought," contributed Higgins. "Somebody right outside, she'd maybe had a little fight with. It could be. Some hairtrigger character—the gas-station attendant giving her the wrong change, or—" he paused.

"And there is the old saw, *de mortuis*," said Hackett. "All these people telling the Wilcox Street boys, sure, she was a saint on earth. Maybe—"

"Look, Arturo, Barth and his boys are experienced cops too. You think they didn't take that into account? Think of it?" Mendoza brushed his moustache the wrong way and back again. "It's just a funny little mystery, *seguramente que sí.*"

"So we go back and cover the same routine all over again?"

"You never know, something may show up the second time round," said Mendoza meditatively.

The ticket-seller at the Mexican movie house, Annie Sanchez, wasn't too much help to them at first. She was a nice honest girl and sorry, she told Landers and Palliser, she didn't know any more to tell them. They'd found her at home, an old turn-of-the-century house on Antonio Avenue the other side of the yards, and she told them they were lucky to stop by just then, she'd usually be at work but she'd had to take Mama to the doctor's this morning.

Fat, placid Mama Sanchez sat and rocked on the porch, beaming at them, and benevolently offered them a little glass of wine.

"No, thank you, Mrs. Sanchez," said Palliser. "We just want to ask Miss Sanchez a few questions—"

"No harm, a little glass good wine. You fellows, a plenty hard job you got, such times, these terrible *ladrones* all over. Do you good. I get—"

"No, really, thanks very much but we're not allowed—" They finally got that across to her and she looked astonished.

"Not allowed a simple little glass nice homemade *vino?* A terrible job you got, you poor fellows. I feel sorry in my heart for you. Try to catch the *ladrones,* terrible, and not even a little glass good wine." She shook her head.

"Mama—" The girl was a little embarrassed. "I guess they'd like to talk to me private. You know the doctor said you better keep your leg up—" Mama was gently urged into the house. "But if it's about that Luisa, I don't guess there's much I could tell you, at that. She only worked at the theater a couple of weeks, I didn't know her, to say *know.*"

"Well, did you talk with her much at all?" asked Landers. "She ever say anything about a boy-friend, her family?"

"Well, no, she never," said Annie. "Now wait a minute. I just remembered that—it'd be about the first week she was there, I saw her meet somebody when she went off at nine o'clock. Yes, a man. I didn't pay much notice, I mean why should I, she was pretty, I guess a lot of fellows might've been after her. I was waiting for Jimmy—Jimmy Cortez, we're engaged, he usually walks me home nights. All I could say, this fellow Luisa went off with, he was kind of tall. I didn't see him real good, didn't hear her call him anything. She never said anything about him."

"Do you know where she lived?" asked Palliser.

"Sure. I wouldn't, only she happened to say when we were in the ladies' room together once. She said she could walk to the theater, it was only a couple of blocks from Boyd. Oh, and that time too, she said—" Annie thought. "I don't know why she did, it hadn't nothing —anything—to do with what we'd been saying—I just remembered that too. It was funny. She was combing her hair—she had real nice hair, you know, blacker 'n mine, and shiny as could be, she must've washed it nearly every day—and she wore it long, just tied back like—and she said, Gee, it sure was good to get let alone, nobody at her day 'n' night, where'd she been, what'd she done, and all like that. I thought it was a funny thing to say," said Annie earnestly, "because, gee, what'd a person *feel* like without somebody to care where you went and what you were doing or feeling? A family? But Luisa—well, I guess she was only about twenty, and she didn't seem very—very grown-up like. Like a kid."

"Do you know if she had another job? She couldn't be getting along just on what she made three hours a night at the theater?" asked Palliser.

Annie shook her head. "Doesn't seem as if, but I don't know. Like I said, I work nine to five at Kress's over on Broadway—I'm saving like I can for when Jimmy and me get married. But Luisa never said about that. She was kind of a funny one."

They went back to Palliser's Rambler and drove up to Boyd Street. It wasn't a very long street and they started out with the two houses that advertised *Rooms* with signs in front windows. They got the right one on the second try.

Mrs. Baumgartner said indifferently, "Fantini, yeah, that was the name she said. Eyetalian. Little dark girl, an' I thought maybe no better 'n she should be. But why in time are cops around? She do something?"

"She's dead," said Landers.

"Dead? Well, if that don't beat all," said Mrs. Baumgartner mildly. "She couldn't've been more 'n twenty or so. What? Yeah, she'd been here about a couple weeks. I don't know nothin' about her atall. She

27

paid me twelve bucks a week for the room, all I'm interested in—o'
course if she'd brought *men* in, anything like—but she never."

"Did she say where she'd moved from?" asked Landers.

"Nope, why should she? Why, yeah, I s'pose you can look at the
room, you want. I never noticed she didn't come back, last couple o'
nights. I don't bother climb the stairs no more."

They went upstairs and looked at Luisa's room, at the rear of the
old house. The house hadn't been thoroughly cleaned in a long time,
and a vague smell of dust, mice and old wood hung over it. The room
Luisa had rented for the past two weeks was about nine by ten. There
was a painted wooden bedstead with a thin mattress, worn sheets, a
cotton blanket and bedspread. There was a painted chest of drawers, a
straight chair, a braided rug covering a patch of the old pine floor, and
a small cardboard wardrobe in one corner.

In the wardrobe, perhaps two dozen dresses crowded together on
hangers: some long evening dresses, more bright prints and revealing
chiffons and silks. A dozen pairs of high-heeled shoes tumbled on the
floor of the wardrobe. In the chest, a jumble of new-looking lingerie,
mostly black lace and nylon.

"I'll be damned," said Palliser suddenly. He'd been going through the
bottom drawer of the chest; he straightened. "Look at this, Tom."

Landers looked. On Palliser's palm, a little strip of brown paper. The
kind of little strip banks used to fasten sizable sums of bills together,
usually with a notation of the amount on the outside. There was a notation on this little strip, in ballpoint print. $1000, it said simply.

"I'll be damned!" said Landers. And then he said, "So—all these
clothes—most of 'em look new. And the rest of it—shoes and under-
wear. So, had she used up the thousand bucks and that was why she
got a job?"

"What kind of a job, for God's sake?" said Palliser. "Five bucks a
night? And how do we know how many grand she had? That she didn't
still have how many of these wads fastened with the brown paper?"

"Then why the job?" asked Landers.

"Suitcases," said Palliser suddenly. "She must have had suitcases."
They looked, and found three suitcases stashed under the bed. Two
were old, brown leather bags, old-fashioned; the third was a smart
new airplane-weight aluminum case. And that one had a little tag in
one corner of the lid, *Fraser's Sporting and Leather Goods*, it said,
Bakersfield, Calif.

"Well, a lead of sorts," said Palliser. He shook his head at the strip of paper. "This is a funny one, Tom. A thousand bucks cash. They always use these little strips for cash, don't they? Did she land here from Bakersfield two weeks ago?"

"We ask Bakersfield," said Landers, "if they know her. Or if this store knows her."

"I don't suppose a photo of the corpse would be very much like her alive."

"We have to go through the motions," said Landers. "Come on." They put a seal on the door and started back for headquarters.

They had to go on looking for answers on Luisa Fantini; by the autopsy report that was a homicide, of whatever degree.

Mendoza had sent Hackett and Higgins up to Castaic Drive in Nichols Canyon, to talk to Harriet Hatfield's neighbors again, and then to her friends; they had read the statements by then. As Hackett said, there was always the *de mortuis* bit; but Barth would know that too.

And right now Mendoza was thinking that *de mortuis* didn't enter into Wilma Tanner's orbit. Maybe it was instinct that had led him to Wilma Tanner first.

She was a big woman, buxom but not fat, with brown eyes and salt-and-pepper hair and a good-humored mouth. She didn't look any younger than her age, which would be about Harriet's age, but she was neatly dressed in discreet navy blue, with makeup as discreet. The eyes, which normally might hold wit and amiability, looked at him sadly and rather anxiously.

"None of us can make any sense out of it at all, Lieutenant," she said. She had taken him from the very plush, very feminine, very expensive-looking front shop of Tanya Creations (gold-veined marble walls, Victorian décor, and subtle fluorescent lighting) to what she called her office, a cluttered little room with a large desk taking most of the space, large ashtrays and two comfortable chairs. "Cathy's out to lunch—she takes the first hour," she said absently. "I suppose you'll want to see her too." She looked troubled. "It's just—a thing that couldn't happen, Harriet getting killed like that. Only it did." She lit a cigarette before he could snap his lighter, and sat back and blew a long stream of smoke. "Such a nice girl, Cathy. And I think quite talented—reason she wanted to work with me." She cast an experienced glance at Mendoza. "You look as if you can see farther through a millstone than most, as they say. That other officer—well. I knew Harriet all her life, Lieutenant. We went all through school together—from kindergarten on up.

If anybody knew Harriet—!" And her eyes were honest and frank on him. "I know what you have to think. Was there some personal reason? But there's nothing—just nothing."

"We have to ask," said Mendoza. "And hope we'll get straight answers, Mrs. Tanner."

"Yes. Miss," she said. "I took my maiden name back after the divorce." She passed one strong spatulate hand over the pepper-and-salt hair in its severe cut. "They're such a nice family," she said. "Harriet was—it's a terrible word for it—nice. An ordinary nice woman, Lieutenant. Ordinary—that's a wrong word too, but what else can I say? Tell you? That other officer—he said you'd decided it couldn't be just a burglar, I don't know why, that seems to me the only way it could have been. He kept asking personal things about Harriet, but—" She made an impatient gesture. "Silly. So silly. Harriet was—was just a nice decent woman with a nice family she loved, and they loved her." She wouldn't have known about Howard Hatfield's brief lapse. "She'd done her best to bring up the children well, and they're all good kids. Responsible. Reliable. They didn't always have so much money, when the children were small, you know—Howard started out as just one of the staff chemists with the company. They had to be careful, and save—Harriet was a good manager. And Howard saved to buy some stock in the company, and got promoted—" She put out her cigarette. "How many thousands of American families like them, Lieutenant? Harriet—Harriet was my friend, and it sounds—priggish?—but she was a good woman. Honest. Gracious. Kind. A good wife and mother. I—maybe it's not such a good idea for a woman to be really interested in a profession, a career. I know in my case, that was what broke up the marriage—what it amounted to, I was just more interested in the job than in Brian." She grimaced. "But Harriet never wanted anything but what she had, you see? It was her only interest—take good care of her family, her home. I'm afraid I was rude to that other officer, Sergeant somebody—asking about other men—just silly! So silly. Harriet—"

"I see," said Mendoza. He got the nuances from people always, and he was seeing Harriet Hatfield, at a little remove. Not an intellectual: an intelligent enough woman: domestic: a good wife and mother, probably.

Wilma Tanner opened her big leather purse that she'd dropped on the desk, and fumbled at a bulging billfold. "I don't know if you've seen a picture of her," she said. "That's Harriet."

Mendoza looked with interest at the color snapshot. It was a fairly close shot of three people seated on a couch: a man and two women. "Howard and Harriet," said Wilma Tanner, "and Linda." The man had a thin intellectual face, thin brownish hair, rimless glasses, a rather miserly-looking mouth. The girl Linda was blonde, the ash-blonde hair that would turn mousy in a few years, an insipidly pretty girl. Harriet Hatfield (he remembered that battered bloody face) had had a roundish face, medium brown hair in a simple style waved off her brow, friendly blue eyes; she seemed to have kept a good figure.

"My God," said Wilma Tanner, "if Rabbie had still been alive—! It was the first thing I said to Howard when—"

"Rabbie?"

"Their old collie—he just died last month. They'd meant to get a new puppy, but not right away—"

And the Brownlees' dog next door hadn't barked. Mendoza felt frustrated. A door opened and shut, and Wilma Tanner said, "That'll be Cathy. You want to see her, I suppose."

Thirty seconds later Mendoza stood up to face a tall, slim, very dark girl dressed very smartly in, probably, a Tanya Creation. She had an unusual face, not quite pretty but arresting: high cheekbones, large dark eyes under sharp-arched brows, a wide mouth made for smiling. "Miss Hatfield," he said.

"I just don't know what more any of us can tell you," she said. Tears came into the dark eyes. "It just seems impossible—Mother. The other man—who talked to us before—he said, not a burglar, because nothing was stolen, but—there just isn't anything more to tell you—"

Mendoza was still feeling frustrated when he dropped into Federico's for a very belated lunch and ran into Hackett. "What's happened to Jase, by the way? I haven't laid eyes on him today."

"He's chasing down that Guy Godfrey. I left George to go see a few more of Harriet's lady friends. So far, it all checks out just the way Barth made it. You get anything?"

"*Nada.* Or rather more than I want," said Mendoza. "I saw this Tanner woman. And Howard."

"I had," said Hackett, "another thought about Howard. If he once took up with the extracurricular girl-friend, why not another? Or three?"

Mendoza sat back and grinned sardonically. "I may have you beat by a few years, Arturo—"

"Six."

"—But that just means I've had more experience. I read Howard

Hatfield like a first-grade primer, *amigo*. The all-business, all work and no play, dead serious fellow. I'd have a guess he's slightly more ignorant about females than the average man in the street, and I would also have an educated guess that that was the only time he stepped off the straight and narrow."

"About that kind of thing I trust your judgment, boy."

"I'd also have a guess that the girl—what's her name, Bobby Sarsfield—isn't a very subtle piece of goods. She wouldn't have to be to gather in Howard. Don't they say it's a dangerous age? He—"

"*Cuidado, compadre.* You're not far off it yourself."

"*¡Vaya al diablo!* I'm the exception that proves the rule," said Mendoza with dignity.

"What about her?" asked Hackett.

"Harriet? *Impossible.* From all I gather—and Wilma's an honest woman, she wouldn't cover up. Not when it's murder. It's a little mystery, that's all. Funny." Mendoza started on his steak sandwich. Hackett sighed and drank black coffee.

"There's still the routine to do. Covering the same ground. Waste of time."

"I don't know. The second time round—" Mendoza poured himself more coffee absently. "Did I tell you that damn mockingbird is back? Building another nest, *Dios.*"

"You and your livestock," said Hackett.

Landers had typed a follow-up report on Luisa Fantini while Palliser sent the indicated teletype up to Bakersfield. A query to the lab told them that no photograph was available of the corpse's face. "Why the hell should we have taken one?" asked Scarne. "So you want one now? We haven't got anything to do up here, of course, but run around taking special shots for Homicide. All right, all right, I'll see what I can do for you. Say by three, O.K.?"

They went out to lunch, and when they came back a teletype was waiting from a sergeant up in Bakersfield. Luisa Fantini was not in their records. If L.A. would send up a photo, inquiries would be made at the sporting and leather goods shop. They hung around waiting for the photo, and Grace came in towing a sullen Guy Godfrey, so they helped to lean on him, and as might have been expected got nothing useful at all.

Chase was, said Godfrey with varied obscenities, talking through his hat. He didn't know nothing about that break-in up in Hollywood.

32

He knew even less about the murder of Mrs. Reiner and the blackjack game. He drew them a graphic outline of Sam Chase's lineage, personal habits, and probable fate. After a while they got tired of him; they'd try him again later. They would probably never make the charge stick, and have to let him loose. Which meant that nobody would get tried for Mrs. Reiner.

By then the close-up photo of Luisa Fantini's dead face was waiting; not a very good one, but it should be recognizable to anyone who'd known her. She had been a good-looker: the regular small pert features suggested that in life she had been gay, sparkling; and maybe, as Annie had said, not quite grown-up.

Landers and Palliser went out again, armed with copies of the photograph, after wiring one up to Bakersfield. They went out on the tiresome legwork, asking all around that rooming house, all around that theater, in bars and restaurants and stores, if anybody had ever seen this girl, with somebody or alone.

Landers asked the questions with half his mind a few hours ahead in time. To when he'd be parking in front of the apartment house where Phil O'Neill lived, in a clean shirt and his best suit, to pick up his girl in a pretty dress and the perfume like lilies, and take her out to dinner. He wasn't really much interested in Luisa Fantini, or how she had come to fall over that balcony. There was just a faint curiosity at the back of his mind about that little strip of bank paper.

At five-forty-five he landed back at headquarters and met Palliser just coming into the lobby. "You get anything?"

"Not one glimmer. You?"

"Nothing. A great big blank. Of course it could be a better picture."

Just as the elevator door swung back silently, three men came up beside the two men from Homicide. They were all strangers to Landers and Palliser. The big balding stocky man they had seen around the building: neither of them knew his name, nor that of the plainclothesman with him, but both, to any cop, wore the familiar aura of fellow police. The third man was different. His right wrist was cuffed to the left wrist of the second officer. He was a thin man about forty, with small pebble-gray eyes and a long sharp nose. He looked unhappy.

The five men got into the elevator. Palliser looked at the big man politely. "We're Eight," he said.

"Four."

Palliser punched the Four button. "If you ask me," he said to Landers, "it'll get tossed in Pending eventually."

"Probably," agreed Landers absently.

The thin man peered round at them. He looked surprised. "Oh," he said, "so you dropped on him too. That one." He gave Landers a sly half-grin. "Cops smarter 'n you thought, hah?"

"What?" said the big man. He turned and looked at Landers.

"Well, that's him, dint you know?" said the thin man. "Him. The one I tole you about, Cap'n. One o' them runnin' the whole thing, them hot cars."

"What?" said Landers.

The thin man said, "He's the one the other guy called Speedy. I tole you. How'd you pick him up so quick?"

3

The twins' baths had been supervised, and promises extracted for two Just-So stories before bed—"*El Gato* all by himself!" insisted Johnny, Terry trying to outshout him on demands for *el elefante pequeño*—and Mendoza had just taken his first sip of coffee when the phone rang down the hall.

"Don't tell me," said Alison.

Mendoza swore mildly and went to answer it. "Mendoza."

"Lieutenant—" Sergeant Thoms, and he sounded peculiar. "You're not going to believe this, but—and my God, there's an I.A. man listening to this call, for God's sake—and they took Tom up to—well, Palliser went with—but—"

"Take a deep breath and start from the beginning, Bill. What the hell is I.A. doing sniffing round my office? . . . *¿Quién?* . . . *¿Cómo dice? ¡Jesus y María!* What the hell—*Tom?* You're not making sense—*¡es ridículo!* What? Did—"

"This damn Van Allen, he's Auto Theft, stranger to me, of course he doesn't know Tom—and the Feds are in on it, and the damn I.A. men took them all upstairs, but Palliser said to call you—"

"I should think so indeed. *¡Es imbécil! ¡Allá voy*—I'm on the way!" Mendoza slammed down the phone and made for the bedroom after his hat. Twenty seconds later he tripped over their shaggy dog Cedric slurping water from his bowl on the back porch. The Ferrari roared to life and backed violently down to the fork of the circular drive.

"Just like being married to a doctor," said Alison resignedly.

"Ah, well," observed Mrs. MacTaggart, "there's one thing about a nice plain stew, *achara*—you can hot it up time after time without spoiling it. I daresay he'll be wanting it when he comes back."

• • •

Mendoza came past the door labeled *Internal Affairs* fast and found John Palliser sitting in a chair flanked by a grim-faced man at a desk. "What the holy hell is all this about, John? Where's Tom?"

Palliser opened his mouth and the man at the desk said, "Uh-uh, Sergeant. We keep it all formal."

"Formal be damned!" said Mendoza angrily. "You home-grown Gestapo—"

"Now, now." Another man came in from an unmarked door at the side of the office. "You needn't call names, Mendoza. We've got a thing here and we'll work it according to Hoyle, just to be sure. And you know that as well as I do."

"You're holding one of my men—"

"For good and sufficient reason," said Captain Macklin gently. "This could be quite a thing, Mendoza. You haven't heard all the details yet."

"Details be damned, the thing's ridiculous."

"I said it's crazy," said Palliser. "Just crazy."

"We've got to be sure," said Macklin. "You know that."

Mendoza dropped his hat on the desk and brought out cigarettes, gave one to Palliser, lit one himself. "So I'll hear your Goddamned silly evidence," he said sharply.

"An eyewitness—"

"*¡Vaya por Dios!* Any cop with a year's experience knows what that's worth!"

Macklin looked a little annoyed. "Identification of a ranking detective as a—"

"Which is the reason, isn't it?" Mendoza took him up. "All the trappings— Where have you got Landers?"

"You know how we operate, Mendoza. This Horace has fingered two other fellows he says will back him up. Some of Van Allen's men are out hunting them right now. We don't want Horace to lay an eye on Landers again until it's in a regular lineup. Sometime tomorrow, with luck. Lieutenant Wright and Southey are in there questioning Horace now—"

"My God," said Palliser suddenly, "I never called Robin—"

"Is the sergeant allowed to phone his wife, Macklin?" asked Mendoza. "You don't tell me. So very damn careful we have to be to inform

36

the pros of their rights—who's in there representing Detective Landers?"

"Well, this has caught us all on the jump—"

"Aren't you right. One side, I'll sit in on this. You show Sergeant Palliser a phone he can use. And I'll see Landers when I've heard the ins and outs of this—this farce." Mendoza walked past Macklin and opened the closed door.

It was thirty minutes later that the scene he'd interrupted was resumed. The three I.A. men, Van Allen, and three Feds had looked at him in annoyance, but admitted he had a right to some background. It was Van Allen who gave it to him, baldly.

"This hot-car ring. It's been a going concern for months—we've had cooperation from Philly and New York and Chicago and St. Louis, where the cars got spotted. By what we turned up—and the Feds—it's based here. The cars heisted, by men hired for the job, late model Caddys, Imperials, Chryslers, Lincolns—repainted, fitted with new plates and registration, and ferried back east. Sold to the honest dealers, and one hell of a job it's been to trace those we've spotted. Philly thinks they've spotted a drop there. We've been looking at everybody here with a pedigree in that line, and we spotted the garage last Monday by putting a tail on this Jack Horace—he looked hot for it, he's been hired as a dauber before. Durfee's Garage over on Virgil. Al Durfee's in Records too—ours, and downstairs as a strong-arm man for a gambling house Gardena shut down five years back. So we pick up Horace, and he comes apart and fingers two others—Rodney Dunne and Bill Byron —they're two who've been heisting the cars, Horace doing the repainting. We were bringing Horace in to get a formal statement from him when he recognized your boy right off. He just said, 'So you picked him up too.' Just like that." Van Allen eyed Mendoza truculently. "He wasn't two feet away from him. And I wouldn't say this Landers is a nonentity who'd be hard to remember."

"¡Vaya!" said Mendoza to himself. "But it's ridiculous, for God's sake! Landers—he's been at Homicide for five years, since he made rank—I know him inside out. It's—"

One of the I.A. men, Southey, spoke up: a tall dark serious fellow. "Lieutenant," he said, "we'd expect you to speak up for one of your men. But you don't know. We don't know. It's not very often we get a man on this force going wrong, but it does happen, if once in a blue moon. And when it does, we want to find out. That's what we're here for, Lieutenant."

Mendoza met his eyes angrily. "We know why you're here, damn it." Internal Affairs—

And one of the Feds looked at his watch and stood up. "We're interested in the ring, boys, so anything you get on that—but I guess the rest of this is your own private fight." He collected the other two with one glance and they filed out quietly.

Internal Affairs, LAPD: the first department of its kind: police to watch police. This was a crack force, and they wanted to keep it that way. Internal Affairs, keeping its careful eye on the personal and professional behavior of LAPD men, occasionally got a little puritanical: maybe that was only to be expected. Most of its work lay in investigating charges on the police by the citizenry: in an average year they might look into a couple of thousand such complaints, and find maybe eight or ten valid, and issue official reprimands to that many officers. As Southey said, it was a very rare occurrence for an LAPD man to turn out a bad cop or something worse. The last case like that Mendoza could remember had been twenty-three years back when he was just a rookie: a bunch of officers at the Valley Station pulling the burglaries on off time. That had been quite a thing: a nine days' wonder in this force.

Something turned up, I.A. had to look—just in case.

They didn't, thought Mendoza unreasonably, have to be so damned serious about it. As if Landers—Landers of all men—

Palliser hadn't seen Landers since they were shepherded up here, until the desk-sergeant grudgingly led him into an anteroom down the hall and indicated that he could use the phone there. Three sides of the anteroom were paneled: the fourth was glass from waist-high to ceiling, and as Palliser picked up the phone he heard tapping and turned to see Landers on the other side of the glass. Landers was looking tremendously relieved to see him; he also looked rather wild, tie pulled loose. All these rooms would be soundproofed; Landers just gestured at him imploringly. Was he locked in there? Palliser wondered. He gestured back inquiringly.

Landers was scribbling in his notebook. He held it up. A phone number in large print, and below, *Call and apologize—can't make date*.

Suddenly Palliser felt absurdly relieved, for no reason. It somehow made all this seem more mundane: just a missed date with a girl. He nodded violently, copied down the number. He was conscious that Landers was watching him as he called Roberta and made a hurried explanation. She said resignedly she'd expect him when she saw him. Dialing the other number, Palliser looked back to the glass: Landers had disappeared. Had they taken him somewhere else?

He hadn't given Palliser any name: when a cool contralto answered the phone, Palliser said, "I'm—er—calling for Tom Landers, Miss—uh. Something's come up, he can't make your date, and he says to apologize—"

"Oh," said the contralto. "Something broke all of a sudden?"

"What?" said Palliser. "Well, no, it's—" he was craning his neck looking for Landers on the other side of the glass: what were they doing with him in there? "It's sort of involved, we're stuck up here in I.A.—" He wasn't paying much attention to what he did say, and he wasn't prepared for the naked shock and astonishment as the contralto caught him up sharply.

"*I.A.? Tom?* Who is this? What on earth do those obnoxious do-gooders think Tom—"

"What? This is Sergeant Palliser, Miss—"

"O'Neill. Sorry, you didn't know. I'm down in Records, Sergeant. I suppose you can't tell me what's going on."

"I don't think I'd better." What was Landers doing, dating a female officer?—though she did sound, well, female.

"If not before, I'll get the story on the grapevine tomorrow. Listen, Sergeant—do you have any idea when he might get away?"

"No. I don't— No."

"Well, you tell him to come round here if it's before midnight."

"I will if I see him," said Palliser uneasily.

"I told you straight all I know," said Jack Horace. He looked at them stubbornly, stolidly: big beefy Van Allen, the three I.A. men, Mendoza. A silent uniformed sergeant took shorthand notes. "I ain't so sorry you dropped on me, no lie, on account I didn't like that Rosso guy. He could be a mean one, I figure. About the other one, the other mastermind you picked up, I couldn't say—I only saw that one like maybe three-four times. Rosso was the one came around, look over the cars in, bring the new plates. You didn't ask questions with that guy. Do what you're hired for, that's it. I'm hired to paint the heaps, I don't ask about the operation, but I can guess this 'n' that. The heaps went back east, I know that much—how I woulden know. There'd be guys back there to take 'em, hafta be. But all I know is, Rosso was the guy here. The guy in charge. And that other one."

"About that one, Jack," said Southey. They hadn't told him anything, naturally: but he sensed dimly that something new and important was going on, different cops questioning him; he looked wary. "The fellow you recognized—or thought you did—in the elevator. Was—"

"Oh, that's him all right," said Horace. "I only saw him that three-four times, like I say, but I had it figured he's maybe the contact for the back east setup. Rosso arranged for ever'thing here, payoff for the heaps, and the paintin' an' the new plates. But from just talkin' on the quiet like with the other guys—like Dunne and Byron I tole you about—it was the other one come move the heaps out, with a couple other guys I don't know nothin' about, see. I figure he's the one knows the drops back there, sets up the shipments, see. I kinda think—I don't *know*, but just somethin' Rosso said to him once, I got it in my head the money come from some operators back east, see. Harder to trace the heaps way across country."

"O.K.," said Southey casually. "You know that other one's name?"

"Nope. Don't you? You got him. Like I say, he only come by—while I was inna garage, workin' on the heaps—that three-four times. With Rosso. No, I don't know Rosso's front name. I just heard Rosso call the other guy Speedy, a coupla times."

Southey offered him a cigarette. "You had a pretty good look at him, though—when you spotted him right off just now."

Horace looked from one to the other of them as if he suspected a trap. "Well," he said, "he's got a face you'd kinda remember, don't he? First thing I noticed about him—this Speedy—he looks so awful young. Younger than I guess he is, because it seems, way he acts and talks, he's been around awhile. Around period. Not a kid. But he looks young. And the long jaw on him, and the way his hair grows straight back—and his eyebrows real straight, don't curve like most people's—well, yeah, I reckanized him easy."

"Remember when you saw him the last time? At the garage?"

"Sure. It was last Friday afternoon about five. He was only there about ten minutes. In the office with Rosso."

"All right, Jack." Southey got up. He said to Van Allen cryptically, "On ice. Solitary. See what shows tomorrow." Van Allen grunted and put a hand under Horace's arm and led him out.

"And just what the hell is that worth?" asked Mendoza hardly.

"Well, you know what it might be worth," said Macklin. "Just like the man said, Landers wouldn't fade into a crowd. He's over average height, and he's—noticeable, in a kind of way, because he does look younger than he is. And how many men do, Mendoza—that much younger than their real age?"

"¡Por Dios!" said Mendoza. "I don't understand this—" He brushed his moustache back and forth angrily. Horace had come out with that so unhesitantly, so readily. "So what now?"

"We wait to pick up these other witnesses Horace fingered. He says they saw this Speedy too. Can probably make him. Meanwhile, Horace doesn't see anybody but the jailer. When we get Dunne and Byron, we hold the lineup with Landers, see what they say."

"The cards all neatly stacked, heads you win, tails we lose," said Mendoza. "If they say yes, you believe them. Eyewitness evidence from the pros."

"Not necessarily," said Southey. "But it would kind of weigh down the scale, wouldn't it? Then, we look further."

"You might," said Mendoza acidly, "have a look at Landers' record as well. Just to throw in the wild card. And now I'll see him."

Landers said, "I just can't take it in, that's all. It's crazy. How the hell could this—*me*? I know they say everybody's got a double, but—"

"That's got to be the answer, Tom," said Palliser forcefully. "Somebody like you. Looking enough like you that— Look," he turned to Mendoza, "what this Horace said, it was in that garage he saw the fellow. Maybe not very good light. And anybody Tom's height and build—with dark hair and—"

Mendoza didn't say it wasn't quite so simple as that. Looking at Landers there, in a rumpled gray suit and loosened tie, he kept hearing the echo of Horace's voice: *he looked so young, younger than he is.* That, probably, was the first thing anybody would notice about Tom Landers. The fresh complexion, the misleading ingenuous look of youth. When he spoke, in a good baritone voice, and you looked twice at his dark eyes, you saw he was older: was, in fact, thirty-one. But at first glance you noticed that young look.

"Where were you," he asked Landers abruptly, "at five o'clock last Friday afternoon?" By the grace of God, Landers out questioning a witness, typing a report in the office, out on something with another man, this whole thing knocked down flat right then.

"Friday?" said Landers. "Friday's my day off." He thought. "Let's see, I went out to pick up some stuff at the market—that was earlier. I guess I'd have been just starting to fix dinner, I was going out and then I got interested in a book—"

"¡Mil rayos!" said Mendoza.

"But, my God—I can't *understand* it," said Landers. "I just can't—"

He was still saying it to Phil O'Neill an hour later, pacing the living room of her neat small apartment. She'd given him a drink he disposed of in three swallows, and insisted on fixing him a healthy sandwich; he felt a little less hollow after that. She was curled on the couch in a starched blue housecoat, her blonde head shining in the lamplight, and listening to him.

"—A lineup!" he said. "Me! To see if these Goddamned small-time pros can identify me—me!—as one of the masterminds of this damn hot-car ring! I swear to God, this is just a nightmare I'm having—it can't be real. My God, they told me—told me not to leave town, and not to report to the office tomorrow—just stay home! Me! I wouldn't like to bet they haven't got a tail on me!" He stopped in front of her looking white and shaken.

Phil uncurled herself and took the glass from him. "You need another drink." He followed her to the kitchen while she measured Scotch, added water and ice cubes. "They say everybody's got a double. But—" She handed him the glass, studying him seriously.

"But? My God, you don't think—"

"No, I don't think, idiot. But I can't understand it either." She sounded puzzled. "It's not as if you—well, had an *ordinary* face."

"That sort of sounds like a lefthanded compliment," said Landers with a forced smile. "Once seen never forgotten?"

"Well—" she considered. "Something like that, anyway. I don't understand it at all."

Landers took a swallow of his drink. "And, my God," he said suddenly, "don't I know I.A.! They'll be poking around in my history back to first grade, and likely questioning Mother and Dad— My God, what could I tell them? I'm in trouble with the law? Me, a ten-year cop?"

"You'd better call them anyway," said Phil practically. "Warn them. It's Fresno, isn't it?"

"But I just can't understand any of it," said Landers. "It doesn't make sense, Phil."

"It doesn't seem to make much. If there's anything I can do—you know my vacation starts Saturday." But her eyes were still puzzled and —was it speculative?—on him.

42

For the first time since this nightmare had started, Landers stopped feeling surprised and angry, and began to feel a little frightened.

Mendoza went home, to be fussed over and fed by Máiri MacTaggart, and blew off steam at Alison.

"It is simply impossible, that's all. Landers, I ask you, *cara!* He made rank at twenty-six, there's not a mark on his record, he's an efficient, reliable, experienced man. And this shifty little pro saying— *¡Porvida!* But how the hell—"

"You're either saying too much or not enough," said Alison, watching him. "What bothers you, Luis?" She stroked the tangle of two cats on her lap, Sheba and Nefertite, automatically. Bast the matron was coiled on the sectional, and the miniature lion El Señor brooded to himself on the credenza.

"Well, damn it," said Mendoza, "he's not a man you would forget if you'd seen him a few times. And that Horace saying—he sounded so damn positive, and it's just not possible. I need a drink."

Inevitably. El Señor reached the kitchen ahead of him for his ounce of rye in a saucer. Mendoza swallowed rye, swore at the glass, and went down the hall to call Hackett and then Higgins. They both said the same things, after initial indignant exclamations, about nearsighted pros and the damn suspicious I.A. men.

"But, you know, Luis—" said Hackett.

"I know, I know. Rather a distinctive fellow in his own way. But—"

"But when you come to think, Luis—" said Higgins. "He isn't just an ordinary-looking guy, Tom. I should think—" He stopped, and Mendoza could see him rubbing his prognathous jaw.

There wasn't any more to say about it then.

Before looking at the reports on his desk on Thursday morning, Mendoza called Southey. The other witnesses, Dunne and Byron, hadn't been picked up yet; but Van Allen was planning a raid on that garage this afternoon. Nobody there knew that Horace had fingered them; with luck they'd pick up most of the ring's employees; with more luck, Rosso. Whoever he was.

"You'll let me know," said Mendoza. He started to go over the reports, and all of them came in at once—Hackett, Higgins, Grace, Palliser, Glasser, Piggott. The rest of them had the gist of the story from Palliser, but they wanted to kick it around, and the same things got said. Piggott concluded gloomily that it was just more of the devil's machinations against honest men. Hackett and Higgins were both supposed to be off, but aware that the office would be a man short, had come in voluntarily.

"Look, boys," said Mendoza at last, "it's wait and see right now. What Auto Theft gets on that raid—what the other witnesses say. It's a bastard and I don't like it any better than you, but there it is. And there's work to do, damn it."

By chance, the first report he picked up was signed by Landers: a follow-up report on Luisa Fantini. Like all Landers' reports, neatly typed and correctly spelled. Landers the efficient and reliable. . . . At the moment, Mendoza wasn't interested in how Luisa Fantini had come to fall over the balcony. But there'd been that inquiry to Bakersfield—

He went out and asked about that. Bakersfield had sent a reply overnight. The sporting and leather goods shop vaguely remembered, in the person of a clerk, a girl who might have been Luisa Fantini coming in to buy a suitcase, maybe two, three weeks or a month back. If it had been Luisa, she must have paid cash for it: a search of checks accepted by the shop for the last month didn't turn up her name.

Which said nothing at all.

There was also Harriet Hatfield. Just how had Harriet Hatfield, that ordinary matron, good wife and mother, come to be battered to death in her own living room?

Mendoza asked Sergeant Lake to fetch some coffee, and sat back over it and ruminated. He could just see—only just—a possible answer on Harriet Hatfield. Barth had said, and they had agreed, that the time of day, the time of death, and the undisturbed valuables, ruled out the casual break-in. Maybe not, thought Mendoza. Suppose it had been the j.d.—from the neighborhood or not—pulling the break-in on impulse. Maybe supporting a habit. If so, jittery and easily panicked. One like that, maybe riding a little high, might conceivably have battered Harriet Hatfield to death, the unnecessary violence a mark of the breed, and then fled in panic without attempting to take any loot, afraid the noise had been heard. It was just conceivable.

Only why hadn't the dog next door barked?

And if it had been one like that, no way to go hunting him. Unless they found one like that living in the neighborhood. There hadn't been any strange prints in the house. . . .

Mendoza stabbed out his cigarette, his mind inevitably going back to Landers. He felt guilty at even speculating—he could not believe in that so-confident identification—but there was the hard fact: not exactly an ordinary face, Landers'.

"But," he said suddenly aloud, "but— *¿Qué sé yo?* Talk of fantastic— but it could be—"

Down in Records, Phil O'Neill was feeding information into a computer. She hoped that if she looked busy and brisk, the sergeant would assume she was working on some legitimate request from upstairs and not bother to check.

She had put together all of the salient physical features of Thomas Michael Landers, as they appeared on his official description. The computer supposedly would present her, eventually, with the names of any individual males in L.A.'s records who matched the description. It was a place to start.

Caucasian, male, five-eleven, one-sixty, hair black, eyes brown, thirty-one, complexion medium, appendectomy scar, no marks. Details of education, exam-scores, didn't matter.

The computer muttered to itself for some time and presently handed her nine names. The pedigrees varied from burglary to narco dealing to rape.

All nine men had mug-shots on record. Phil went and looked them all up.

Not one of them bore any faint resemblance to Tom Landers.

Descriptions, she thought, staring into space, didn't really say much: could be misleading. Even the precise police-type descriptions. You could, for instance, describe Phil O'Neill and her sister Kitty in much the same way: they were both small and blonde, Kitty only two years older at twenty-seven; blue eyes, fair skin, appendectomy scars and tonsils out and straight noses and that awful tendency to freckles—but they weren't really alike at all. Not to anybody who knew them. They didn't even look much alike, and Kitty was more like Dad—impulsive and given to sudden enthusiasms—while Phil O'Neill, however deplorably, was an intensely practical and common-sensible female.

It was funny about genes, thought Phil vaguely.

Hackett, worrying about Landers, had gone out again to look some more at the Hatfield thing. He had had, belatedly, the same idea about it that Mendoza had, and he did the patient legwork all through that neighborhood up there, looking for the hypothetical j.d., possibly with the habit. He got nothing. Most of the residents were older people; few young people around. But the more he thought about it, the more convinced he was that that was the only possible answer; and it needn't

45

have been a j.d. from around there. Just anybody with a habit, looking for the wherewithal to support it; and that was a neighborhood of big expensive homes. Where the loot might be had.

But of course there was nowhere else to go on that idea. Harriet Hatfield, even as Barth had predicted, would probably end up in Pending.

He came back to the office at a quarter of twelve and found Jason Grace feeling frustrated about Guy Godfrey and indignant about Landers. They'd never nail Godfrey for that, said Grace; all they had was Joe Chase's statement, worth nothing, and they'd had to let Godfrey loose. And what the hell was going to happen about Landers? "I know we've got to realize these I.A. men don't *know* him," said Grace, brushing his dapper moustache in unconscious imitation of Mendoza, "but anybody who knows him—my God, of all the crazy things—"

"Crazy is the word," said Hackett. "Where's the boss, Jimmy?"

"Arguing with I.A. on the phone."

"I seem to remember Seventy-seventh thought they'd spotted that Jenknown double killer, which was why the fliers had come to Homicide. there." The phone buzzed; Lake manipulated plugs. "Headquarters,

"False alarm. Maybe it was him—he'd gone by the time they got there." The phone buzzed; Lake manipulated plugs. "Headquarters, Homicide . . . O.K., sit on it, somebody'll be there . . . New body. The Spring Hotel over on Temple. Probably natural death."

"Oh, hell," said Hackett. "I'll take it. If George calls in, tell him I'll meet him at Federico's at one."

"I just don't understand it," said Grace complainingly as Hackett went out. "Positive identification of Tom—it's out of *Through the Looking Glass*, Jimmy. Of course, this cheap little pro—have they tested him to see if he's got twenty-twenty vision, I wonder. It's got to be a crazy mistake of some kind."

"Let's hope to God," said Lake seriously. "The damn I.A. men always so quick to jump the gun." Mendoza came out of his office looking annoyed, and asked if anything new was in. He looked more annoyed to hear about the new body and Guy Godfrey.

"More paper work. And that Goddamned Macklin—"

The phone buzzed. "Headquarters, Homicide . . . Right away! O.K. —Spring and—we're on it . . . Bank job," said Lake tersely. "Spring and Ninth. The guard jumped one man—squad car's there now."

"¡Condenación! All right, come on, Jase."

Higgins and Palliser were just getting out of the elevator down the hall, so they went along too.

4

THEY GOT TO THE BANK about the same time as the Feds—Mendoza had finally got round to having a siren installed in the Ferrari. There wasn't, as it turned out, much for them to do at the bank: the guard had jumped the lone heister and a couple of male tellers piled out to subdue him. He was sitting in a chair behind the railing labeled *New Accounts*, surrounded by the heftiest bank employees, one of them brandishing a gun. One of the Feds took that away promptly; it was an old .45 automatic with a full clip.

The bank-robber looked at all the law men and said despondently, "It was tryina do a job alone, that's where I went wrong. I shouldn't never've tried it. But I don't know nobody out here."

And the Feds took a second look at him and were pleased. The bank-robber was Lloyd Jenkins, on the run from a murder rap in Chicago. It wasn't the first time he'd killed—he'd hit more than a dozen banks, with a little gang of pals, through the Midwest, and once shot a bank guard —but the Chicago rap was first degree. He had caught his best girl with another boy-friend and shot them both, back in March.

When the guard heard who it was he'd jumped, he looked ready to pass out.

L.A. couldn't hold Jenkins; there'd be extradition. They stashed him in the Alameda jail. The Feds went back to whatever they'd been doing, and the Homicide men went to Federico's for a belated lunch.

Everybody but Mendoza ordered pre-lunch drinks. The waiter brought Mendoza black coffee with the others' drinks, took orders efficiently. Mendoza lit a cigarette and said, "I've had one of my far-out ideas, boys."

"A hunch?" Grace cocked his head.

"No hunch. Just an idea. That Horace"—Mendoza looked meditatively at his coffee—"came out with all that so pat. So prompt. Drop the coin and click-click, out comes the confident identification."

"What's in your mind now?" Higgins swallowed Scotch and water.

"Could it be a frame? A deliberate frame? Horace knowing what Tom looks like, primed with that description? By somebody?"

"Who for God's sake would want to frame Tom?" asked Palliser blankly.

"That I couldn't guess at. It's just a thought."

Palliser drank bourbon and shook his head. "I don't see it. I'd like to buy it, because it could be the only logical answer, but—I was there, you know. When that Horace first spoke up. If I'm not a genius, I don't think I'm all that stupid either, and all I can say is, that sounded damn —spontaneous."

"Sometimes they're good actors," said Higgins. "I'd like to buy that too, Luis. It struck me that it was all—like you say, pat. Rehearsed? I'll say this much. I wouldn't bet I could just tell somebody, for instance, what one of you looks like, even a detailed description, and trust him to pick you out of five or six men. Unless the rest were all midgets or something. But it'd be very damn easy for anybody to describe Tom so he'd be picked out right away."

Palliser and Grace stared at him. "Now that never struck me," said Grace. "But you are so right. How'd you describe John here, so a stranger might recognize him? Any tall dark fellow in his thirties 'd fit that description. But Tom—"

"And you know," said Mendoza dreamily, "that was the very first thing Horace said. He said that was what he noticed first—he looked so young, this guy. The first thing any—mmh—third party would have told him about Tom Landers."

"But—" Palliser thought. "But look, how does this hot-car thing tie in? Why all of a sudden, in the middle of something that isn't Homicide's baby, the frame—if it is? Not even Horace knew Auto Theft was going to drop on him, on that. What the hell would anybody in on that deal know or care about Tom Landers?"

"I couldn't say," said Mendoza. "I just say it could be, that's all. And then, you know—the pros don't get picked up every time on the same count."

"Which means what?" asked Palliser.

"Oh," said Higgins. "Yes. Well, we can ask Tom—"

"Ask him what?" asked Grace.

"About somebody maybe he picked up once—on something to do with Homicide—who nursed a little grudge on him," said Mendoza, regarding the steak sandwich set in front of him. "Who may now be—what story am I building, George?—just maybe—"

"Yes," said Higgins thoughtfully. "Who may now be, say, in competition with this Rosso—whoever he is—in dealing in hot cars. Who may have got to Horace—and possibly these two pals of his, he seems to have parted with their names a little fast, didn't he?—killing two birds with one stone. Put Rosso out of business and frame Tom at the same time. Like all your stories, it's a little bit complicated, and the pros aren't, very, as a rule. But it *could* be. And if it is, Tom will likely remember who might have laid any threat on him, for what."

"Or didn't," said Mendoza. "Just nursed the grudge." He poured himself more coffee. "I'll commit myself this far. If Dunne and Byron make the positive identification, all as confident as Horace, I'm going to have triple doubts that that's for real. Damn what I.A. may think, that would say to me it's a frame."

"I might think so too," said Higgins. "But damn it, Luis, how many times do we hear it? I'll get you, cop. And how many times do they do anything about it?"

"There's always the exception that proves the rule. . . . Have you got anything on that girl, John?"

Palliser sighed. "A cooperative witness," he said, "who gives us nothing at all—or not much."

There was the routine to be done, cases to be worked. They still didn't know much about the Fantini girl, and Palliser had been out most of the morning armed with that photograph, looking for anything on her. He had started on the premise that if she had met a man once after work at the theater, she might have done so often, and they might have gone to one of the bars or cheap restaurants on up from there.

At a bar five blocks up Main from the theater, he finally struck pay dirt.

"Her," said the bartender, glancing at the photograph. "Yeah, sure I seen her in here. That's a hell of a picture of her, though. She's a lot prettier 'n that."

"Did she come in alone or with somebody?" asked Palliser.

"Why, she come in with Duke, acourse. She's Duke's new girl."

"I see," said Palliser. "And who's Duke?"

"You said you're a cop? Neither of 'em done anything, have they?"

"Not that we know of," said Palliser truthfully. "Who's Duke?"

"Well, he's a guy. Just a guy, comes in here sometimes. Duke's O.K., he works downa street at the men's store. What? Well, I don't know his right name, everybody calls him Duke account he's a sharp dresser. Duke Wagner."

Palliser went down to the men's store, a cheap little place with a couple of gaudy sports-coats in the window, and asked for Duke Wagner. The owner looked at his badge, did a little fawning, and told Duke he could take whatever time the officer needed, we had to cooperate with the force, didn't we?

He talked to Duke over a muddy cup of coffee in the drugstore on the corner. Duke Wagner was a little too good-looking and a little too conscious of it: the Greek profile under wavy blond hair; he was tall and well-built, in a gay plaid sports-jacket, a flashy tie. He had a very winning smile. Not one to be satisfied with the cheap men's store on Main Street, thought Palliser: he'd have ambitions. On the make, but very cautious of his own skin. Ambitions toward TV?

Wagner turned a frank gaze on him and answered questions readily. "Luisa, sure, a good kid," he said. "She's only been here a little while. I met her in Dinty's bar one night. Oh, maybe three weeks back. She's a real looker, you know? Yeah, sometimes I'd meet her at that theater and we'd have a few drinks."

"When did you see her last?"

"Oh, last Saturday it was, why?"

"If you'd been going around together, didn't you expect to see her in the next few days after that?"

Wagner looked a little flustered. "No," he said. "No, I didn't. I—why all the questions, anyway? I don't get it, Luisa hasn't done anything, has she?" Palliser showed him the photograph. Wagner stared at it and asked, "What—what's wrong with her? This picture—she sick or something?"

"Or something. She's dead, Wagner."

"Dead!" said Wagner. He went a sickly gray. "How can she be dead? Luisa—what happened, how—"

"Never mind," said Palliser. "Just answer a few questions, Mr. Wagner. Did you have a date with her after Saturday night?"

Wagner shook his head blindly. "No. No. I—tell you how it was. I—it sounds funny, maybe, but it's how it was. Luisa—well, sure, I picked her up that night, she's a looker, maybe an easy lay—you know how you do. But, see, we get talking, we kind of thought about things the same way, and we felt—I got to explain how it was—kind of friendly. How we're both out to get somewhere, you get me? This crummy neighborhood—old Jackson and his cheap little store, my God, sixty-five bucks a week—Look, I picked her up for the usual reason, but it was funny—after a while we felt just friendly, you get me. Like, sympathetic." He tasted the word on his tongue, experimental. "Like that. Luisa told me about herself. You want to hear that?"

"I would. What did she tell you?"

"Well, see, she was raised on a farm way up north, I think she said outside San José someplace. Her pa was awful strict, you know how some of these Italians are, they seem to think kids belong to 'em, order 'em around however they want—not just Italians I don't mean, old-country people like that sometimes. He'd beat her too, beat up on her and her ma and the other kids. Anyway, there wasn't never any money, he's a kind of miser, and she has to work like a dog all the time, and so she ran away. She stole some money out of her pa's pants one night and ran away. Came here on the bus, and she's got ambitions, see, she was going to get somewheres however she can. Poor kid, she was only twenty, my God. How did—"

Palliser took that with a large grain of salt, thinking of that little brown strip of paper from the wad of cash. "I see. And how was she planning to get somewhere?"

Wagner was silent. "It's not so easy for a girl, you got to sort of make allowances," he said at last. "I—well, I tell you all I know. If some bastard hurt her some way— Well, I tell you, see, she was looking for some—some guy loaded, to make up to. Like that. I said I'd meet her, a couple times, we'd have a couple drinks—but a lot of nights, she'd get all dressed up and hit places uptown, looking for the rich guys. She told me some about it."

"I see. What luck had she had?" asked Palliser.

"Well, not the kind of deal she was after. See, she'd bought herself some nice clothes with her pa's money she took, she was real class when she got dressed up. Sure, she met up with the eager johns, but it was the permanent deal with somebody really loaded she wanted, not the one-night stands, she wasn't that kind of girl," said Wagner earnestly. "But last Sunday afternoon, I only saw her a few minutes, I met her on the street. She told me—" he shook his head. "She was all lit up, sort of sparkling—excited, you know?—she said, night before she'd met up with a real high-class guy, not so young maybe but he looked like a good deal for her. It was at some bar out on Beverly, something to do with gypsies the name was—no, she didn't say what the guy's name was. Just that it looked like a good deal. She was going to meet him that night. And that's all I could tell you. I never saw her again."

Palliser thought. If that was so, and it rang true, he didn't think Luisa would have revealed her shabby background by taking the john to Boyd Street. Pretty evidently, by all that, she'd been posing as the high-class call-girl. If she'd made a deal with the john, it would be at his place, or some hotel. He foresaw more legwork around the bars uptown, and sighed.

He passed that on to Mendoza at lunch; Mendoza didn't think much of Luisa's sad tale of an ill-used childhood either, but they'd ask San José anyway. The rest of it rang a little truer.

After lunch Palliser looked in the phone book for bars on Beverly Boulevard. He didn't find any gypsies mentioned, but he did find the Tzigani Room, so he drove out there to show the photograph and ask questions. It was just open, but frustratingly, of course, the bartender and waiters on duty after nine P.M. weren't there now. And that probably meant some overtime tonight.

He went back to the office and began to type up a report on what Wagner had told him.

Piggott and Glasser were doing the dogged routine on the Carolyn Katz case. They had looked in Records for the pedigrees of men picked up on similar assaults, and gone out to look for the first batch of those that showed. It was boring and unrewarding, because even when they found those men and brought them in to question, very few of them could produce alibis, and there was no evidence at the scene to link to anybody.

Up to noon they had found and questioned three men from the list. All of them denied knowing anything about Carolyn Katz, none of them had alibis for the relevant time, and any of them could have done it but there was just no evidence.

"You know, Henry," said Piggott over a drugstore sandwich, "I think it'd be a shortcut if we just put this thing into Pending right now. We'll never get anywhere on it."

"I wouldn't doubt you're right, Matt," said Glasser. "But we have to work it some, after all."

"That thing about Tom—it's crazy. Just crazy. I wondered if it could be a frame," said Piggott, his thin dark face morose.

"How the hell? What I heard, what the Lieutenant said, this pro claimed to recognize him right off. Oh," said Glasser. "Oh, I see what you mean. Somebody could have described Tom to him—"

"When he acted so positive, way I heard it. Bearing false witness," said Piggott. "It's almost got to be, Henry, because Tom—well, we've both worked with him awhile."

"Yeah," said Glasser. "That's so, Matt. I'd take an oath he's as straight as they come. But this Auto Theft deal—how the hell could anybody mix Tom in with that? Setting up a frame?"

"I don't know. But I do know that the devil is—like the minister was saying just last Sunday—full of wile and subtleties. All too true, Henry. And always watching for ways to catch the honest men."

"Well, I'll tell you one thing," said Glasser thoughtfully. "If I.A. goes after Tom, to try to break him, the Lieutenant—as they say, Matt—will be neither to hold nor bind. Like a tiger after those damn suspicious do-gooders."

A gleam of slightly unchristian satisfaction showed in Piggott's eyes. "Oh, that he will, Henry, that he will. And more power to him."

Mendoza had been fidgeting around the office ever since he'd come back from lunch; he knew I.A. probably wouldn't be calling until at least three o'clock, but you never knew—and with Van Allen's raid on that garage— He sat swiveled around looking out over the view across the city, the Hollywood hills a blur on the horizon this slightly overcast day, and smoked too many cigarettes.

A new body turned up on a park bench in MacArthur Park. Palliser had just finished typing a report, and went out to look at that. At three o'clock Hackett came in and said he'd come round to agreeing with Barth that Harriet Hatfield posed a real mystery. Seeing that Harriet and everybody connected with her looked so upright and respectable.

"You're unsold on the hopped-up j.d.?" asked Mendoza inattentively.

"On account," said Hackett, "of the dog. I got to thinking about that dog, Luis. The Brownlees' dog next door. Call it fifty feet between the two front doors, and the back yards adjoin each other. Ornamental wooden fence and a hedge between 'em." He sank his big bulk in the chair beside the desk. "Dogs," he said, "are funny. If you didn't know. Breeds."

"¿Y qué?"

"Well, I just got to thinking about the dog. And I went and saw Mrs. Brownlee. The dog is a Dalmatian."

"So?"

"They're not barkers," said Hackett, "as a rule. She said the dog always barks, just once or twice, at strangers anywhere near. To let her know the stranger's around. Well, George said dogs have better ears. The dog would probably have heard any stranger—intruder—on the property next door. And barked. The dog was in the Brownlees' back yard all afternoon."

Mendoza swiveled around and looked at him. "Q.E.D.?" he said softly.

"Well, call it ninety percent yes. The dog didn't bark."

"So it wasn't a stranger next door? You're telling the story, Art."

"It's kind of logical to say so, isn't it?" said Hackett reasonably. "It was somebody who'd been to the Hatfield house before. Somebody the dog next door knew was—all right. But how could it be, Luis? Such damned upright people— Oh, well, I know that says nothing really. But—"

The inside phone rang and Mendoza snatched it up.

"Lieutenant?" Southey. "We've got Dunne and Byron—and a couple of others. We're ready to set up the lineup now."

"I'm on my way," said Mendoza tersely.

They were being even more careful on this than they ordinarily would be on arranging the completely equitable, fair showing. The lighted platform up there in front was isolated from the darkened space here, and this area was soundproofed: no word spoken here could be heard by the men on the platform.

And Macklin was saying rather fussily now, "This is quite irregular, Mendoza, I hope you realize that. Ordinarily no outsider would be allowed to be present with the witnesses—and you can stay only if you give your word to remain absolutely silent—the witnesses will not be influenced in any—"

"All right, all right! But I'll hear this at first hand, Macklin. Speaking of influence—"

"Are you accusing—"

"I'm not accusing you Nice Nellies of anything but jumping to conclusions," said Mendoza irritably. "Have you taken the trouble to glance at Landers' record?"

"We've seen that, yes," said Southey. "You know we don't jump to conclusions, Lieutenant. We just want all the facts in."

"Facts," said Mendoza, unconsciously stating one of his deepest convictions, "mean damn all when you're dealing with human people."

54

A grunted expletive turned him around to face Van Allen. The Auto Theft captain looked slightly contemptuous at that overheard remark; there was unconcealed dislike in his eyes on Mendoza's beautifully-tailored silver-gray dacron suit, the gold links and heavy gold ring.

"So here they are," he said.

The two men with him were rather typical of the pros cops saw a lot of. They weren't unintelligent or even without skills: just lazy. They'd rather get it the easy way. Both of them had pedigrees of theft, break-ins, shoplifting. The job they had just been picked up for must have been one of the easiest they'd ever had: hopping cars on order, getting paid for ferrying them to the Virgil Street garage.

Dunne was twenty-six, a weedy young man with a too-small mouth and hard eyes. Byron was much bigger, sandy, a little too fat, trying for an arrogant swagger.

Southey gestured, and the uniformed man who had come in with Van Allen herded the two over to the other side of the room. "What did you get?" asked Southey quietly.

"Four of them," said Van Allen. "The little guys—like these. The other two hired to hop the cars too. Six new shorts in for processing. This Rosso wasn't there." He looked like an angry bull.

"Durfee?" asked Southey.

"Or him either. Damn it, it was just the odds," said Van Allen. "We might have dropped on the whole ring—it was just the way the ball bounced."

"Coincidence!" said Mendoza, and laughed. "It doesn't enter your head that that might say Rosso and Durfee knew the whistle had been blown, and made tracks to cover?"

"It was just the way the ball bounced," repeated Van Allen doggedly. "These four we picked up know we've got the goods on 'em. They've got no reason to shut up on anything—not when they know Horace's already split. No, for God's sake, they haven't laid eyes on Horace, naturally. I told 'em he'd fingered them and they came apart. They give us Rosso too. Just the name. Description of sorts. I never asked one question about the other one, but they told me there is a second man. The other two never saw him. These two give us just what Horace did—the second man wasn't there often, at the garage. When he was, usually at night, in the office with Rosso. And usually just before a shipment moved out. These two started to tell me what they knew about him, I stopped 'em."

Careful, so careful to be fair, thought Mendoza sardonically.

Southey nodded and went over to Dunne and Byron, Macklin beside him. "Now I want you to listen carefully," he told them in his quiet voice. "You're going to look at a number of men up there in the light. All we want is for you to tell us whether you've ever seen one of them before. If you have, we'll ask you some questions about that. If you haven't, that's just too bad. But we'd like you to be very sure about it, you understand?"

Both men nodded jerkily. "All right," said Southey. There were chairs down there in front of the platform; he led them there. Mendoza sat down directly behind Dunne; Southey and Macklin flanking the two, Van Allen behind Mendoza.

The light on the platform brightened suddenly. A uniformed man came out first, and after him, rather slowly, a file of eleven men. I.A. leaning over backwards, thought Mendoza: eleven men, all of a general type.

Landers was the sixth man in line. All the men were between five-ten and six feet. They were all dark, or darkish. They were all clean-shaven. They were all in the late twenties or early thirties. They were wearing suits and white shirts. And Mendoza knew who they'd be, too. Men on the force, men picked as that general type, possibly a couple of prisoners from the Alameda jail. In silence they filed onto the platform, in silence stood there.

And in that file of men, for the one reason, Tom Landers stood out. He looked, at first glance, so much younger than any of the rest.

Dunne moved suddenly. He said, "That's him—the other guy. Isn't he the one, By?"

"Don't consult with each other," said Southey in the darkness, "please."

"Yeah, that's him," said Byron. "He was in the office with Rosso once, I brought in a heap. I never heard what his name is, but Jack told me—"

"That's right," said Dunne. "I only saw him twice, but he's a guy you'd remember."

"Which one?" asked Macklin. The men in line stared straight ahead; under the light Landers looked pale.

"The sixth one," said Dunne. "Sixth man in from the left. I reckanized him soon's I saw him, on account he looks so young. Not as old as I guess he is, but I wouldn't know how old he is."

"That's right," said Byron instantly. "You'd spot him easy, on that account. Even if you only saw him once like I did."

And Mendoza said loudly, "*¡No faltaba más!* All dovetailed nice and

56

neat—as if I needed any more convincing it's a Goddamned frame!"
Macklin turned on him furiously.

They wouldn't let him see Landers alone; at least it was Southey who
stayed in the room with them.

Landers was looking angry again now, and that was a good thing.
"Listen, Lieutenant, a lot of good it does to say it, but—"

"Skip that," said Mendoza. "We haven't got much time. I think this
is a frame, Tom, and if so we're going to find out all about it—"

"Excuse me, you won't be allowed to do any investigation in this
matter," said Southey. "It's I.A.'s business."

"I've been on this force, for my sins, twenty-four years this month,
Lieutenant," said Mendoza icily, "and as a rule I decide what's my
business and what isn't. At the moment you're an observer only. Tom,
I want you to think back and try to come up with anybody—anybody at
all—who might have any reason to set a frame on you."

"Well, but offhand I can't—"

"I don't want offhand. Think about it. Motives are sometimes damn
small. Now in the meantime these—officers," said Mendoza, "are going
to be questioning you hot and heavy. As a fellow officer—"

"Detective Landers is suspended from duty," said Southey.

"Temporarily," said Mendoza between his teeth. "Now you're not
guilty of anything so they're not going to find any evidence. So you're
going to cooperate with them any way they ask."

"Sure," said Landers. "God knows they can look—for one thing, these
operators must have been taking a lot of loot at that racket, and they're
not going to find any attached to me."

"*De veras*. We're both feeling damned annoyed about this," said Mendoza, "as well as—mmh—surprised—"

"That you can say again."

"—And you might feel even more damned annoyed at some of the
personal questions they're going to be asking you. I just want you to
remember something, Tom. We swear at I.A. and sometimes we laugh
at it—but this is the top force anywhere—and you come to admit it, I.A.
is one of the reasons. If we have got a bad one carrying a badge, we
want to know."

"And amen to that," said Landers seriously. "All right. I know that.
I just can't figure this at all, but there's got to be some logical answer.
A frame—I don't know."

"And, damn it, other things to work," said Mendoza. "But we'll be in

57

touch, boy. We'll find out what's behind this damned farce—" Southey cleared his throat and Mendoza's grin tightened. He gripped Landers' arm. "Whatever the hell *is* behind it. You just mind your manners with these fellows."

Landers gave him an anxious smile. "I'll do that. Thanks, Lieutenant."

And he had known what to expect, in a general way, but if Mendoza hadn't said all that to him, he might have lost his temper. As it was, he hung onto it tight; he cooperated, remembering what Mendoza had said.

He gave them his bankbook, his keys. He told them how he spent his money, what he saved, that no, he didn't have a safe-deposit vault. He explained the florist's bill they found when he emptied his pockets; he was surprised to see it still there—flowers for his mother's birthday last month. They asked him about girl-friends, and it was the queerest damned thing, he had to stop to think to remember the last girl he'd dated before Phil O'Neill. He didn't mention her name at all, afraid to get her in trouble with him.

They asked him the hell of a lot of personal questions, all right, but he went on hanging onto his temper. The fact that three men had identified him as a pro crook he'd just stopped thinking about: that was just nightmare, an impossible thing. There must be a logical explanation somewhere, but that was just too much to think about right now. He clung to the facts he knew: he wasn't guilty of anything, so there'd be no evidence for them to find, no ill-gotten loot, no secrets.

With the impersonal, inexorable voices going on at him, Landers kept his temper. He answered the questions. After a while he lost any impulse to anger, resentment; he was just concentrating on answering truthfully, fastening all his hope to what Mendoza had said.

He had no idea what time it was when Southey straightened and said to him formally, "As I told you, Landers, you're suspended from duty pending the outcome of this investigation. You are not to leave town. You'll hold yourself available for questioning at any time. Right now you're free to go home."

And Landers knew how the grapevine worked, too. Some version of this all through the headquarters building by now.

My God, how and why was all this happening to him?

They'd given him back his keys. Looking at his watch, he found it was ten minutes to nine. A few hours ago they'd taken a break, given him a sandwich and coffee; his stomach was growling now, but he felt faintly sick.

The Corvair had been dusted for latent prints. They had wiped most of the powder off, but he could tell.

He drove home, to the rather shabby apartment on Fountain where he'd lived ever since he'd come to L.A. and joined the force. The apartment had been searched and dusted too. Everything was in place, as he'd left it, but he knew that. He had never realized before what a feeling of—violation—that could give you, your private place looked over by alien eyes. By searchers.

He felt empty, but he didn't want to go out to a restaurant, and he didn't have the energy to make a sandwich or put a TV dinner in the oven.

He went out and got back into the Corvair, and he'd driven up Fountain to Normandie and turned left there before the thought entered his mind: was he wearing a tail?

To bring Phil into this Goddamned mess—

He slowed and pulled in to the curb, watching the rearview mirror. Cars passed him, apparently unconcerned. Landers thought tiredly, yes, and make some obvious maneuver to shake off the possible tail (*him*, with a tail!), just double the suspicion in their minds—

After debate, he went down to Ardmore. That was a side street, empty at night. No cars turned after him; he parked, but no lights showed in the mirror.

He turned back to Normandie, down to Melrose, and down that to Kingsley.

She came unhurriedly at his ring to open the door. She was wearing the starched blue house-robe, primly high at neck, full around her ankles, and it showed her slim neat figure. Her short blonde curls shone in the light.

"I shouldn't have come—"

"Well," said Phil, surveying him calmly, "one good thing may come of all this mess, now I take a look at you. You look at least five years older already, you realize that? You also look as if you'd been through a wringer. Have you had anything to eat?"

"I don't remember—a sandwich a while ago—"

"I've got creamed chipped beef left over. Whole wheat toast. Asparagus or Italian beans. But I think," said Phil, "you need a good stiff drink first."

5

THE CORPSE ON THE BENCH in MacArthur Park looked to Palliser like one of those things that might create more than paper work. The ambulance was waiting when he got there; the squad-car men holding off a little knot of curious people. The interns said the man had been dead at least eight hours; presumably he'd been taken for a sleeping bum until somebody sat down beside him.

He was an elderly man, and his clothes looked expensive, a gray suit, white shirt, new shoes. The interns said it looked like an overdose of some kind, at first glance. There wasn't a thing on him but an empty prescription bottle in his breast-pocket, and that bore only a doctor's name: Dr. William Bartlett, an address in Beverly Hills. Palliser let the interns take the body, and drove out to Beverly Hills.

Dr. William Bartlett had his own smart little clinic building, and the offices were closed on Thursdays.

Great, thought Palliser. He went back to headquarters and typed up a report. He had, belatedly, realized what Landers had: damn that ridiculous identification, there wasn't going to be any evidence for I.A. to find on Landers, so it would be O.K., just—as the Lieutenant was saying —the attempted frame that fell apart.

And he'd be doing some overtime tonight, so he went home a little early, to the house on Hillside Avenue that was too big for them now. He told Roberta about the frame. "It'll be a tempest in a teapot," he said. "Naturally there won't be any evidence on him, it'll blow over. But I wonder what was behind it."

His lovely dark Robin gave him a rueful smile. "You've given me something new to worry about now. Besides all the trigger-happy thugs. Your own private watchdogs jumping on you for any little thing."

"Well, not just any— I suppose they have to look, damn silly as it is to anybody who knows Tom. But it'll be all right in the end," said Palliser. "Rough on Tom for a couple of days, that's all."

At nine o'clock he went out again, to the Tzigani Room. The Tzigani Room was attached to a new and large and expensive-looking chain motel, and it was crowded. Palliser was patient, and a harried headwaiter, impressed by the badge, cooperated. The ninth waiter Palliser talked to, looking at the photograph of Luisa, said he wouldn't like to get anybody in trouble.

"Do you know her?" asked Palliser. "This is police business, Mr.—"

"Smith," said the waiter surprisingly. All the waiters were dressed in somebody's idea of gypsy attire, tight black trousers, white shirts with billowing sleeves, and red silk ties. This one was swarthy enough to look the part. "George Smith. Look, it isn't like the manager lets B-girls in here, but people behave O.K., how do you throw 'em out? For all I knew she was stayin' here."

"All right, when did you see her? With somebody?"

"She was in Friday and Saturday nights last week," said Smith reluctantly. "I didn't say anything to the head. Why should I? She was a pretty girl, she was dressed nice, nothing too sexy or—you know. Blue lace dress she had on, nice dress, and a kind of white cape across her shoulders—and she acted O.K. How should I know she didn't know the guy before?"

"Who?" asked Palliser.

"Well, Mr. Silverman. He's stayin' here. He's kind of regular, he'll be here—stayin' here I mean—maybe a couple of weeks every three, four months."

"Is he still here?"

"Look, you don't need to tell him it was me told you? I don't want no trouble—we aren't supposed to talk about the guests—well, that's him in the corner booth, but—"

Mr. Harold Silverman, looking at the badge, was a little flustered. "Police?" he said. "Why the hell are police interested in me?" He was a big man about forty-five, not a bad-looking man, with thick curly gray hair and a Brooklyn accent. "Why you asking?" He wore two diamond rings.

"You know this girl, sir?" asked Palliser, holding out the photograph. Silverman looked at it.

"What's this about?" he asked in a quieter voice.

"The girl's dead."

"Dead? That little— Well, I will be good and Goddamned," said Silverman blankly. "So that's why— How? What happened to her?"

"It looks as if she was murdered. You did know her?"

Silverman looked shocked. "Oh, my God. I hope to God you're not going to connect me—the papers—my God, Jacob would have a fit. So that's why she never showed. I'll be damned."

"If you'd just tell me what you know about her—"

"Sure," said Silverman almost absently. "Buy you a drink? Well, I guess I'll have another. My God, this shakes me. In the midst of life, all right."

Silverman was the high-class john Luisa had picked up on Friday night. He was partner and chief salesman in a big jewelry-manufacturing company in New York; he was fancy-free, divorced, with plenty of money to spend, and Luisa had looked like a real fun girl to him. He had about a week's worth of business to finish up in L.A., after which he proposed that they spend a couple of weeks in Acapulco; meanwhile, he'd get her a room at the motel. "That is," he said to Palliser, "I'd give her the money to. They're particular, they don't put up with funny business." She'd been supposed to meet him for dinner at seven-thirty on Sunday night, but she hadn't. He didn't know where she lived, any way to get in touch with her; he'd been mad about it. She sure looked like a girl you could have fun with. . . .

Palliser thought about that autopsy report. Luisa dead maybe as early as eight o'clock that night, falling over that theater balcony: or shoved over. Why had she missed keeping her date with her high-class john?

And Silverman, mad at being stood up, had gone out and picked up another girl along Hollywood Boulevard. Had gone back to her apartment with her. "I don't know if she'd say, Sergeant—I don't figure she's a pro, and—"

It didn't matter. Silverman was alibied by waiters here up to nearly ten on Sunday night. Palliser asked Silverman to come to headquarters in the morning to make a statement. "My God, this isn't going to come out in the press? I want to help you guys, Sergeant, but—"

"No, sir, it's just for our records."

It was, however, funny. Luisa on the make for a john with money, so when she found one she stood him up. Why?

Mendoza was wakened just after dawn by faint and then more definite sounds from the alder tree in the yard.

Coroo, coroo. Awk. Yankee Doodle came to town came to town—
AWK!

That damn mockingbird. The cats were huddled at the foot of the king-size bed. El Señor got up and walked over his mother and sisters to stare out the window. A sudden flash of gray-white beyond that: the mockingbird was up early, intent on his nest-building.

Mendoza pulled the sheet over his head. Alison was sound asleep. It was no use; he was awake for good. Half an hour later subdued sounds from the kitchen galvanized the cats into action. El Señor, standing on his hind legs, rattled the doorknob until he tripped the latch, and all four cats vanished down the hall toward Mrs. MacTaggart and breakfast. . . . Five minutes later the mockingbird began to scream raucously, and an amiable bark informed Mendoza that their shaggy dog had been let out into the yard. Three minutes after that, the twins erupted down the hall shouting.

Alison sat up. "Why on earth did we, *amado?*" she asked sleepily. "Get into all this?"

"It was strictly your idea," said Mendoza.

He landed at the office at ten minutes to eight. The grapevine had, of course, carried the tale of I.A.'s investigation to every office at headquarters, and the night men Schenke and Galeano had hung around to ask him what went on. "I think it's a frame," said Mendoza, "and a fairly crude one too. But there'll be no evidence for I.A. to find. I only hope to God they'll come to the same conclusion."

"Those guys briefed to identify Tom?" asked Galeano. "Who'd try a thing like that? Without any more to back it up—"

"As I said, crude," said Mendoza. "We just wait and see what shows."

It had been a quiet night: nothing new for Homicide. He read Palliser's report on the body in MacArthur Park: nothing to do on that until they got the body identified through that doctor.

When Hackett and Higgins came in at eight-fifteen, he beckoned them into his office with a crooked finger. "You two are on special detail. I want Al Durfee—if possible, before I.A. gets hold of him. I'd like Rosso ditto, but that's a little more difficult."

"Just a little more, the man says." Hackett looked at him. "Are you just pining for a vacation, *amigo?* You're not careful, you'll find yourself alongside Tom on suspension. So you want Durfee. If we find him, and fetch him back to master like good dogs, you know what's going to happen?"

Mendoza grinned. *"Pues sí.* We may lose part of the ninth floor when

Southey and Macklin explode. I'll take the risk. I'm just a dedicated officer trying to help out those dedicated I.A. men, that's all—business is a little slack here for once and I'm just being helpful, turning my two senior bloodhounds onto Durfee. You find him, we'll send him up to I.A. like good boys."

"Straight up, I don't think," said Higgins.

"Well, after I've had a talk with him," said Mendoza, shutting his eyes and leaning back in his desk-chair. "It's not that I don't have—mmh—faith in these dedicated I.A. men. Not at all. They're cops too. But they're not, at the moment, operating on the premise that there's been a frame, and I feel they might be *muy cortés* to Mr. Durfee. Such little gentlemen they are."

Hackett laughed. "I don't know Durfee. You think a little less politeness might open his mouth wider?"

"*Es posible.* When and if you pick him up, you two savage-looking cops can stand over him and tell him, we know all about the frame, come on, who put you up to it. Etcetera. I'd just like to hear what that might produce. We can always say," said Mendoza placidly, "that we couldn't get through on the phone, or something."

"I keep having this feeling," said Hackett, "that we might end up getting suspended too. You know how touchy I.A. is. And that's up in the air, we haven't found him yet. And I.A. and Auto Theft are both looking for him too. And Rosso."

"If you run into any of them," said Mendoza, "you can just look surprised and say, What a coincidence. The sooner you start to look the sooner you may get results. *¡Vamos!*"

Higgins and Hackett looked at each other and went out resignedly.

Mendoza hadn't said it to them; and he wouldn't have to say it to any other man in the office, because they'd see it for themselves once they thought about it. They had said, after the first little shock, I.A. mounting an investigation and Landers suspended from duty, that it would blow over: frame or mistake or whatever, there'd be no evidence for I.A. to find on Landers, no illicit loot or a tie-up to pros—so it would fizzle out. When they thought it through, as Mendoza had, they'd see that it couldn't.

There the ugly little fact stood: three pros, presumably with no personal ax to grind, had identified Tom Landers positively as the second operator running a hot-car ring. So, no solid evidence, I.A. couldn't ask for his resignation, couldn't do a thing to him. No proof. But there the mark would be—forever a question mark. And so, when the

64

chance for promotion came, Landers—who had passed the sergeants' exam with the top grade—would be passed over. Probably passed over from now on. The LAPD didn't promote officers with question marks on their records.

If this couldn't be definitely proved to be a frame—or of course a mistake—it would hang like a Sword of Damocles over Landers the rest of his professional life.

And there were the current cases, legitimately Homicide's business, to be worked. Harriet Hatfield. Carolyn Katz. The Fantini girl. That new body.

Mendoza swore softly to himself, took up his hat and went out to the anteroom, where Sergeant Lake was gloomily studying *How To Stay Slim.* "I'll check in by noon, Jimmy."

Palliser had gone out looking for that doctor in Beverly Hills; Piggott and Glasser were doggedly pursuing their hunt through Records for Carolyn Katz's killer, and Grace was in court covering the inquest on Luisa Fantini. Nobody but Sergeant Lake was in the office when Lieutenant Carey of Missing Persons came in and said he'd got that new corpse identified for them. A description had been sent down to his office yesterday.

"The people called in yesterday morning. I didn't see the description until an hour ago, it rang a bell so I called them. They've just identified him at the morgue. One Wilson Guilfoyle, address in Beverly Hills. I gather he'd been going a little senile—he was nearly eighty, had had strokes. It looked like suicide?"

"I couldn't say," said Lake. "Palliser was on it, and he's out."

"Damn," said Carey. "Well, if he calls in or comes back, let him know, hah?"

He had just gone out when Harold Silverman came in, looking nervous, looking curiously around the Homicide office, and said Sergeant Palliser had asked him to come in to make a statement.

Lake hadn't any idea what that was about; he felt a little indignant at Palliser; but he'd just noncommittally asked Silverman to sit down when the outside phone buzzed and it was Palliser.

"Anything up, Jimmy? I've got that body identified, the doctor—"

"Yes, so has Carey. You needn't have gone chasing off. And a Mr. Silverman's here wanting to make a statement."

"Oh, hell, I'd forgotten him," said Palliser. "I'll be in in twenty minutes."

65

Both Auto Theft and I.A. had been before them—long before them —in Records. The grapevine stretched to Records too, and Sergeant O'Brien eyed Hackett and Higgins curiously; but he didn't make any comment. He produced the pedigrees without question and Hackett and Higgins looked at them.

Albert Joseph Durfee didn't have too long a pedigree or too bad a one. He had a little j.d. record of hopping cars; after that, nothing until he was twenty-seven and charged with grand theft—he'd stolen some expensive tools from the garage where he was working. He was a skilled mechanic. He'd got into law trouble again five years later, a burglary charge dropped for lack of evidence. Then, his arrest for assault at that gambling house where he'd apparently been an unofficial bouncer. That was all. He was now forty-seven, and from somewhere since five years back, he'd got hold of the money to start buying the garage on Virgil. His mug-shot showed a heavy-jowled man with a sullen mouth and heavy eyebrows.

"Suppose we do find him?" said Higgins. "He looks like a tough customer, Art. Could you get the truth out of him at all? Even our Luis?"

"No bets," said Hackett. There was a recent address—he was only off parole since last year—on Second Street past Hoover.

Rosso, of course, was another thing. None of the witnesses in that case knew his first name, or said they didn't. As they'd all said too that he was a mean customer, all business, it was only natural they hadn't known. There were fifteen men named Rosso in the current LAPD Records; it took a while to get particulars on them. When they did, it turned out that six of them were presently incarcerated here and there, from Atascadero to the county jail, on various counts. Four of the others looked like very small-time pros by their records. Three others had done time for embezzlement, rape, and forgery, which somehow didn't sound close to operating a hot-car drop. The last two, however, sounded quite possible. Victor Rosso, forty-seven, had done time for fencing, possession of stolen goods. Paolo Rosso, forty, two arrests and one charge on receiving stolen goods. There had been a man charged with him on that, one James Herbert Saunders, and just to be thorough they looked him up too.

And looking at Saunders' pedigree, Hackett said, "I'll be damned. Does this say something, George?"

Saunders was described, five years back, as Caucasian, male, twenty-four, five-ten-and-a-half, one-seventy, complexion medium, hair dark brown, eyes blue, no marks.

"You're thinking, an honest mistake," said Higgins, looking at that. "On the surface, vaguely like Tom. He's got brown eyes but who notices that close? I think we go looking for these birds, Art."

"Durfee first."

On their way out of Records they passed a good-looking little blonde in neat uniform, making for the computer. "Getting some cute junior officers these days," said Hackett idly.

Mendoza, with an effort putting Landers at the back of his mind, had gone to see Howard Hatfield again. There wasn't, he had decided yesterday, anything at all in that little lapse of Howard Hatfield's, to tie up to this murder. He had decided that after ten minutes' talking with the shallow-eyed pseudo-redhead Bobby Sarsfield in a plush office on the Strip. She hadn't remembered Hatfield's name at first; she didn't like cops, but she wasn't smart enough to have faked that.

Hatfield was in his office on the top floor of the three belonging to Hollywood Girl Cosmetics, in a tall building on Wilshire Boulevard. He polished his glasses slowly as he answered Mendoza; he looked older and graver than when Mendoza had first seen him only a few days ago.

"It's the little things that one notices," he said with a twisted smile. "I—we never thought about it, at least I suppose the girls—but, the house all run smoothly, the marketing done, dinner waiting when we— And now, well, the girls both working, they do their best, but—Harriet was always a little house-proud, as they say. Kept things just so. And a—a good cook." He was silent, and then he said, "It's just a terrible mystery. We can't imagine what could have happened—why. That other man—Sergeant Barth—he explained why you don't think it was just an ordinary burglar, but I just don't know what other explanation there could be."

"Mr. Hatfield, did you and your wife discuss most things together? What I'm getting at, if she had had a quarrel, an argument, with some-one—a personal disagreement—do you think she'd have told you about it?"

Hatfield looked surprised. "Why, I imagine so—I'd have heard about anything like that. It would have been unusual—Harriet wasn't a—a secretive person. But anything like that—it'd be impossible. Someone she knew—Harriet didn't—didn't have arguments with people, Lieuten-ant. She was—easygoing. And nobody would—" He put his glasses on, looking at Mendoza curiously, incredulously. "I'd been very busy," he said suddenly. "We're bringing out a new line in the fall, and I'd had a good deal of overtime work here. But I'd surely have heard of anything like that. Harriet—you can't be thinking—"

"We don't know, Mr. Hatfield. We're just asking."

"Her friends—most of her women friends, I know their husbands —we'd entertain them—dinners, Sunday lunch." He looked at his clasped hands. "All just ordinary nice people, Lieutenant. Beth and Tom Lederer—the Novaks—the Townbridges— You can't be thinking—"

Mendoza had seen Hackett's report on those people. Hackett might look like the big stupid cop but he got nuances from people too. Those couples, closest friends of the Hatfields, were impossible, said Hackett. From Homicide's point of view. Ordinary people: Mendoza was tired of that word. And all of them, as it happened, were firmly alibied for the afternoon Harriet had been battered to death.

The children, he thought. The grown-up children. Was there possibly anything there? The girls had boy-friends. John in college: had he got in with some friends the Hatfields disapproved? Sniff around them, their personal lives.

The dog wouldn't have barked at any of the Hatfields' friends, coming frequently to the house.

He opened his mouth to ask Hatfield about the girls, about John.

Palliser took the statement from Silverman before he called Carey. By that time Grace had come back from the inquest, and went to sit in on the new one with him.

Mrs. Alma Swift and Mr. Wilfrid Guilfoyle, Junior, had still been in Carey's office making statements; they were voluble to the Homicide men.

"He'd been getting a lot more forgetful lately," said Guilfoyle earnestly. "Poor old Uncle Will. He realized it, and he minded like hell. Alma could tell you." Guilfoyle was about thirty, very natty indeed in pale fawn slacks, a sports-jacket with the faintest of brown shadow-plaids, a white silk scarf draped inside the jacket in lieu of a tie.

"Well, he had," said the woman. She was middle-aged, angular and plain, gray hair pulled back to a knot; she wore a long-sleeved black dress that gave the effect of a uniform. "I've been housekeeper for Mr. Guilfoyle for over twenty years and it was a terrible thing to see him failing like he had been since his last stroke. He always had such a sharp mind."

"I gather," said Palliser, "that Mr. Guilfoyle was—er—quite well off?" The doctor had said, filthy rich: very much the self-made man, and still wearing the pants, so to speak, if the strokes had slowed him down.

"Oh, yes, sir. But to think of him doing such a thing— Such a turn it gave me, when I went up with his breakfast yesterday morning and there was his empty bed!" She sniffed into a handkerchief. "To think of him—that other man, he said the doctors thought he'd taken an overdose of his heart medicine—the bottle—but I don't see how it could be, Mr. Guilfoyle'd never do such a thing on purpose— And way downtown here—I just don't understand it!"

"Well, I suppose I'd better tell you this," said young Guilfoyle in a subdued tone. "It just didn't cross my mind that he meant anything by it, but— Well, you see, I live—lived with him, and I used to take him his coffee after dinner, he liked to sit in the library then, and"—he smiled—"you know, I'd talk with him, try to cheer him up. He was crotchety, poor old uncle, the way old people— And just a few times lately—I never said anything to you, Alma, because I never thought he really meant it—when I'd be settling him in his chair, get his footstool, he said to me life was getting to be a damn nuisance, he'd be better dead. Well, I tried to josh him out of it, but—"

"I see," said Palliser. "He knew that if he took all those tablets at once it would kill him? The digitalis tablets?"

"Oh, dear!" said Mrs. Swift, and burst into tears. "Oh, my dear goodness! Anybody'd know that, wouldn't they? But to think of him—poor old Mr. Guilfoyle—getting up in the middle of the night and—"

"That would be Wednesday night," said Palliser. "Did either of you hear anything? Anybody else sleep in the house?"

She shook her head. "He wouldn't hear of a nurse—the doctor said— but, to think—"

"Well, it seems a rather peculiar thing for him to do," said Grace in his gentle voice. "To go all that way from home to—instead of just quietly taking the overdose after he went to bed. And how did—"

"I thought about that," said Guilfoyle abstractedly. "Since you called —that other officer that is, and—we found it was uncle." He looked up at them earnestly. "You see, he wouldn't have wanted to make any—any unpleasantness in the house. It was one of the things he minded about getting old, having to depend on other people, being a—a care, you know. And he never would ask for help unless he had to—he was, well, considerate like that. You can say that, Alma."

"Oh, dear, that must have been it—yes, he was always so kind—it was just since his first stroke he'd got—a little difficult, and it fretted him so when he couldn't remember things—"

"Well," said Palliser, "but how did he get down here, Mr. Guilfoyle? There wasn't any money on him—"

"Oh, Mr. Wilfrid! Your *car!*" exclaimed Mrs. Swift agitatedly. "Do you—do you think—he *could?*"

"He might have," said Guilfoyle. "My car's missing from the garage at home. In the upset of finding uncle missing, I didn't discover it until—"

"Did he drive?" asked Grace.

"He hadn't in some time—about ten years—but he knew how, of course."

"Did he have access to your keys?"

"Well, I keep a spare set in the drawer of the chest in the front hall. He knew that. I—" Guilfoyle blinked. "I never dreamed he'd—well, how could we? But—"

"What's your car?"

"Oh, it's a Triumph—open sportster. I've got the license plate written down somewhere—"

"Thanks very much, sir, we'll have a look around," said Palliser. "You understand there'll have to be an autopsy."

"Oh, *dear!*" Mrs. Swift subsided into her handkerchief again. "That dear good man—"

A call to Traffic told them that the Triumph registered to Wilfrid Guilfoyle had been towed into the garage this morning after accumulating twenty-four hours' worth of overparking tickets. It had been parked on Park View Street, abutting one side of the park.

Palliser and Grace went down to look at it. It looked perfectly clean, and there was no suicide note left in the glove compartment or on the seat. They called the lab to come and give it a going over.

On the way back upstairs, Grace said, "You know, John—this fantastic thing about Tom. Even if they don't turn up any evidence, which they can't, there'd always be the—implication."

"I know," said Palliser heavily. "I saw that too. Damn it, Jase, the frame sounds just as fantastic—but what else could it be? They say everybody has a double, but coincidence I swallow just so far—a double for Tom showing up right here, out of the blue?"

"But a frame—" Grace was silent, brushing at his moustache. As the elevator started up he added, "But I really did not take to Wilfrid with his precious silk scarf."

"Neither did I, with bells on," said Palliser.

Mendoza had come back to the office while they were still downstairs, and asked if Hackett or Higgins had called in. "Nope," said Lake. Mendoza looked annoyed.

Five minutes later he was sitting at his desk neatly stacking the deck of cards and dealing himself a crooked poker hand when the phone buzzed at him. Lake said economically, "Tom." Mendoza picked up the outside phone.

"How're you doing, Tom?"

"Not so hot," said Landers. "I've been trying to think—what you asked me—I didn't get much sleep. But I can't come up with one damned thing. About a frame—that's got to be wild, Lieutenant."

"They were all so very damned—pat," said Mendoza. "Which is what put it in my mind. Sure, that's him—and coming out, excuse me, with the one salient point of your description which would be the first point anybody—" He had balanced the phone on his shoulder, was shuffling the deck: an honest shuffle this time, just to keep his hands busy on the cards. He always thought better with the cards in his hands.

"But it doesn't add," said Landers. "Look, Lieutenant. The only office I've been in, since getting into plainclothes, is Homicide. Not that that says anything, any department operates the same way. You said, a frame—somebody with a grudge on me. And, sometimes a very damn small motive will trigger a thing like that. And I guess you're right. But, how could any motive, damn what it might be, be aimed at me personally? Sure, we go doing the legwork alone, we've never got enough men —but on a charge, on questioning witnesses, there's always at least two of us on it. Isn't there?"

Mendoza's hands paused on the cards, ready to start dealing a hand. "*¡Demonios!*" he said to himself. "And of course you're quite right. Me, the veteran the damn press is so fond of calling me—missing the trees for the wood. But—"

"Even if, for God's sake," said Landers, "you want to hark back to my days riding a black-and-white, it was all in Seventy-seventh and Central divisions where there's two men to a car. If anybody's got a grudge on me from then, he's also got a grudge on twenty men I rode with as partners—or, in Homicide, any man I ever worked a case with, which is all of 'em."

"*¡Caramba!*" said Mendoza vexedly.

"It's no help, I just thought I'd pass it on. Do you still think—"

"I don't know what I think, Tom. Just that there's got to be an answer, a sane answer, somehow." Mendoza began to deal the honest, random hand of poker.

"Even if they can't find any evidence—just those damned eyewitness identifications—"

"There's an answer, damn it. I'll find it," said Mendoza; and stared at the hand he had dealt himself.

Random chance. Ace, king, queen, knave and ten of hearts. A royal flush.

Good omen? He said, "Don't fuss, *amigo*. Matt would tell you that force-for-good is always active on the side of virtuous men."

Landers laughed rather forlornly. "I don't know that I'm all that virtuous, Lieutenant."

6

It was nearly noon but Mendoza wasn't thinking about lunch. He had, again following in the footsteps of I.A., seen the pedigrees of Byron and Dunne. Byron's only relative was an uncle in Camarillo; Dunne had a family, over in Boyle Heights.

Mendoza went to see whoever was home. He found a slatternly middle-aged woman who told him at length it was just misery and grief, try to raise kids, no thanks from them you get, and if it wasn't the damn kids bringing the fuzz down on a respectable woman it was the old man. "Lyin' in there right now drunk again, and more fool me to stick around atall."

He found, a little more to the point, Rodney Dunne's kid brother Jerry, who already had a pedigree started at seventeen. Auto theft, shoplifting. Jerry answered questions sullenly. Yeah, he'd known a little about that job Rod was on, heisting shorts for a ring of some kind. Easy money. Rod never said no names, the guys running it, only that the top guy looked sorta mean.

"The top guy. He said there was more than one?"

"Yeah. I guess. First he thought it was just the one guy and then another one showed, like he was in it with the other one."

And just why he'd wasted time getting that— Mendoza swore, heading the Ferrari back for North Broadway. The vague thought had just crossed his mind, if it was a frame, had there been a second man in that racket at all? Really?

If Durfee and Rosso had known the ring was fingered—or was going to be fingered— Or if somebody else had fixed Horace to finger it— Conceivably the frame (given somebody with the grudge on Landers) had been a bonus: side money.

It was something to think about.

Landers hadn't started to think about lunch when a Sergeant Slaney of I.A. came to fetch him in for another bout of questioning. They rode all the way down to headquarters in silence, Landers in the back seat. By the time the car turned into the parking lot Landers was burning with resentment. The damn I.A. men seemed to have turned the phrase around: guilty until proved innocent.

Upstairs, Southey and Macklin wasted no time on the formalities. They sat him down in a chair, the inevitable uniformed man taking notes, and Southey held out his hand palm up. "Your key?" he asked conversationally.

Landers stared at the key on the square palm. It was a long, thin, flat key, silvered metal. "No," he said. "That looks like— No, it's not mine."

"That's funny," said Macklin. "It was on the shelf in the closet of your bedroom, Landers."

Landers said flatly, "That's impossible. I never saw it before. I don't—"

"You told us," said Southey, "that you don't rent a safe-deposit box."

"No, I don't. I don't need one, why would I? I don't have any valuables to—"

"Such as cash," said Macklin. "You say this isn't your key. Then what was it doing in your bedroom closet?"

"I never saw it before," said Landers, feeling confused. "I don't know how it could be. I don't—"

"On the closet shelf," said Southey. Landers looked from one to the other of them—Macklin big, broad-shouldered, dark, Southey slighter with a thin face and very shrewd blue eyes. "There wasn't anything else on the shelf except a Colt .22 revolver and some ammo for it. In a box."

"That's all I thought was on the shelf," said Landers. "I use that some-times when I go home—target practice, my father's got a gallery in the basem—"

"Your home's in Fresno?"

"Yes—no, I live here. My parents live in Fresno. I—"

"Your father's a veterinary surgeon with his own hospital there. And your sister, Mrs. Jean Kelvey, also lives in Fresno."

"Yes." God, if they'd been nosing around up there—upsetting the family—

"And you don't know anything about this key?"

"No, I don't. You ransacked the place," said Landers, "so you know —or ought to guess—that I don't use that shelf in the closet, damn it. I don't own a hat, and I've got nothing to put there, no reason to use it. I stashed the extra gun there because it was out of the way."

"You ever have a nickname?" asked Macklin.

"Not that I remember." And as he said that, a funny vague memory stabbed him: there had been a name, a funny pet name, his mother had used to say in fun when he was very small, but he couldn't remember what it was.

"Never been called Speedy?"

"No, for God's sake. Why would I be?"

"People pick up some funny nicknames sometimes, that's all. This key—"

"I never saw it before."

But he knew what that damned key was: the key to a safe-deposit box in a bank vault. Mendoza said, a frame: had it been carried that far, had that key been planted on him? What possible reason anyone could have—

When they finally told him he could go, he had to take a bus back to Hollywood. He collected the Corvair and went out to the nearest coffee shop for lunch.

Lieutenant Robert Southey felt academically sorry for Landers. Those positive identifications were not evidence, of course; it remained to be seen whether any solid evidence would show up. Macklin liked the key; Southey, thinking all round the thing, didn't much. It didn't strike him as a very likely place to keep a single key, not even on a chain: a key you might be using rather often. The key had been pushed way to the back of that shelf, where even a man as tall as Landers would need a kitchen stool or ladder to reach it.

Landers' Corvair wasn't in the apartment lot or in front. (He had finished paying for it a year ago, they knew now; he wasn't in the habit of running up bills, and at the moment he didn't owe anybody anything; and he hadn't been throwing any cash around.) Southey rang the bell of the first right front apartment where the manageress lived. This was one of the first apartments that had gone up on Fountain Avenue, twelve or fifteen years back, when the new modern ones began to be built. Scattered along here still were the old shabby garden-courts, the equally shabby four-family places dotting this long narrow street that snaked through Hollywood; but this was a newer Spanish-style building.

"Oh, it's you again," said Mrs. Burgess. They'd showed her the search warrant yesterday, and she didn't much like them.

"Just a few more questions," said Southey. "You told us that Landers has lived here for nearly ten years?"

"That's right."

"That must be nearly as long as this place has been up."

"It was built in nineteen fifty-seven," she said shortly. "I've been here since it opened."

"So you can tell me who rented that apartment before Landers."

"Well, what on earth you want to know that for—I s'pose I can look. I keep records." She didn't ask him in. He waited on the step until she came back and said, "I remember him now—Mr. Kenneth Lowry. He was here about two years. Just like Mr. Landers, nice quiet young man, no trouble, rent on the dot. He worked at a theater somewhere, he ran that projection machine, they call it. He left when he got married."

Southey thanked her and went back to his car. He met Captain Macklin for lunch at an unobtrusive bar and grill out on Third that specialized in steaks. Macklin was a teetotaller and already halfway through a T-bone; Southey ordered one to match and a Scotch-and-water first.

"Foley came in just after you left," said Macklin. "It's a model the Security-Pacific banks use for safe-deposit boxes. He left a copy with them, they'll try to trace it for us. Hell of a job."

"There may be a shortcut," said Southey. "All right, he's lived there ten years—we could see he doesn't use that shelf. Bachelor living alone —it was damn dusty. As if nobody'd been near it in weeks. That key could have been left there, by accident or loss, by another tenant years ago. I know you're supposed to turn 'em in when you give up the safe-deposit box. People don't always bother, and anybody can lose a key. Anyway, I got the name of the tenant before. He was a projectionist —may still be—if so, we can probably trace him through the union."

"I can hope you're right," said Macklin. "Landers has got a very clean record. I'd hate like hell to find out he's gone wrong. But how do we get round those damned positive identifications, Bob?"

Southey shook his head. "I've got no ideas on that," he said soberly.

There wasn't much Palliser and Grace could do about the Guilfoyle thing until they got the autopsy report and a lab report on the car. They had by default gone back to Luisa Fantini; both of them thinking about Landers but not mentioning that.

Since they hadn't been in on the Fantini thing at the beginning, after lunch they went back to the office and looked at the first reports Landers had written and the lab photographs of the corpse *in situ*.

One thing struck them both at once. "What was she doing in the theater like that?" asked Palliser. "She was supposed to meet Silverman at seven-thirty, and it looks as if she was all dressed up for that." The photographs of the sprawled slender body on the dusty thin old carpet of the theater aisle showed it wearing a black-lace-and-chiffon evening gown, low cut front and back. The gown had crumpled around her where she fell, pulled up to show twisted slim legs in sheer smoke-gray stockings, high-heeled black patent pumps. A little velvet clutch-bag lay near the body.

Palliser rummaged and came up with the list: contents of bag, comb, powder puff, costume gold compact containing such-and-thus brand of face powder, neutral-beige tone, one brand-name lipstick labeled True Persimmon, one ten-dollar bill. Jewelry from body, one costume pearl necklace, value about three bucks, one ditto pearl ring, one costume gold bracelet, one pair pearl stud earrings.

"She was all dressed for her date," said Palliser. "A seven-thirty date. By the autopsy she didn't go over that balcony until eight or later. And come to think, what brought her to the theater that night? From what we've heard, she'd walked off the job. She'd have got dressed in her room, wouldn't she?"

Grace brushed his moustache. "Funny, all right. But she was a good-looking girl, John. Probably attracted men like flies. Jealous boy-friend? You said Wagner sounded on the level. Sympathetic, as he said. She'd found the high-class john, good luck to her. But—"

"So he did. She hadn't been here very long, if she bought that suitcase in Bakersfield not more than a month back. Of course the jealous boy-friend could have followed her. Wagner said she told him, from somewhere around San José. There's no tracing her back on that—too vague."

"Um," said Grace. "But what was she doing in the theater that late? Nothing in Tom's reports on that?"

"Not a damn thing. Of course we've found out all this since. I think we go talk to Hernandez again."

They found Hernandez in the manager's office at the theater; it was just open, at two o'clock. Another girl than Annie Sanchez was in the ticket-booth, which they ought to have known; Annie had told them she had a regular job.

"Well, I thought it was a little funny myself," said Hernandez. "I told one of the policemen that—I think I did. I think one of the men that come first, in the car, but I couldn't swear— She hadn't come in the night before, see. To work. This Fantini girl. I asked Annie if she'd said anything to her, but she hadn't. So I figured she'd just walked off the job. These girls. I don't bother with another one—just the girls to sell tickets. It's not worth it. And then next morning, I come in like usual, place all dark, the house I mean, but the lights on in the lobby so's I can see my way, I spot something down there—so I look, and there she is. My God, dead. And all dressed up like for a party. I couldn't figure it. I don't figure it now."

They exchanged exasperated glances. The flustered Hernandez, babbling that to a uniformed man who had probably said, Save it for the detectives; and no detective hearing it at all.

And it looked all the funnier, of course.

They said they wanted to talk to the girl selling tickets. "So go ahead, so long as you don't stop her taking the money. She wouldn't know nothing, she never laid eyes on the Fantini girl, far's I know."

But she had. Her name was Nita Valdez and she was a very young seventeen, in her first job and conscientious. She was a nice girl, respectful to police officers, and she said to them in a soft, frightened voice, "I wondered if maybe I ought to tell. Mr. Hernandez or somebody. Because it was so terrible—poor, poor Luisa, an awful sad life she had, and to die like that—it was awful, wasn't it?"

"You knew her?" asked Palliser.

It all came out in her gaspy little voice. Luisa had come round to the theater one afternoon, just after she'd started to work there Nita guessed, and said who she was so Nita'd let her in. She said she'd left her compact in the ladies' room that time—but, they could read between the lines, Nita naively worshiping the glamorous Luisa, the credulous admirer, and Luisa would have basked in that. Enjoyed telling the dramatic tale and getting the sympathy, the admiration.

"It was just awful," said Nita. "She hadn't any mother or father, just this awful old uncle who beat her and made her work like a slave— and he didn't give her enough to eat either. What? Oh, it was a farm someplace over by El Centro, I seem to— But she was so brave, you know, she ran away from him, but she didn't have any money and —and she met this man and she thought he was going to give her a job, but it turned out he was"—Nita blushed—"you know, he wanted her to do bad things—and she ran away from him too, and finally she got here and—"

"That's interesting," said Palliser. Luisa had told fancy stories.

"And she was *nice* to me—she was just so nice, like a—like a princess, she was so beautiful—and I guess she saw I liked her—and I didn't think anything about it only then—" suddenly Nita started to cry. "I thought—maybe I ought to tell—"

"About what? Nobody's going to do anything to you, miss," said Grace softly. "She wanted to go in the theater daytimes? Why?"

"Oh—oh—oh!" sobbed Nita. "She said—she said the people where she had a room weren't honest—and there wasn't a good lock—and she was afraid they'd steal—and she had a—a—a hiding place inside the theater —oh—oh—oh—"

Palliser and Grace looked at each other. "For what, Nita?" asked Palliser. "What did she have to hide that was worth stealing?" The remnants of a wad of cash?

"I—don't—know," wailed Nita.

"Or where the hiding place was?"

She just sobbed, shaking her head.

"So, a little work to do," said Grace sadly. It was a good-sized theater. There was no point in turning the current customers out, starting a search now. Anybody might have stumbled on Luisa's cache in the five days since her death; or she might have cleaned out whatever was there. Or, of course, her killer might have taken it. But just in case, they would look. Tomorrow morning when the theater was closed.

"Rope the lab in on it," said Palliser tiredly. He didn't think Luisa Fantini was any great loss. But it was Homicide's business to work the cases, whoever the victims had been.

Hackett and Higgins had spent a completely profitless day looking for Al Durfee. It was, they agreed, adding insult to injury that wherever they went, both Auto Theft and I.A. had been before them. "Oh, more cops," the owner of Dick's pool hall on the corner up from that garage had said. "Tell you whatever I can, like I told the other cops, but I don't know much about him."

Durfee had come in there sometimes for lunch, to play a few games with anybody else in. Everybody had thought the garage was a legit business. Durfee seemed like a nice enough guy.

They tried all the likely places near the garage, where Durfee might have been known, and then they split up with the short list of Durfee's known pals listed in his pedigree. They met at Federico's at one-thirty for lunch and compared notes. They had only found two of the pals, both also with pedigrees, both on parole, and both of them claimed not to have laid eyes on Durfee in weeks.

"But I heard this and that," said Higgins, after a preliminary swallow of his drink. "Durfee's a gambler—"

"I heard the same thing," said Hackett. "And according to this guy, anything goes with him—the ponies, poker, whole works. And what's that worth in locating him, George? He's long gone, if you ask me. Either he was tipped off about the raid or lucky in not walking into it —he's on the run, and God knows which direction."

"By what we've heard," said Higgins, "that ring was operating for months. They must have been taking a nice piece of change out of it, Art. Maybe it was burning a hole in Durfee's pocket."

"Oh," said Hackett. "Vegas?"

Higgins shrugged. "Or Reno—Mexico City. Do no harm to ask 'em to take a look around for him. And what do you bet Auto Theft and I.A. both already have?"

"Well, just in case they haven't, we will. Meanwhile, I suppose we go on making bricks without straw, to convince Luis we're earning our keep."

"Is that one of his for-real hunches—the frame?"

"I don't think so. It's—the wrong shape for a frame," said Hackett. "Or—I don't know . . . He's going to get himself in trouble with I.A., if he goes on horning in like this."

"That won't worry him," said Higgins amusedly. "Point is, he's going to get all of us in trouble too."

"And I can't say that'd worry me," said Hackett, "if we turn up something to get Tom out of trouble."

After lunch they went, as the only place left to go, to the place on Second Street where Durfee had rented a room. Either Auto Theft or I.A. had put a seal on the room door; that couldn't be helped, but it was annoying. No knowing what had been in the room, leads to Durfee's other pals, whatever. At least they did know he wasn't driving his own car: the Ford registered to him had been in the garage. They talked to the woman who owned the house, Mrs. Blessing, a fat benevolent-eyed old lady who said, "Oh, you're policemen too. About poor Mr. Durfee. Seems like he was just born to trouble, that man."

That was one way to look at it. "When did you see him last, Mrs. Blessing?" asked Hackett.

"Why, let's see, it was sometime on Thursday afternoon. I was out at the side watering the roses when he come out with a suitcase, but I didn't pay much mind to that, just thought he was going off for the weekend like he's done before. Then when the other policemen came —my, my, the things that poor man gets led into!" She looked at Hackett. "You put me in mind of my boy, sir—he's a big one like you, takes after his dad, and nice blue eyes like yours too. That first policeman come askin' questions"—she sniffed—"I sort of took against him, some reason. Real abrupt-like he was—" That would be Van Allen all right, thought both Hackett and Higgins—"and I figured, he's so interested in poor Mr. Durfee, let him go look how he pleases. Putting a great big wax seal on that door! As if to say I'd go snooping in other folks' things! But you been real polite. Why don't you go see Mis' Durfee?"

"What? His wife?"

"Well, ex. But she's a nice lady, she feels sorry for him, getting in trouble all the time. It was when they split up and he moved in here, she come to me and says, now you just let me know, he gets to hittin' the bottle or in some fix, see? And I said I would. Once or twice, last year, he got behind on the rent and I called her and she come right around and paid me. You like to go see her?"

"Er—yes, ma'am, we would," said Higgins. "You didn't mention this to the other officers?"

"I did not. Let 'em find her theirselves, they want. But I'll tell you. She's right over on Grattan Street. Mrs. Alice May Durfee. I even got her phone number," said Mrs. Blessing, beaming at Hackett.

In the Barracuda, Higgins said, "Just like the moral maxims say, Art, politeness does pay off."

Hackett smiled fondly on the slip of paper with Alice May's address. "At least we've stolen a march on I.A."

Mendoza got home in the twilight, to the usual uproar just increased by Cedric in the back yard barking at the alder tree and the mockingbird madly using the remaining light to carry twigs nestward, breaking off to dive-bomb Cedric. Inside, the twins were bathed, powdered, and pajamaed, and descended on Daddy like twin hurricanes, clamoring to be read to.

"¡El Gato! ¡El Gato, Daddy! Read los cuentos 'bout El Gato and— and—and El Rinoceronte!" Johnny clutched his tie.

"¡No Rinoceronte! El elefante pequeño!" Terry yanked on his collar excitedly.

"*¡Bastante!*" said Mendoza. "Quiet! Let go of me, *monstruosos*, or I'll have no breath to read anything! *¡No me molesten!*"

Alison and Mrs. MacTaggart hastened to the rescue, tripping over cats. "Now Daddy's tired, let him have his dinner in peace—*¿comprenden?* Be good now—you can have *los cuentos* after a while—"

"And the man will be needing a drink to whet his appetite—" Mrs. MacTaggart hurried to the kitchen, hotly pursued by El Señor intent on his drink of rye.

"I thought you said something," said Mendoza to Alison over breaded veal chops, creamed potatoes, and Mrs. MacTaggart's special scones with her own jam, "about using one language or the other until they learn the difference."

"Don't nitpick," said Alison. "After the day we've had, with that damned mockingbird—and the twins watching his every move, and Cedric convinced he's a burglar and barking at him—*¡Dios!*" She smoothed her hair absently. After six months of letting it grow, she'd got impatient coping with it, and these days looked like the Alison he'd first known, the red hair in a short feathery cut, and very becoming too. She was, for once, wearing the two-carat solitaire diamond earrings he'd given her for her birthday last August. He reflected a little ruefully that it took some time for the people—like both of them—who'd grown up minus much money, to get used to having it. . . .

But with *los cuentos* duly read and the twins hopefully drifting to sleep, he paced the living room worrying about Landers. "It's a bastard," he said. "Damned if you do, damned if you don't. So I.A. doesn't come up with any evidence, there are still those damned identifications. All right, so pat, so glib, but—there."

"And what do they say?" asked Alison tartly, looking up from where she was rubbing El Señor's shamelessly exposed fat stomach. "You're not thinking simply enough, *amado.*"

"*¿Qué es esto?*"

"The trappings," said Alison. El Señor uttered a querulous comment; he liked his stomach massaged, the harder the better. "This Horace—he takes a glance at Landers, and there's some superficial resemblance to this crook, so Horace comes out with that, so they picked him up too. And comes the reaction, and at second glance Horace sees it isn't the crook, but it is a cop. And he's naturally pleased to get a cop in trouble, so he goes on saying it is too this crook."

"And I wish it was just so simple," said Mendoza. "The flaw in that reasoning, my love, is that there are also Dunne and Byron. And Horace was very much incommunicado until after they'd made the positive identification too."

"Oh," said Alison. "Oh. I didn't— I see what you mean."

Higgins went home and with an effort paid attention to his second-hand family, Bert Dwyer's kids. Laura had a new piano piece to play for him, and Stevie—now with the brace off and the limp almost gone —had just finished *The Man Without a Country* and was enthusiastic about it.

"Gee, that's an awfully great book, isn't it, George? You ever read it? I'm going to ask the teacher if I can do a report on it instead of that awful old thing she gave me."

"It's a good book, Steve."

"You know I just can't hardly wait, George," said Laura. "For the baby. It's a whole four and a half months more, Mother said. Before we'll *know*—I mean, if it's David George or Margaret Emily."

"I know, Laurie. It won't matter really."

And after dinner, with the kids settled down to homework, Mary's gray eyes on him. "You're fussing about this thing."

"Damn it," said Higgins, "can I help it? If they don't turn up any evidence—still the damn implication, on his record. Luis saying, a frame. I wonder. If Durfee didn't know they were fingered—and what the hell his ex-wife might give us, if we do find her—"

"Since a couple of months ago, George," said Mary tranquilly, "when you got away from those three toughs with nothing worse than a cold, I've been convinced that just lately Providence is being a little more alert about looking after the good guys. Something will turn up."

"And I hope to God you're right," said Higgins.

Hackett went home, to Angel concocting a new recipe, and four-year-old Mark imitating a jet plane, and his darling Sheila, these days navigating somewhat less like a candidate for A.A., and worried aloud about Landers. "Luis saying a frame—it doesn't smell that way to me. Like Palliser said, how could Horace come out so damn spontaneous— but what else could it be, for God's sake?"

Angel gave him a quick glance, her mountain-pool eyes sympathetic, and said briskly, "Don't bring the office home, Art. Have you weighed today?"

"I'm down three pounds," said Hackett gloomily.

"Well, maybe some benefit to worry," said Angel. "Don't pull pussy's tail, Mark! Now, if he's innocent, surely something'll turn up to say so—"

"And I hope to God you're right," said Hackett.

Phil had called Landers at six o'clock. "It's very forward of me," she said coolly, "but I think you need cheering up. I could bear to be taken to dinner."

He took her to the Frascati's out on Sunset. He told her about his latest session with I.A. "This damn key," he said. "I never *saw* it before. *I* don't know where it came from. Shelf in my closet, they said—of all the damned things, I never use it for anything, but don't I know how they read that! The damn key could have been there since I moved in, but they'll say, well, I've lived there ten years, how could I have missed it?"

She had made him drink a double Scotch. She looked at him consideringly there opposite her, at one of the outdoor tables on the terrace. She was slim and neat in a sleeveless blue cotton dress with a full skirt, little pearl earrings, high-heeled white sandals. She said, "You said you've got a sister. Any cousins?"

"What?" asked Landers, surprised. "Well, a couple. Why?"

"Nothing really," said Phil. "That key—you know, I think that Lieutenant of yours is all wrong. I don't think it's a frame at all, Tom."

"What? It sounds crazy, sure, but when the Lieutenant said—"

"Mmh," said Phil. "The great Mendoza. With his crystal ball. I've heard. Even geniuses have off days." She sipped her martini; the waiter came up and she said she'd have the herb omelette, please. Landers ordered a steak without consulting the menu. "My vacation starts tomorrow," said Phil.

"Oh. Yes. You—going anywhere?" asked Landers with an effort.

"I don't know. I think so," said Phil absently. "I rather think I am . . . I've just got a new car, did I tell you?"

7

LANDERS HAD CALLED MENDOZA overnight and told him about that damned key. "When I got home last night, Mrs. Burgess came over—the manageress. She said one of the same men who searched the place had come asking about the last tenant. But my God, that'd be ten years back, Lieutenant—how could—"

"And who was it?" asked Mendoza.

Landers told him. Looking at the scribbled note on his desk, on Saturday morning, Mendoza thought about those so-careful and thorough I.A. men. They had this key linked to Landers, and they were going to follow that up through every channel, checking back with the banks—the banks just as precise and a damned lot slower—and only after every avenue had been explored would they possibly start to think about another explanation.

Mendoza thought it might be helpful to take a little shortcut here.

This and that had turned up overnight: reports on his desk. A prostitute strangled over on Temple, probably by a customer. A knifing in a bar on Main. A new unidentified body on the Row. He shoved the reports aside and hauled out the five telephone directories. Various people liked to accuse him of having the tortuous mind: once in a while it went somewhere more directly.

In ten years, of course, Kenneth Lowry might have moved to New York, or died. It was just worth a first cast.

There were nine Kenneth Lowrys and fourteen K. Lowrys in the phone books. Mendoza started phoning. He had only the one question to ask; it wouldn't take long. Hackett looked in, and Higgins, and then Palliser; he waved them off impatiently.

He found the right Kenneth Lowry on the nineteenth try, at an address in Seal Beach. Rather he found Mrs. Lowry, who said yes where everybody else had said no. She also asked questions, but reluctantly told him where to locate Lowry—the Drury Art Studio in Long Beach.

Mendoza got his hat and told Rory Farrell, sitting in for Lake, that he probably wouldn't be back that morning.

On the way down on the freeway he wondered whether the Drury Art Studio produced real pornography or plain nudes. It turned out to be a prosaic project of conservationists which turned out nature studies and wild-life documentaries. Kenneth Lowry, in his mid-thirties, balding, with myopic eyes behind horn rims, was very surprised to see him.

Mendoza took shortcuts. "The apartment on Fountain Avenue. Before you were married, Mr. Lowry."

"That's a while back," said Lowry. "We've got three kids now. What about it?"

"Did you rent a safe-deposit box at a bank then?"

"What *is* all this about?" asked Lowry. "Police—well, it's beyond me why you're asking but I'll play. No, I didn't. I didn't have any reason to. But—"

"But?"

"Well, for God's sake, talk about ancient history," said Lowry. "I had a key to my father's box. We both had access to it, that is. Yes, then —when I lived there."

"Still have it?"

"No. Dad died just after Ruth and I were married."

"What happened to the key?"

"I—" Lowry stopped. "Well, I hadn't remembered that till just now. There was the usual red tape to go through—probate and so on—a seal on the box. I didn't keep it on, we weren't living in Hollywood. But when they asked for the keys back, I could only find Dad's."

"Yes," said Mendoza. "So you could. You kept it separate from your other keys. A key you didn't use often."

"I don't think I ever did use it—it was just a—a convenience, in case Dad was sick. Yes—"

"What did you keep on the closet shelf in that apartment, Mr. Lowry?"

"What?" Lowry looked confused. "Why—how should I remember?— oh, I guess I'd stash summer things there in winter, and—"

"Yes." Let I.A. get all the details. Eventually the bank would identify the key. Save I.A. some time and effort. "I'm sorry, Mr. Lowry, but I'll

86

have to ask you to come back to headquarters and make a statement."

"What? What in God's name is all this? Look, we're *busy,* we're just cutting this thing—"

"I'm very sorry," said Mendoza. "This is important too, Mr. Lowry. You're a good citizen—all we can do is apologize for asking you. But a man's career is—mmh—in danger."

"Oh, hell," said Lowry, shrugging. "Be kind of interesting to see the inside of that place up there, at that."

He didn't see much of it. Mendoza took him up to the Internal Affairs office and marched him in on Lieutenant Southey while the uniformed sergeant in the anteroom protested. "All right, Southey," he said briskly, "here's a shortcut for you. Mr. Kenneth Lowry, former tenant of Landers' apartment. That safe-deposit key you turned up probably belonged to his late father's safe-deposit box, and between you and the bank you can sort it out and identify it. Thus unlinking Landers with the key."

"Look here," said Southey angrily, "what do you think you're up to, Mendoza, interfering with this investigation? You've got no business—"

"Why, I'm just being neighborly and helping you boys out a little," said Mendoza.

"Damn it, you're interfering and it's a breach of regulations as you damn well know!" said Southey. Macklin came in the open door wearing a scowl; he had obviously heard that exchange.

"If you want to get included in this investigation we can oblige you, Mendoza. You know you're to keep strictly hands off on I.A. matters—"

"And you don't know me well enough, Macklin, to know that I don't sit and twiddle my thumbs when one of my men is in trouble!" said Mendoza hardly.

Southey opened his mouth, shut it, and said, "Sergeant."

"Sir."

"Would you—er—take the witness out, please. If you'll just wait a few minutes, Mr. Lowry— So, you're implying that we'd try to railroad a man, Mendoza? You're accusing us of bias and covering up evidence, by God? That charge we can take right to the top—and I've heard this and that about you stepping outside the rules too—" They were both glaring at him.

"Now let's stop calling names," said Mendoza with a thin smile. "I'm not accusing you of one damned thing. All I'm saying to you, and occasionally the fact needs underlining, is that you watchdogs are so damn chary of showing any bias, you tend to lean over backward to avoid bias toward the cops. May be salutary in a general way. You're not going to tell me that you were even thinking about former tenants until you'd bloodhounded that damn key back to the factory that made it. So I took a shortcut for you. There's Lowry to unlink Landers with the key—use him." He turned on his heel. "You needn't bother to say thanks."

"I wasn't planning to," said Southey. "And you can damn well keep your nose out of this from now on, Mendoza!"

"Just until I find you dragging your heels again, *amigo*," said Mendoza. He went down to his own office and called Landers to tell him the key had got itself explained away. "Where is everybody?" he asked Farrell.

"Palliser and Jase took everybody someplace to search a theater," said Farrell.

"*¿Cómo?* What the hell's all that about?" Mendoza hadn't seen Palliser's overnight report.

"I couldn't say," said Farrell comfortably. "They had a warrant, and I think they turned out some lab men too."

"*¿Y después?*" said Mendoza. "What next?" He started to read reports.

It wasn't, as theaters went, a large one, but as a place to be searched there was a lot of it: some thirty-five rows of seats on the main floor, divided into three sections by two aisles, and the main lobby, offices and cubbyholes and cupboards, the area behind the curtain and screen. And they hadn't any idea of what they were looking for.

"We know she told whoppers," said Grace at the outset. "This could be just another one, John. A hiding place in the theater—I ask you! What kind of valuables could she have had? All right, that little strip of bank paper, the thousand bucks cash. Luisa wasn't an idiot—she wouldn't hide that in here, instead of stashing it in her handbag to keep an eye on it. And no sign of cash, maybe she'd spent it all."

"It doesn't sound very likely, the rigmarole you said she gave Wagner and then this Nita," contributed Higgins dubiously.

"Then why did she want to get into the theater at odd times?" said Palliser. "I know it sounds silly, but this isn't such a hot part of town, George. If she had something valuable, she just might have found a handy cache for it somewhere here—and checked up on it now and then."

"So we go wild-goose hunting," said Piggott. "Well, it's more interesting than all the boring legwork on Katz. Where do we start?"

Nobody had any ideas on that. "Check the ladies' room first," suggested Palliser; but that proved to be fruitless. It was a bare tiled place, three toilet-cubicles, no possible hiding place. They fanned out into the theater, starting with the front row of seats.

"Wild goose you can say," said Grace to Palliser. "She wouldn't have dared leave anything—like what?—in the body of the theater. A public place, people coming in, fiddling around with the seats—"

But they looked. With the house lights all on, Hernandez watching interestedly. They looked everywhere there was to look, and turned up a lot of dust and nothing else. Hernandez told them the place was swept out twice a week. "People are pigs," he said. "The things the janitors find—" But there certainly weren't any valuables anywhere here now.

Palliser took time out for a cigarette and Higgins came to join him. "As if we needed any more exercise," he said.

"Wait a minute," said Palliser. "The balcony—she was up in the balcony. Late for her date."

"So you said."

"She was going to move into Silverman's motel—probably the next day. She hadn't packed her clothes yet. But she had apparently walked off this piddling job. Hadn't come to work. Had she come here to pick up what she'd cached away? Maybe followed by X? And anyway— if she did have a hiding place here, it seems more logical it might have been up in the balcony. I wouldn't think many customers here use it."

"You're right," said Hernandez promptly. "We don't get a full house often. Kids wanting to neck pick the last row of seats."

"So let's try the balcony." They moved the hunt up there, and went on training flashlights under seats, turning up seats, for some time without finding anything.

"She wouldn't have taken the risk," Grace was saying again, when one of the lab men stood up and his flashlight swung an arc around, up the wall, before he snapped it off.

"Hold it!" said Palliser sharply. "Hold—we're damn fools. The balcony was searched after she was found—"

"Well, we looked around," said Scarne, "sure. But—"

"That door's got to be left unlocked by law." Palliser went over to it: the door leading to the fire escape. He shoved the heavy bar down, the door opened, and sunlight streamed in. They looked, the lab men crowding up.

A little steel platform, and the stairs going down to the right. And lying on the platform just outside the door, a cardboard box: a shoe-box. Palliser bent and looked at it. "That won't take prints," said Scarne. Palliser bent to pick it up; it resisted, and he found that it had been bound with twine to the open steel strip of the landing. He cut the twine carefully, preserving the knot, and straightened. He took the box top off.

Something had been Scotch-taped to the bottom of the box, and violently pulled away. While he contemplated what was left, Higgins took the box top.

"McKellar's Fine Shoes, Lompoc, California. So both the tales she told were phony."

"Yes," said Palliser absently. A piece of Scotch tape, in the bottom of the box, still held a good-sized piece of brown paper—"Manila envelope," he said. He worked the tape loose.

Caught inside the wedge that had been a corner of an envelope were two more triangular bits of paper. One was tinged faintly pink and showed part of a rather fancy engraved border. The other was stiffer paper, heavy and thick, and bore an ornate letter T in black print.

They stared at the pieces. Higgins said, "You know something? I think that pink thing could be a corner torn off the pink slip on a car."

"But what the hell?" said Palliser blankly. "Luisa's valuables? And somebody killed her for them?"

"Whatever they were," said Grace.

Hackett had been feeling—he had cast around for a word and come up with one. Redundant, he thought. This Hatfield thing. It was there, it had to be looked at; and it was annoying in at least two ways. First, there was Landers; they were all a lot more concerned about Landers than anything else, though (and that was annoying too) they had to keep hands off and let I.A. do the investigating. Though if an idea occurred to Mendoza about where to look, that wasn't going to stop him. Second, the Hatfield thing was annoying because it was so meaningless —so shapeless.

Hackett had gone back over ground Sergeant Barth and the men at Wilcox Street had already covered, looking for something overlooked, and had found nothing. Luis had said, what about the Hatfields' grown-up children?—these days, kids getting into bad company, something like that—but that had been off the top of his mind. If he hadn't been thinking about Landers, he'd have known that Barth would have covered that.

Barth and his minions had checked everything they could check. The Hatfields' grown-up children were reliable, responsible young people. Catherine's fiancé, Owen Hartigan, had a clean record, would begin practice next year after finishing his internship. Both girls had good reputations; the Hatfields had never disapproved of any boyfriends; both girls were working in apparently congenial jobs among upright people. The boy, John, had a clean record too, and seemed to be a good student at his engineering course.

In a way, of course, thought Hackett, the dog next door made it into a kind of locked-room puzzle. What the evidence of the non-barking dog said (shades of Sherlock Holmes) was that whoever had battered Harriet to death was known to the dog: had visited that house next door before and been admitted freely. At least an acquaintance, if not a friend.

At which point, checking back on all the statements and reports Barth had turned over, Hackett had a sudden brain-wave. With his mind half on Landers, he had been idly thinking back over cases they had all worked together, and quite suddenly remembered that messy one—the child murders—and heard an echo of Mendoza's voice talking about the familiar strangers. Really strangers but not thought of as such by many children—or adults.

He sat back and lit a cigarette and thought. Laundry truck drivers. Bakery trucks. Fuller Brush men? Milkmen? In neighborhoods like that, the milkmen might come round to collect at civilized times of day—or did they? Anyway, someone like that was possible. A familiar figure, known, coming to the house on legitimate occasions, so the dog not barking.

Grasping at straws, he thought. He went out to the Barracuda in the lot, got on the freeway and drove up to Castaic Drive in Nichols Canyon.

Hatfield wasn't at home, presumably still busy over Hollywood Girl Cosmetics' new fall line. Everybody else was: the boy home for the weekend. Harriet had been buried at Forest Lawn nearly ten days ago.

"It isn't that we can blame you for—not finding out," said Catherine rather bleakly. She had ink on her fingers, a smear on her chin; she wore a smart blue smock over blue slacks. She wanted to be a designer, he remembered. A very pretty girl, in an unusual way: so dark, and oddly Slavic flat-planed cheeks. "I know it can't be—simple."

The other girl was dressed to go out; she excused herself in a thin voice when the doorbell chimed. A clean-cut young fellow appeared, shaking hands with John, respectful to Hackett; a terrible thing to happen, he said earnestly, Mrs. Hatfield such a nice person.

When they had left, John Hatfield said to Hackett, "Of course you don't get over a thing like this—just so soon." He shook his head. "You come home and—just without thinking—you expect Mother to be there like any time. And then you remember."

"Yes, I know," said Hackett. A nice family. And what with the dog next door, no shape to the sudden death striking here. "I've got just a few more questions, if you don't mind."

"Anything we can tell you—"

And except for one small thing, he got nothing at all. They didn't send things to a laundry: had a washer and dryer. Mother hadn't bought from a bakery truck, she went to a bakery down on Sunset. She didn't buy things at the door. (Habit, thought Hackett: they hadn't always had money, she'd got into the habit of thrift, and things bought at the door were usually a little more expensive.) She did buy eggs from a man who had his own chicken ranch in the valley, because they were so much better than the eggs at the market. But neither of them knew which day he usually came, once a week.

"But she'd been getting eggs from him for years," said Catherine. "You can't possibly think—"

"Well, I don't know, Miss Hatfield. We just like to check everything," said Hackett. He thought irrelevantly that it was odd how children turned out. Mark probably going to be as big as he was, and luckily Sheila had got Angel's eyes and—but you never knew. If that was a photograph of Harriet Hatfield on the table beside the door, she'd been a nice-looking woman, but only her youngest daughter resembled her at all. Catherine so dark, and the boy square-jawed, sandy-haired—possibly more like the father. "I'd just like to—do you know his name?"

"It's an ordinary name," she said. "Smith—Robertson—no, I don't. But I think Mrs. Brownlee takes eggs from him too, she'd know. But you can't possibly be thinking—"

Hackett thanked her and went down the curving front walk to the street: no sidewalks up here. There was a car in the Brownlees' driveway. He started up that walk, and as he stepped onto the porch the dog barked inside. It was a single amiable bark that said, "Stranger," that was all. Hackett felt unreasonably annoyed at the dog.

Mrs. Brownlee welcomed him in with surprise and pleasure. She was as amiable as the dog, an elderly overfed Dalmation, who came sniffing at Hackett's shoes wagging his tail. Mrs. Brownlee was a plump blonde with dangly bracelets and rather foolish china-blue eyes, and she told him eagerly that she'd just remembered something. "I don't suppose it could be anything to do with what happened to Mrs. Hatfield—of course that was a burglar or even worse, the terrible people running around these days—but that other officer said it was important to tell you everything we remembered, whether it seemed important or not—because after all you men are *trained* to see what is important—"

"Yes, Mrs. Brownlee. If you could just tell me, I think you buy eggs from—"

"But then I thought twice," she plowed on, "and, well, naturally I don't know anything about criminals, but everybody reads mysteries, don't they, and I should think those authors have to write about things the way they really are—*which* is why I was so glad to see you here again, in fact if you hadn't come I'd just about decided to call and tell you—not you personally I mean but the police—because what I thought was, you see, if it *was* a burglar murdered Mrs. Hatfield, which seems to be the only way it could have been, then it could be she was—the way they say it—*casing the job*." Mrs. Brownlee paused impressively.

"What?" said Hackett. "Who?"

"This woman. I just remembered it yesterday, and I'd thought it was queer at the time, but I never thought it might be important until I got to thinking about it again. Yesterday. And I thought—"

"What woman? If you'd just tell me what you remembered from the beginning," said Hackett patiently.

"Oh, certainly. I couldn't be sure of the day when I first saw her, but it was about three and a half weeks back. And of course I don't know if that was the first time she came. Or how often she did come. Only, I just remembered *that* too, that first time I saw her, Captain didn't bark, so she'd probably been there before. I saw her twice, that's all, and I thought it was a little funny then—Mrs. Hatfield had a woman come to clean, twice a month, but her I know, Mrs. Rawlins, I have her myself and besides she drives a Chevrolet—"

"Mrs. Brownlee, if you'd— What was funny about it?"

"Why, she was walking. She came up the street walking, and we're quite a way up the hill here. Practically everybody's got a car now, don't they? It looked queer, you see—because she wasn't from anywhere around the neighborhood, I'd have seen her before, and she was on foot, and she must have walked all the way up from the boulevard—or farther. There's a bus-stop there," said Mrs. Brownlee vaguely.

And what was this? "You saw her twice. She went to the Hatfields'?"

"Yes, that's right. The first time was about one o'clock, I was watching out for the mail. The next time—oh, it was about a week later, I think, or not quite so much, I was just going out to get my hair done, and I always have a three o'clock appointment so it'd have been about a quarter to. She just rang the bell and Mrs. Hatfield let her in."

"Could you describe her?"

"Oh, let's see now, I'm not very good at that—I didn't see her close to—but I'd guess she was about medium height, and thin—not very well dressed, I just got that *impression*—I couldn't say how old at all. She walked as if she was tired, but my goodness, anybody would be after climbing that hill, walking—"

Hackett regarded her with veiled exasperation. He couldn't imagine what this odd little jigsaw piece might add to the case; it was probably extraneous.

"And it just occurred to me—if it *was* a burglar—that she could have been an accomplice, *casing the joint,*" said Mrs. Brownlee, "and so I thought I'd better tell you—"

And so who was Jane Doe? An old acquaintance fallen on hard times, Harriet dispensing private charity? Or—

He thought he would lay the odd jigsaw piece before Luis. But first—

"So I asked Catherine and John," he said to Mendoza "and they didn't know who it could have been. So I went and asked Hatfield at his office and he didn't know either. So you can ruminate on it and produce a hunch."

"*Extraño,*" said Mendoza. "I scarcely think, Arturo, that Jane Doe was a burglar's moll casing the joint."

"Neither do I. But who was she?"

"I haven't the slightest idea," said Mendoza. "For a change, you can try your deductive powers on what the rest of the boys turned up on Luisa Fantini," and he told Hackett about that funny little find.

"A pink slip. Also *extraño,*" said Hackett.

"And I think," said Mendoza, making a steeple of his long hands on his desk, "having looked at it, a legal document of some kind. That kind of paper."

"Luisa's valuables," said Hackett, and yawned. "Have we got anywhere on the Katz thing?"

"*En ninguna parte.* I told Matt to shove it in Pending—he and Glasser were looking overworked. At least we've got Tom unlinked from one piece of trouble," and he told Hackett about that.

"And you needn't tell me what names the I.A. boys called you. Are you still thinking, a frame?"

"I don't know," said Mendoza abstractedly. "Damn it, it could be just as simple as Alison said—malicious mischief—get a cop in trouble, fun and games—if only Horace hadn't been incommunicado. . . ." He got up abruptly. "*¿Qué significa eso?*" he said to himself. "There was that time Tom had his pocket picked and the stupid jailers wouldn't believe he was a cop. Yes, making assurance doubly sure. I suppose you can find something to do, Arturo. I'm going down to the jail."

What Hackett found to do was more follow-up on yesterday's little break. He ran into Higgins doing the same thing.

They had heard about Alice May Durfee, the sympathetic ex-wife who had kept tabs on former hubby, from Mrs. Blessing, yesterday; but they hadn't found her yet. She rented a single apartment at the Grattan Street address, but none of the other tenants knew much about her or where she worked. The night men had gone over to try again at ten last night, with no luck.

She wasn't home now, at three-thirty on Saturday afternoon. Hackett and Higgins asked around the shops up the street on Olympic Boulevard, but no one seemed to know her. They were ready to head back for the office when a shabby maroon VW turned into the curb in front of the apartment house and a buxom hennaed female got out of it.

"Somehow," said Hackett, "that looks like Durfee, female version." He loped after her. "Mrs. Durfee?"

"Well, I don't use the name no more," she said, turning. "You're fuzz. I s'pose about Al." She sounded resigned.

After listening to her for three minutes, they took her back to the office in Higgins' car. Mendoza was just back; he was sitting at his desk looking annoyed, shuffling the cards. He left the hand he had dealt lying there while he listened to Alice May.

She was pushing fifty and looked it; she wasn't caring, and she was forthright, emphatic. "So Al's a wrong one," she said. "No reason I can see either, he's a good mechanic, get jobs easy. But he gets into things—no willpower, no guts. I don't know but what it's a little bit my fault, which is the reason I"—she shrugged—"looked after him some. You could put it. See, I work hard and I was lucky. I got my own beauty parlors—two of 'em now, I don't say the classiest like on Wilshire Boulevard, but I hire good operators and I do real good. I finished paying off the mortgage on my first place now, own it clear, so it's all profit, except for taxes. I do all right. I guess Al sort of felt it, me doin' better than him. I knew he'd been in trouble when we got married, but I thought I could straighten him out. More fool me." She got a cigarette out of her capacious shabby handbag and Hackett lit it for her. "Thanks. Real gentlemen you fellows are. He was O.K. the first couple years, got a good job all steady. Then, boom, he went—in with the old racket again. I gave him another chance. He's a nice guy, Al. And I guess it was lucky we never had any kids. But the next time, I see it's no go. You get me."

"We get you," said Mendoza. "So you divorced him."

She sighed. Her blunt, not unhandsome middle-aged face was incongruous under the perfectly arranged hennaed hair. "Yeah, I did. I didn't like to. And I felt sorry for him. He's an unlucky guy. A gambler for one thing, he's got a dollar in his jeans he'll bet on anything—and an unlucky gambler."

"Most are," said Mendoza, and Hackett muttered under his breath, present company excepted.

"Yeah, that's so. Anyway, I guess you're interested in this latest thing. I never knew the ins and outs, what kind of racket it was, until Al come to see me—"

"When?"

"Four o'clock last Thursday afternoon," she said promptly. "I suspected he was in a racket of some kind again, most likely something to do with cars. He's good with cars. He come barging into my place— this is my first place, on Hoover, I work there, the other shop's on Beverly and I got a good girl to manage it, right on her toes and better be too, I'm particular about service—he come barging in asking for travel money. I took him in the back—he'd never dared come in my shop before, so I knew it was serious." She smoked fast, and bit her orange lipstick. "If you're goin' to say, helping a fugitive, I can't help it. He told me these guys had been running a racket out of his garage and he didn't know it. He said the fuzz had come down, just then, and he had to go on the run."

"Did you believe him, Mrs. Durfee?"

"My name's Beauchamp," she said. "My maiden name. It sounds classier, don't it? It's spelled with a *p* and all but you say it like Beecham . . . I don't s'pose I did, no. But I—was married to him, Al's the only guy ever— I know he's no good, but—the poor guy just can't seem to help himself, you know? He said he'd got cleaned out in a poker game down in Gardena the week before. That, I believed."

"So?" asked Mendoza.

"So I gave him two hundred bucks. You'll think I'm a damn fool. Maybe I am."

"Few people," said Mendoza, "haven't been damn fools at this and that time. He was—mmh—taken by surprise, the fuzz descending on the garage?"

She stared at him. "That he sure was, mister. He said he hadn't known about the racket, that was just a tale for me—damn fool Alice May, always the right side o' the law, *which* he knew. But he was caught with—well, he didn't have any notion the fuzz even suspected anything, way he talked. He'd been out shooting some pool, came back to find the place lousy with cops. So he ran. To me."

"For travel money. He couldn't even get his car—it was in the garage," said Mendoza. "Where was he heading and how?"

She shrugged again and stabbed out her cigarette. "Would I know? Just away. And you want him. You're never going to make him any different, but— If you want a guess, he headed for Vegas or Reno. He said something about a guy named Ricky, they didn't pick up either. Maybe they went together. Maybe this Ricky had a car, I don't know."

"Oh, really," said Mendoza. He looked at Hackett. "I think, Art, that you and George will now escort Mrs.—er—Miss Beauchamp up to Internal Affairs, also informing Captain Van Allen, and explain that we—mmh—just stumbled across her by pure coincidence—"

"I can hear what Macklin will say," said Hackett.

". . . and that we're just being cooperative. Knowing they'll be interested."

"I think it might be more to the point," said Higgins, "to explain that Art's bonny blue eyes prompted Mrs. Blessing to open up to him. She took a notion against Van Allen."

"For valid reasons," said Mendoza, looking amused. "*¡Vamos!* And my compliments to Lieutenant Southey."

8

"DAMN IT," said Mendoza, pacing the living-room floor, "the hell of it is, no guarantee there wasn't a mix-up at the jail. And jailers have tongues too. Added to which, there's a grapevine in jail just as much as at headquarters, and anybody could have known that Horace—" He caught Sheba as she leaped for him from the back of the sectional; she scrambled up on his shoulder.

"You're not making much sense," said Alison, who was trying to read while Bast washed Nefertite on her lap.

"But, damn it, even so," said Mendoza, "even granted that—all Dunne and Byron could have known was that Horace had fingered a cop. Not which cop."

"Which you said before. *¡Bastante!*" said Alison as Bast and Nefertite started to wrestle. "Enough is enough—off! But, Luis—"

"*¡Demonios!*" said Mendoza. "What I would give for an hour alone with Dunne and Byron!"

"Those I.A. men are detectives too."

"Granted. And I do not imply, if you were wondering, that being little gentlemen they wouldn't press that pair too hard. But they're leaning over backward not to show bias—they always do. And at the moment they're concentrating on Tom. Which I know is just the wrong place. Hell! If I could have a free hand to question those two, lean hard enough on them, with Art and George to make faces and scare them— By God, could they have been primed? They both came out with that so damned—spontaneous."

"*Amado,* you know he's completely innocent, so—"

"Pure hearts protected by guardian angels?" Mendoza laughed. "It doesn't always work out that way, *cara.* I wish to God it did. And I might as well stop wishing, on those two—don't I know it, nobody but I.A. allowed to talk to them."

"You'll wear out the carpet. Worrying never helps."

"That's a constructive piece of advice," said Mendoza irritably. The shaggy dog Cedric came in licking his hairy chops, and Sheba left Mendoza in one bound to invite him to play; Mendoza laughed. "All right, we just hold good thoughts on it . . . but I wish to God I had a hunch on it. . . ."

No hunches came to him. As he opened the window before getting into bed, there came a faint sleepy voice from the alder tree. *Yankee Doodle came to . . . AWK.* "My God," said Mendoza, "we're stuck with that bird for life. I told you so."

Sunday is just a day to cops. Theoretically Mendoza was supposed to have it off; in practice he seldom did. He was in his office, immaculate in silver-gray dacron, as usual at eight-fifteen. Everybody was in except Piggott, who would show up after church.

Glasser went out on the strangled prostitute. Hackett was still mulling over the funny thing Mrs. Brownlee had given them on the Hatfield case. Higgins was discussing Luisa Fantini with Grace and Palliser; Palliser had teletyped an inquiry up to Lompoc yesterday afternoon. That wasn't a very big town; if she had come from there somebody on the force should know it.

"I'll tell you what did come to me," said Hackett. "Mrs. Brownlee said she only saw this woman twice, coming to the Hatfield house. And the dog didn't bark. So I think she must have come a couple more times, and been let in. But what for, and who was she?"

"I don't see any possible way to find out," said Mendoza, "when the family didn't know. . . . And you know, Art, the fact that Al Durfee was taken by surprise by—mmh—Van Allen's raiders argues that his employers were too. Rosso and—er—Speedy. So it wasn't a fingered job."

"So?"

"So, I said, if it's a frame on Tom, maybe a side bonus as part of putting Rosso and Company out of business. But it doesn't look that way."

"But Horace could still have made the mistake, and then stuck to it out of—malice, the way you said. Only Dunne and—" Hackett sighed and lit a cigarette.

"I talked to Tom last night," said Higgins. "He's feeling low. The trouble is, it's all so up in the air I don't see how I.A. can get anything to say a definite yes or no."

"Sword of Damocles," said Mendoza absently. Sergeant Lake came in and said they had a new body—woman out on Severance Street. Hackett and Higgins went out on that resignedly. One of the many annoyances of police work is that, not only being never finished, it necessarily leads men from one piece of routine to another before any conclusion is reached.

Grace was just saying, "That thousand dollars Luisa had—or probably had—did she swipe it somewhere? And whatever else she had in that—" when a uniformed man came into the anteroom and handed Lake two manila envelopes.

"Autopsy and lab reports," said Lake, handing them over. "Guilfoyle, who's that?"

Palliser snatched one and handed the other to Grace. "Hold your breath, Jase. Did we have a joint hunch?" He opened the report.

"I'm the one has hunches around here," said Mendoza. "What kind was this?"

"On Wilson Guilfoyle, poor old fellow going senile—only according to his doctor not as senile as some people may have wanted to— Oh, boy," said Palliser. "It was a hunch all right, Jase. Listen to this. 'Immediate cause of death'—well, it was the overdose of digitalis tablets all right—'indication is that tablets were dissolved in black coffee, to the approximate amount of two cups, two to four hours prior to death. Deceased had eaten a meal consisting of beef, potatoes, green vegetable and vanilla pudding approximately five hours prior to death—'"

"And the lab gives us something too," said Grace pleasedly. "Some dandy latent prints on the steering wheel, gearshift and light-knob of that Triumph. Not the corpse's."

"My God, is he that much of a fool?" said Palliser.

"What are you talking about? I'm supposed to know what goes on around here," complained Mendoza.

"You'll find the gist of it in my reports," said Palliser. "Come on, Jase!"

The house in Beverly Hills was an old one, a big one, on a generous plot of ground, in an older section of town. It was defiantly old-fashioned, with a porch round the front and one side, and dormer windows, and a pane of colored glass in the wide front door. As they climbed the steep wooden steps, Palliser said, "But why the hell did he take him all the way downtown?"

"Maybe that will emerge," said Grace.

The housekeeper, Mrs. Swift, opened the door to them, again in her decent black long-sleeved dress. "Oh!" she said. "Oh, Mr. Wilfrid was going to call you—to find out when we can have the—poor Mr. Guilfoyle's— Oh, come in." She forgot to shut the door, staring at them.

"Is Mr. Guilfoyle Junior here?"

"Why, yes, sir, he is. He's just having breakfast—if you'll come—"

"Just a moment, Mrs. Swift," said Palliser. "You've been here a long time, you said. I wonder if you know anything about the money. Old Mr. Guilfoyle's money—and what money young Mr. Guilfoyle has."

She stared at him. "Why, yes, sir. There isn't any secret about that. Mr. Wilfrid was Mr. Guilfoyle's only relative since his brother passed on some years back. Mr. Wilfrid's father. He didn't have near as much as Mr. Guilfoyle, but it's in trust for Mr. Wilfrid, Mr. Guilfoyle managed it. And of course I suppose his own money will come to Mr. Wilfrid."

"I see," said Palliser. "That's very interesting. And did Mr. Guilfoyle and Mr. Wilfrid get along well together? Any quarrels, differences of opinion?"

"Well—" she stared at him, looking a little confused. "Of course Mr. Wilfrid's young, and my Mr. Guilfoyle was old—set in his ways you might say. He'd go on at Mr. Wilfrid about—well, he didn't like some of his friends, and—things like that, but it was just—" She looked from one to the other of them, surprised and disturbed.

"Very natural, in fact," said Grace.

"Well, yes, I guess so."

"So we'll see Mr. Wilfrid," said Palliser.

He was in the old-fashioned breakfast-room, drinking coffee and smoking a cigarette, and he was again very natty in pale fawn slacks, a blue-green shadow-plaid sports jacket with a faintly green-tinged silk scarf tucked negligently between the lapels. He looked up. "Mr. Wilfrid, it's the police officers, they—"

"You really are pretty stupid, aren't you, Guilfoyle?" said Palliser. "And you must think we're pretty stupid. You might at least have taken the trouble to put his fingerprints on the steering wheel and a few other relevant places."

"What?" Guilfoyle went muddy gray, staring at them.

"It all looked so easy," said Palliser, "didn't it? I don't know your routine here, but we'll be finding out." He turned on Mrs. Swift. "I think Mr. Guilfoyle took his coffee after dinner in the library, didn't he? And you cleared away the meal and probably didn't see him again before he went to bed?"

She put a hand to her mouth. "Why, yes, sir, that's—he hated so to be helped, and he could get to bed by himself—"

"In fact, not at all senile," said Grace, "if he did forget things now and then. So you brought him his coffee, Mr. Guilfoyle, only you'd gone upstairs first and got his digitalis tablets and dissolved them in it—"

Guilfoyle sprang up so suddenly he knocked over the chair. *"What is this?* You can't—you damn nigger, walking in and saying—"

"If we're calling names there might be a couple for you too," said Palliser. "Deliberately killing an old man who trusted you. I don't—"

"Killing?" said Mrs. Swift in a muted shriek. *"No—"*

"I don't know whether your prints are on record anywhere, but with the evidence we have we'll be taking them, you know, and I rather think they'll check out as identical with the prints on the wheel—and other places—in your Triumph. As the last one to drive it. What about it, Mr. Guilfoyle?"

"No, I—we told you how he— He'd threatened to kill himself, I told you how—"

"Unfortunately you seem to be the only witness to that," said Palliser. "And it was easy—up to a point. He passed out rather soon after drinking the coffee. This is a big house, and you weren't afraid that Mrs. Swift would hear anything and wonder. I think—considering all that shrubbery shielding the drive from the street out there—you ran your car down the drive and just carried him out to it. He wasn't a very big, heavy man. If he had any wallet on him, you took that, tucked the medicine bottle in his pocket, and off you drove downtown to Mac-Arthur Park. It'd be a deserted area by ten o'clock—no trouble getting him in, leaving him on the bench. Why, Mr. Guilfoyle?"

"Why—why— There *wasn't* any reason for me to— No, you're all wrong, I—"

"Oh, my God!" said Alma Swift, and sank into a chair and started to cry.

"I didn't mean why about that," said Palliser. "We can guess why you did it. He disapproved of some of your habits, and it was possible—seeing that he was far from senile—that he wouldn't have left you any money at all." Guilfoyle had both hands over his eyes; he rocked to and fro. "But why MacArthur Park? Why ferry your uncle's body all the way down there?"

"I think maybe I can answer that," said an interested voice behind them. Palliser and Grace turned. A big man in a rumpled gray suit, a man with a face as craggy as Higgins', came a few steps into the room. "Captain Ward, local force. You're LAPD? That's very interesting, what you were saying. Excuse me—the door was open, I just walked in. I've got a warrant for Mr. Guilfoyle's arrest."

Palliser introduced himself and Grace. "Charge?"

"Narco possession." Guilfoyle suddenly made a wild dash past them for the hall, and Ward collected him handily. "Just for that, I think we use the cuffs."

"Listen, you can't do this to—"

"You'll be surprised," said Ward, and added, "Somebody ought to do something for the lady." They looked, and Alma Swift had fainted ungracefully onto the floor. Grace went to find the kitchen and a glass of water.

They sorted it out at the Beverly Hills police station, with Wilfrid in a temporary detention cell. "I guess that's half your story," said Ward. "We know Wilfrid—and the old man knew that too, because last year we got Wilfrid on five counts of D.-and-D. within about six months. He's been running with a few unsavory characters on our beat—"

"Fags?"

Ward shrugged. "Your guess as good as mine. He knows some. Most of them he knows are users. We can have a guess he is too, if not all the way hooked or he wouldn't still be going for the liquor. But knowing Wilfrid, and the old man, we'd have taken a long hard second look at the situation if the old man had just been found dead in bed. Which I suppose Wilfrid guessed. He must have figured you boys downtown are maybe too busy to take much notice of one more corpse."

Grace grinned. "That's possible."

"I'll say this," added Ward. "The old man was a character, not much education but a smart fellow in his time, and I happen to know that a couple of months ago he hired a private shamus to watch Wilfrid. It'd be kind of poetic justice, wouldn't it, if he'd already made a new will and cut Wilfrid out? You think you've got him solid on a murder first?"

"It looks pretty good," said Palliser. "If the prints in the car are his, and I'd take a bet."

"That's the hell of a thing," said Ward. "Just get him out of the way, hell-bent for the money. I'll keep my fingers crossed that the old boy had cut him out."

They took Wilfrid back to L.A. headquarters and tried to get something out of him, after reading him the piece about his rights; but he just turned sullen and silent. After a while they took him down to the jail and came back to apply for the warrant. They would get a search-warrant for the house; there might be some evidence there, and they'd requisition Beverly Hills' records on him. The D.A. didn't, by law, have to show motive in a murder charge, but it was always nice to be able to show one.

By that time it was twelve-thirty and they went up to Federico's for lunch.

Southey phoned Mendoza at noon. "Thank you so much for Mrs. Durfee," he said icily.

"Quite welcome. We thought you'd find her interesting."

"We did. To a point. I'd be more interested in hearing about the strange coincidence which caused Homicide to stumble across her."

"It's a long story," said Mendoza.

"I'll bet," said Southey. "How many times do I have to tell you—"

"Don't bore me," said Mendoza. "You careful boys trying not to show bias—the wrong direction. Such gentlemen. I'll lay any amount you name you haven't done any serious leaning on those witnesses yet, to get the slightest glimmer as to whether they're lying—"

"We are not mind-readers up here."

"Oh, for God's sake! Any five-year man in uniform can make the educated guess about that!"

"We all have opinions," said Southey, his tone dropping in temperature by the word. "You will keep your paws off this business, I told you."

"Yes, I know you did," said Mendoza. "I remember it distinctly. I presume you've got fliers out on Durfee to Vegas and Reno."

"You can presume what you damn well like," said Southey, and hung up.

They all landed there at the same time—Hackett, Higgins, Piggott, Palliser and Grace—and took the big table at the front of the room near the hearth. They were starting to hear about Guilfoyle when Mendoza came in, sweeping off the black Homburg, and joined them.

"I.A. is annoyed at us," he said.

"Do we looked surprised?" said Hackett. "At least John and Jase have tied up something." They heard about that one while everybody but Piggott had pre-luncheon drinks.

"Nothing in about Luisa," said Higgins, finishing his. "That's almost as—as shapeless a thing as Hatfield. I think we'll end up with both of them in Pending."

"The devil," said Piggott, "is getting around these days. Making mischief. That Katz girl—not a pretty girl, or very smart maybe, but she didn't deserve to die like that. And there wasn't a smell. It could have been anybody we looked at out of Records—"

"Or somebody making mischief for the first time," said Grace.

"And there is now the new one," said Hackett, settling his bulk more comfortably; the chair creaked. "Oh—the low-calorie plate," as the waiter came up. "Damn it, I was up two pounds this morning . . . Mrs. Anna Shaw. Over on Severance Street—one side of an old duplex. It looks like—run of the mill. Par for the course. She was sixty-nine, a widow, lived there with her daughter, Wanda Shaw. Middle-aged spinster. Daughter was out at a movie last night, came home about eleven, took it for granted Mama was asleep—she usually went to bed about nine-thirty. Didn't find out anything had happened until this morning. Mama dead in bed, place ransacked, back door forced. Not much gone, but there wouldn't have been much there. Daughter's a salesclerk at Bullock's. What's gone, a portable TV, old lady's watch and a little jewelry, odds and ends."

Mendoza grimaced. "*¿Qué más?* The little lout's doing what comes naturally. Mama made a little noise, he biffed her one?"

"Looks like. Daughter was all broken up. If only she'd looked when she came home—but she didn't want to disturb the old lady, just put on enough lights to get to her own room." Higgins put out his cigarette with a sigh. "Not that it'd have made any difference—the interns said the old lady probably died right then. Knocked over the head with our old friend the blunt instrument."

"So, another little job just like the one you stashed in Pending yesterday, Matt. Back to Records for the M.O.'s," said Hackett. "But on Harriet Hatfield, Luis—"

"Don't mention the name to me. There is just nowhere to go on that. As for locating your Jane Doe—" Mendoza shrugged and sat up as the waiter approached. "Food. I am starving."

Hackett looked balefully at his low-calorie plate. "But I'd like to know the answer on Harriet. What the hell could have been behind that?"

"I'm a little more interested, Arturo, in what the hell could be behind this fantastic thing about Tom."

They kicked that around awhile, but they'd said all there was to say about it. They were all feeling frustrated at the necessity to keep hands off and let I.A. handle it. Even with Mendoza not giving a damn about what I.A. said, there wasn't anywhere for them to go looking, to show it was a frame, a mistake, about Landers.

And to put the thing on the lowest basis, it left Homicide a man short.

When Palliser and Grace came into the anteroom at one-thirty, Lake handed Palliser a teletype.

"From Lompoc," said Palliser. "They don't know her either. Luisa."

"But that box—well, of course, I suppose she could have picked up a shoe-box anywhere. Or could she? Could she, John? That's not a very big town. What would be the odds on some outsider buying a pair of shoes in Lompoc and then landing in L.A. close enough to Luisa that she came by the box? Somehow? It wasn't a very old box."

"The box for her valuables. In the hiding place in the theater," said Palliser. "That was a damn silly sort of thing to do, Jase, you know? Just out on that fire escape. She was a scatterbrained sort of female. On the make, but—doing what comes naturally."

"And she hadn't been at that rooming house very long, but you know, we never tried to catch any of the other roomers home to ask questions. She also seems," said Grace, "to have been a talkative female. She just might have let something out to one of the other roomers. Something other than her whoppers."

"And it is Sunday," said Palliser. "Let's go and ask."

At the house on Boyd Street, they talked to the owner, Mrs. Baumgartner, again, but she didn't know anything about Luisa. She rented out six rooms in the house, and four of the roomers were in.

Mr. James Turner, recovering from a hangover, told them frankly he'd have liked to make time with that girl, but she'd turned up her nose at him. He'd seen her a dozen times maybe the while she lived here—Mr. Turner was out of work and not too concerned about hunting a new job while he was getting unemployment compensation. He said airily, what the hell, some girls fell for his line and some didn't, there it was.

Mrs. McSorley, fat, sixtyish and woolly-minded, said she hadn't noticed the girl much. Not to notice.

Miss Lila Weaver, prim and mousy and notably nervous of anything male, told them in a near-whisper that she'd never spoken to that girl, a real fast sort of girl she'd looked, and it only showed how right she'd been, that girl ending up murdered.

Miss Cora Foley, however, told them something they hadn't known. It didn't lead them anywhere and in fact it was no use to them at all in finding out what had happened to Luisa Fantini, but it was interesting.

Miss Foley was a hard-eyed blonde about thirty, a waitress in a cheap restaurant on Main, and she told them in a brassy voice that she didn't poke her nose into other people's business. "Do unto others," she said, waving her hands in the air to dry the garnet nail-polish she'd been applying when they knocked at her door. "I only noticed that girl a coupla times, she had the room right acrost, you know. I'm out a lot, and it wasn't no skin off my nose what she was doin' or not. I don't think she had a job, though, not right off, she'd come 'n' go different times, when I was here to notice. What the hell? But one thing I can tell you."

"What's that, Miss Foley?" asked Grace.

"Well, the one time I seen her close, I was just goin' out one night —she hadn't been here long then, I don't think, maybe a week. I had the evening shift and I was just leavin' like I say, when she come out of the room acrost. And the only reason I noticed, hall's usually dark but my door was still open, so there was some light. All dressed up she was, nice clothes she had, classy, and she never said nothin' to me or I to her, but she had her hand on the door to shut it and I saw the ring she had on. I useta go with a guy worked in a jewelry store, I know a little bit. And that ring, it had a pretty good-sized di'mond in it."

"Is that so?" said Palliser. "Can you describe it?"

"Oh, I only saw it a second, and off she goes. It was a gold ring— yellow gold, I mean—and it had just the one di'mond. Maybe almost a carat di'mond."

"Well!" said Palliser. He looked at Grace. Something new, but what did it tell them?

Landers was feeling terrible. A big part of it was being at such loose ends. One thing you could say about police work, you might not get rich at it and you might be in a good deal more danger of sudden death or injury, but it kept you busy. For ten years he had been very busy at it, in uniform in a car, and then at Homicide, at least eight hours a day and sometimes a good deal longer; and it felt very queer to get up in the morning, shave and dress and then have no place to go.

Suspended from duty. They had a queer and nasty flavor, those words. Him. Who'd always just tried to be a good cop on this top force.

The daytime programs on TV were impossible, except for a couple of old movies he'd picked up. You couldn't read all the time.

I.A. hadn't come near him again; he kept expecting the polite summons, the same silent contemptuous sergeant to ferry him downtown, the questions.

The damn watchdogs in I.A. just taking it for granted, for God's sake, that those damn small-time pros were telling the truth? *That's the one, that's him, the one they call Speedy.*

Like asking when you stopped beating your wife.

At least the Lieutenant had cleared up that damn business about the key.

Aware that probably I.A. would go nosing around up in Fresno, he had finally called his father last night. He'd said it was just some interdepartmental red tape, not to worry. But of course he'd had to talk to his mother too, and he'd never been very good at covering up things from her.

At noon on Sunday, he called Phil's number; maybe she'd take pity on him and go out to dinner again. But the phone rang emptily in his ear until at last he hung up.

Phil, on vacation, going off somewhere to enjoy herself. Well, what did Tom Landers matter to her? Nothing, obviously.

Feeling very sorry for himself, Landers switched on the TV and watched a so-called comedy hour without smiling once.

Phil O'Neill had a new car; she'd only had it for three months. It was a little bright-green Gremlin, and she had set out in it bright and early on Sunday morning with a bag in the storage-space under the flip-up rear window. She took the freeway through what used to be Dark Canyon Pass over to the San Fernando Valley, and made time up to the Ridge Route. By noon she was pulling into Bakersfield.

It was a good deal warmer in these inland valleys, even in June; she was glad she had put on the new green silk-jersey sheath, low-necked and sleeveless. She had lunch there, and got on the road again. There wasn't much traffic, even on Sunday, and she made good time.

At three-forty-five she came into the outskirts of Fresno. She stopped at a drugstore and consulted the phone book. Elm Street. But just out of curiosity she drove down Union Boulevard first, past a rambling gray stucco building. *Fresno Small Animal Clinic, Dr. John Landers.*

The house on Elm Street was big and old-fashioned, two-storied, set back from the street with two tall maple trees in the front yard. And there were people sitting on the front porch, and a car in the drive.

Phil had not, however, spent four years as a junior officer in the LAPD without losing any shyness she'd ever had. She parked the Gremlin at the curb, got out and marched up the front walk. The four people on the porch watched her coming with surprised interest, the sun bright on her blonde curls.

"Dr. Landers?"

"That's me." The tall lanky gray-haired man rose from the wicker rocking chair. "Can I do something for you, miss?"

Phil divided a brisk friendly smile among them, as interested as they were if she didn't show it, and for a different reason. Dr. Landers was square-faced, more fair than dark complexion, hazel eyes. Mrs. Landers —a faint look of Tom there; she had a long face, dark eyes, crisp short hair still almost black; and she had kept a good slim figure, and her wide mouth smiled at Phil. The girl would be Jean; more definitely like Tom, a thin face, lively dark eyes, humorous mouth. The fair young man would be her husband, Bob Kelvey; Phil thought Tom had said he had his own TV repair shop.

"I'm a friend of Tom's," she said. "I'm on the force too. I came—"

They were hospitable, friendly. They urged her to sit down, and Mrs. Landers brought her a glass of lemonade. They asked questions, interested in her. "Tom called just last night," said his father. "Never mentioned you though, Miss O'Neill. I couldn't make head or tail of what he said—about somebody coming to ask questions. I wondered—"

"And did somebody?" asked Phil.

Mrs. Landers leaned forward. "Tom never could fool me. I thought then he was in some kind of trouble. Do you know anything about—"

"Yes," said Phil soberly. "He's in quite a lot of trouble, Mrs. Landers. Anybody who knows Tom knows it's a lot of silly nonsense, but—well, you see, I.A.—Internal Affairs—has to investigate it. His Lieutenant is furious—"

"Mendoza," said Dr. Landers. A little brief smile touched his steady eyes. "We've heard a lot about that one. What's this all about, Miss O'Neill? Are you from this Internal Affairs department?"

"Heavens, no. I'm just a lowly clerk down in Records. And—a friend of Tom's. You see—"

"That I do see," nodded Mrs. Landers. "And I must say his taste is improving. That last girl he was dating—well, she sounded to me like a little cat—which I shouldn't say, I like cats personally."

Phil laughed. "Well—I've only been at headquarters about two months, we don't really— But anybody who knows Tom—"

"And I refuse," said Jean Kelvey in a warm voice, "to call you Miss O'Neill. I've got a little hunch we'll all be knowing each other better."

Phil explained apologetically about the impossible Phillipa Rosemary. "But that isn't why I came—" and she flushed a little at Jean's mischievous smile. "You see—I'll explain how it happened, and you'll see what a—well, a mess it is, for Tom—these three pros identifying him as one of the operators of a hot-car ring—which is ridiculous but you can see—"

"What damn nonsense is this?" exploded Dr. Landers.

"Tom?" said Kelvey incredulously. "Why, that's the most damn silly—"

"I never heard anything so silly in my life!" said Jean.

"Well, of course it is. But three witnesses—you can see I.A. has to look—"

"Of all the *damned* ridiculous things—"

"Jean," said her mother in a troubled voice.

"Well, it is! Tom? Why, a thing like that—they could discharge him from the force—and you all know he never had any other ambition all his— You don't mean anybody *believes* that?" Jean stared at Phil.

"Well, it has to be looked into, you can see. You know we are the top police force in the world—"

"Which is exactly the reason Tom wanted—"

"Now let's calm down here," said Dr. Landers, "and listen to what Phil has to say. I think she's got something to say."

"You may think it's fairly harebrained," said Phil. "I said his Lieutenant is furious, and saying it's a frame, and I suppose the other men at Homicide are too. But from all I've gathered, the witnesses are—call it simple. Ordinary pro louts. So I just had the thought that maybe the whole thing was—simple."

"How do you mean?" asked Jean.

"Just," said Phil, "a mistake. Only Tom isn't just ordinary-looking. So I came up here to ask you to—tell me something. Show me something."

"Anything we can do, if it's to help Tom. What things?" asked Mrs. Landers curiously.

Phil smiled at her. "Some family history," she said, "and—if you have any—some family photographic albums."

9

About eleven-forty Sunday night the two men riding the black-and-white on that beat, Ferris and Hart, got sent over to an apartment house on Westlake Avenue, to an assault of some kind. They found a weeping young woman and a little crowd of aroused tenants on the first floor, most of them in nightclothes. They were greeted with relief and excitement.

"—Tried to *assault* me!" sobbed the young woman. "Just came up and grabbed me and if it hadn't been for Mr. Gebhart hearing me scream—"

"You all right, miss?" asked Ferris. Her dress was torn but otherwise she didn't look much harmed. "You don't want an ambulance? Well, can we have your name?"

"No, I'm all right—I got away from him and he just ran. I'm Mary Ridgeway, I live in four-oh-five. But I can tell you who he was—and Mr. Gebhart saw him too—"

"That I did," confirmed Mr. Gebhart mushily. "'Scuse me—get my teeth—"

"Say," said Hart suddenly to Ferris, "there was that homicide right here last week, you remember? Another assault, only the girl didn't get away. Maybe the Homicide dicks'll be interested in this, Bob."

And Mary Ridgeway shrieked, "*Carolyn Katz!* Oh! Do you think *he* could've been the *one?* And he just grabbed me— Oh, Mr. Gebhart!"

"There, poor girl," said the manager, less accordion-like with teeth in, "it's all over now."

So on Monday morning they found that report waiting from the night shift, a note signed by Sergeant Galeano. "Identified attacker William Royce, resident apartment building. No record with us. Not at apartment up to 3 A.M. Employed Weideman Interiors Wilshire Boulevard."

"Well, if that isn't a funny one," said Glasser, looking at it. "Just after we throw Katz in Pending, maybe a break. I suppose we go see Royce, if we can find him."

And Piggott said, "An interior decorator, committing an assault? But we'd better check him out, Henry."

Mendoza was already in; as Piggott and Glasser went out past the open door of his office, he was saying to Hackett, "All I'm saying, Arturo, is that we haven't done one damned thing on this Rosso, and I'd lay no bets that I.A. is—yet—and I think—"

"—Get us all suspended from duty," said Hackett exasperatedly.

Weideman Interiors had a whole new building to itself in a smart block of Wilshire; inside the double plate-glass front door, it presented a rather kaleidoscopic panorama of styles, displayed in chopped-off sections. Victorian blood-red plush gave abrupt way past a gilt railing to Moorish tile and Spanish wrought-iron furniture; next to that a chintzy Down East bedroom abutted on an ultramodern bar in zebra stripes. Neither Piggott nor Glasser was impressed.

A brisk dark woman in black harlequin glasses and a tight black sheath covering an emaciated frame came up to them. "I can help the gentlemen?" she asked.

"You can," said Glasser. "Mr. William Royce. We understand he works here. Is he here now?"

"Oh, Mr. Royce. He is here, but I'm afraid he's not at all well. A migraine headache. Mr. Burns has him resting in his office—"

"Isn't that a shame," said Piggott. "I'm afraid we'll have to disturb him." They produced their badges simultaneously, and the emaciated lady let out an ungracious squawk.

"Police? Mr. Royce? Whatever do the police—"

"Which way?" asked Glasser.

William Royce, when they found him sitting on a black plastic couch in the manager's office, looked at them wanly. "I knew she'd tell," he said. "I knew—but I—but I—there wasn't anything to do but come to work—as usual—and all I wanted—" He was a weedy little man with no chin, weak pale eyes, and a thin reedy voice. He looked about twenty-five and actually was thirty-two, they were to find. He described himself as a commercial artist, but didn't look very successful at that either: employed here as a mere copier of other men's work. They told him they wanted to talk to him, and he said he supposed so, and they read him the piece about all his rights and took him back to headquarters. Higgins was just coming out of the sergeants' office and Royce shied back at sight of him as if he'd been a sidewinder.

"Like a witness?" asked Higgins genially.

"It won't do any harm," said Glasser.

But as it turned out, Royce came apart almost as soon as they asked him anything. He admitted he'd been the one last night, but it wasn't an assault, he said drearily. He looked at them standing over him in an interrogation room and he said, "Girls don't like me. They laugh at me. I never had a girl-friend. They laugh at—how I look. But I'm like anybody else inside! I—I'd—just like—to have—a—girl-friend. And Mary's a pretty girl—she came home just ahead of me last night and—and—and all I wanted to do was kiss her! She might've let me—that was all I wanted—but she screamed as if—as if—"

"Royce," said Piggott tiredly (it took all a man's time to keep up with the machinations of the devil), "what about that other girl, last week—Carolyn Katz? Did you want to kiss her too?"

Royce looked down at the floor. He said, "She—she wasn't so pretty. You see, I thought—I thought maybe she was like me. Like me. Wanting —friends, and not—not having any. Because she wasn't pretty, or so awful young I—thought—maybe she wouldn't mind. If I—kissed her. When she didn't expect it. That was all I ever—meant to do."

"And so what happened when you tried?" asked Glasser very gently.

Royce looked up at them slowly. "She," he said, "she—it was all—you don't understand how I felt. Her. Not pretty, but—if she was—a girl— who'd let me—I thought— But she screamed and screamed and screamed —as if I was a monster of some kind—her, a girl like that! As if I was a *monster*—and all I wanted—just like any human being, but she—" He pounded one fist on his knee, just once. "I—wanted to hurt her, then. Acting as if I was a *monster*, when all—"

That was about all the coherence they got out of him; it was probably enough. They got it down and he signed it in silence and Piggott took him down to the jail while Glasser started the machinery on the warrant.

It was funny, clearing up the Katz thing so unexpectedly.

"Have any guesses as to whether they'll stash him away in Atascadero?" asked Piggott.

"Probably they will," said Higgins. "If he isn't legally nuts he's heading that way. And at that you can feel a little sorry for him. At least that's one off our minds."

Hackett had argued with Mendoza to no avail. "I.A. will be hunting this Rosso eventually, Luis—and Auto Theft. Very much their job, and they're cops too. Who knows whether they got any prints in that garage as leads?—we've got nothing. All I say—"

"And all I say is," said Mendoza, "you came across a couple in Records who just might be this boy. Follow them up as you can and see what you get."

"Listen," said Hackett, "I know we're all concerned about this, but there are other things on hand—and I.A.—we never got a statement from the Shaw woman yesterday, she was too upset, and sometime today we've got—and there's Luisa—"

But he didn't get to any of their legitimate business until after lunch. Meanwhile he did a lot of tiresome legwork looking for both those possible Rossos out of L.A. Records. Both addresses noted were out of date, and neither was in a neighborhood where the residents particularly liked cops; he did some asking around and got nowhere at all. But he was feeling better about Landers' thing now: the I.A. men weren't fools, and those witnesses had admitted they'd only seen this Speedy a few times. When the principals were hauled in, Durfee and this Rosso, they'd probably give it away that the identification was a mistake. The idea of a frame was too fantastic; it had to be a simple mistake—some superficial resemblance. It was damn tough on Landers but sooner or later it would get cleared up.

And he was a good deal more curious, if possible, about what was behind the Hatfield murder than about the death of Mrs. Anna Shaw —the violent lout breaking in for the little loot—but there was always the paper work to do. After lunch he and Higgins went over to the duplex on Severance Street, and found Wanda Shaw listlessly straightening up the shabby living room, and asked her to come in to make a statement.

"Anything you say," she said. "It seems kind of heartless to be dusting and all, as if nothing had happened, but Mother liked things kept tidy." She was a thin drab of a woman in her forties, with a drooping mouth and defeated-looking tired eyes. She came along silently, in Higgins' car, and upstairs in the sergeants' office they gave her the chair beside Hackett's desk, brought her a cup of coffee. "You're very kind," she said. "What do I have to do?"

"Just tell us again, for the record, what happened when you came home on Saturday night, Miss Shaw—and then about Sunday morning."

"Oh. All over again? Well, you heard how it was. I don't go out nights hardly at all, Mother doesn't—didn't like being left alone. Besides, working all day— Well, I fixed her supper and had mine and did the dishes before I went out, to the movie, and she had her radio right beside the bed—she had her supper in bed, she hadn't been feeling so good that couple of days—poor Mother, she had a lot of troubles—"

"Yes, just take it easy, Miss Shaw."

"Oh!" she said. "If I'd only looked, when I came home! If I'd only just put on the kitchen light, I'd have seen into the living room and noticed the television gone—but I never thought—it was late—" She bowed her head in her hands.

Hackett was taking notes, and looked up at movement to find Mendoza in the doorway regarding Wanda Shaw interestedly. He drifted in and sat down behind her at Palliser's desk.

"I never *thought* to!" she said piteously. "I knew Mother'd be asleep —and any little noise disturbed her, I didn't want to—and I was going right to bed myself, had to be up at six to fix her breakfast, she liked— So I just put on the light in the service porch a second to see my way into the hall—I know the house, of course, we've lived there thirty-two years—and I went into my room and shut the door and—and went to bed, and all the time poor dear Mother was lying there—lying there—" She sobbed into her hands. Higgins pushed the coffee cup toward her.

"Just take it easy now. Drink your coffee. You heard the doctor say she was already— There wasn't anything you could have done if you had—"

"No, but it's just the *idea*. She was always so afraid of burglars, you see. I was always careful to keep the doors locked—but that back door, I guess it isn't a very good lock, old one—I never thought— Oh, when I think of poor Mother there—"

They took her through the relevant details, times and items missing from the house, and Higgins started to type up a statement. He had it ready for her to sign in twenty minutes, and they called a squad car to take her home. "You're very kind," she said again vaguely. "I suppose you'll do your best to find out whoever it was that—"

"Yes, of course we will, Miss Shaw." The uniformed man ushered her out, and Hackett cocked his sandy head at Mendoza, who was sitting back in Palliser's desk chair with his hands clasped across his flat middle. "And did you find that piece of routine business edifying, *compadre?*"

Mendoza stood up and automatically straightened his tie, yanked down his cuffs. *"Piense antes de hablar,"* he said pensively. "I'm always telling Alison that marriage has ruined my well-known talent for women, but maybe I've retained a little at that."

"Meaning what?"

"I'm not too sure myself. And—"

"Don't ask me about Rosso. If either of the possibles in our Records is the one Auto Theft's after, he's long gone. And as if you need reminding, we've got legitimate work to do."

"I saw Henry's report on that whore. Nobody's going to find that X."

"No loss," said Higgins. "But there's still the Fantini girl—"

"And Hatfield. If you want to know, Harriet Hatfield is haunting me," said Hackett. "I've been round and round on it, and there's just nothing. Nothing to say who or why. Such a damned ordinary woman, Luis. And you stand there maundering about Rosso."

"I wasn't."

"You were going to. Look, when and if they do catch up to him and Durfee, it'll all come unraveled. It's got to. They—"

"I'd like to hear the reasoning on that, Arturo."

"Well, for one thing they'll have no remote idea that these underlings have fingered a cop. I.A. being so good at keeping secrets, the press hasn't heard even a rumor. When Durfee and Rosso are picked up, you know how I.A.'ll handle it—the casual intimation that they've also got the number two man, and the casual lineup—and Durfee and Rosso both saying, Hah, that ain't either him, any of those guys."

"Which had also occurred to me," said Higgins.

"Oh, yes?" said Mendoza. "Hey presto, the other three made a little mistake, and I.A. and Auto Theft swallow that right off. It doesn't cross their minds that Durfee and Rosso could be protecting an accomplice—"

"But—"

"The press," said Mendoza, "doesn't have a monopoly on news, *amigos.* There's a grapevine everywhere. A lot of our pigeons offer the info to the other side too—and you both know as well as I how uncanny the grapevine can be. Would you take an oath that it's absolutely impossible—wherever Durfee and Rosso are—that they could have got the word about Horace and the other two fingering the cop? By mistake or whatever? So, would it work quite that way? If I.A. or Van Allen picks up Durfee and Rosso? Wouldn't they be pleased to tell I.A., Sure, that's the guy, that's Speedy."

Hackett massaged his jaw. "You're not exactly a Pollyanna today, Luis. I hadn't seen it quite that way, but—"

"But there's no *evidence*," said Higgins. "Nothing but these identifications—and from who, for God's sake? Three louts of—"

"So they couldn't ask for a resignation on that," said Mendoza. "You know how it'd be. Forever on his record. Sword of Damocles."

"Goddamn it," said Higgins. "There ought to be something we can do—"

The sergeant attached to Internal Affairs who had been sent up to Fresno was a fifteen-year man named Kurt Wengel. He was by nature a thorough and careful man, and he had been briefed by Lieutenant Southey in all the details.

He got to Fresno on Saturday morning, and found a middle-class motel and checked in. In what was left of the morning he located the principal of the high school and politely bullied him into opening the school records to him. Sometimes things showed up in school records that pointed out latent tendencies.

He didn't find much of interest in Tom Landers' school records. Beyond the fact that Landers had been better in English than math, and had taken two years of Latin with a C average, there wasn't anything in the records to offer Wengel a lead.

He tried the school library next—school wouldn't be out for two weeks and the library was open to students studying for final exams—and found, after search, a class yearbook of the year Landers graduated from high school.

Looking through that, he found a couple of items which interested him very much. When he left the high school, mindful of I.A.'s eternal rule of discretion—a rule kept mostly out of fear of harming the innocent—he drove five miles up the road and found a pay phone to call Lieutenant Southey.

"I haven't had a chance to work at that angle yet, Lieutenant, the athletic record. Tomorrow. But another little thing showed. In this yearbook, there was a kid named Rosso in the same class."

"You don't tell me," said Southey.

"That's right. Charles Vincent Rosso. Same age as Landers. The phone book lists a John Rosso, only one, so maybe it's the same family.

It could be that this Rosso had been a school pal, and showed up again down there on the bent, and inveigled Landers into—"

"That could be," said Southey. "We should know about Rosso, with any luck, sometime. We picked up quite a lot of prints in that garage. Durfee's, and some unknown—the Feds are checking to see if they know them."

Wengel drove back to Fresno. He'd only been transferred to I.A. five years ago, after a stint in Bunco, and he often thought that of all dirty jobs a cop came in for, I.A. offered the dirtiest—checking up on fellow cops. It wasn't very often at all that they found a man on this force guilty of anything really bad; but this thing right now was shaping in Wengel's mind as the worst that could happen—a cop going wrong with a vengeance, on the bent with pro crooks.

He had copied down some names from that yearbook, other boys in that graduating class; but he went to look up what he could find about Rosso first. The John Rosso listed in the phone book was a farmer outside of town, living in a prosperous-looking big white farmhouse. He looked askance at Wengel's representation of himself as checking up for Social Security records (all the governmental bureaucrats' snooping provided cops with some useful cover these days) and told him his boy Charles was working in the city. San Francisco. He was with a brokerage there. Oh, yes? thought Wengel. Story for the home folks?

He found some of the other names from his list in town, starting out again on Sunday. Some of those boys had left town. One had a garage, another an insurance business, another was a teacher in an elementary school. And so on. He went on looking, asking questions; he explained his questions by introducing himself as a statistician working on a thesis, and as cover he asked questions about other people in that class too. He was a patient, thorough man, and by Monday afternoon he had built up a picture of Tom Landers, that many years ago, which wasn't going to be much help to Lieutenant Southey.

It didn't tell them anything they hadn't known, for Landers' record was just fine up to now. So was his record all this time ago. None of it said that Landers hadn't recently been tempted by the easy money to joining this Rosso—old school pal or not—in the hot-car operation.

It didn't even say much that Landers and Rosso had known each other casually. It wouldn't have been a very big graduating class—not like a high school in the city—and most of them would have known each other. But late Monday morning he came across, in his dogged search, Mr. Fred Barker, who was the pharmacist-owner of a drugstore on the main street and had also been in that graduating class.

Mr. Barker was a tubby little man already losing his hair, a garrulous little man pleased to reminisce at the drop of a casual question. Wengel told him his sister was thinking of taking a teaching job at the high school, and led him on from there. . . . "Landers?" said Barker at last. "Oh, sure, know the whole family. Been here a long time, they have. Doc Landers, he's got the biggest animal hospital in the county, good man I guess. . . . Yessir, I was at school with their boy—lessee, Bob, Bill, Tom, that's him. His sister's a mighty pretty girl but she never had any time for me—married to Bob Kelvey she is, no kids yet—" And Wengel eventually got him around to school athletics. Somebody had told him, he said, that this Landers had been pretty good at— "Oh, sure," said Barker. "Me, I was never any good at athletics any kind, no coordination—but Landers was a track man—kind of a star that last year in high when we beat Dinuba at the meet—"

"Oh," said Wengel. "Track man, was he? Pretty fast?"

"Oh, I guess so, kind of a star you could say—"

"Did he ever get called Speedy?"

"Why, uh, I don't know but what he might have," said Barker. "Like I say—"

Wengel was a good man, but in keeping with his plodding habits of routine, he completely lacked any imagination; and it never crossed his mind that Barker was just a fat little man who had been an unhappy fat boy in high school, with few friends, and hadn't really known Landers at all, then or now. As far as Wengel was concerned, Barker was an important witness. He noted down that conversation to relay to Southey.

He got round to the family on Monday afternoon. They seemed like nice people, he thought sadly. Dr. Landers was at his hospital, but Mrs. Landers was home, a nice-looking woman, and Mrs. Jean Kelvey was there too, and a friend of hers, a pert-looking little blonde who hadn't much to say, but then she probably didn't know much about Landers if she was just the sister's friend and lived here.

He had by then looked up the family. What he was looking for, of course, was the possibility that there had recently arisen some pressing need for money. He didn't find anything like that; both the elder Landerses seemed to be in good health, the hospital was doing well, Bob Kelvey's store was doing well. There'd be somebody looking down in

L.A. to see whether Landers had contracted any gambling debts or other expenses which might have led him into temptation.

It was very likely that Landers had told the family something about this; Wengel didn't use much camouflage with them. He didn't expect anything useful from the family, and he didn't get anything; if the family knew anything about Landers getting led into a crooked setup, they wouldn't be telling Sergeant Wengel.

The women had evidently been doing some housecleaning or furniture-arranging. Funny, when they must be worried about Landers.

He went away to find a phone and report to Lieutenant Southey.

"Well!" said Jean. "I suppose that's your man from I.A."

"With a vengeance," said Phil.

"Exactly like a Prussian officer," said Jean indignantly. "Asking if Tom likes to gamble! Asking—"

"Well, they have to investigate," said Phil.

"Now, Jean," said Mrs. Landers. "If Phil's idea is at least halfway sensible, we'd better get on with it. The last time I saw your Grandmother Borman's album was when I put it away after Father died— I think it's in that old sewing chest in the attic. I seem to recall it's behind that old wardrobe trunk, and why I didn't give that to the salvage years ago I'll never know—"

They climbed stairs, Jean still muttering about Wengel, "—All he needs are the dueling scars—honestly, asking *such* questions about—"

Phil smiled at their backs. Nice people. They wouldn't hear of her going to a motel, there being plenty of space in the old house. And they had both been interested in the idea, which was so simple—as Phil said apologetically—that it was really no good going to the men in I.A. with it. Or even the Homicide men. Even if they'd pay any attention to a junior officer from Records. "I should think not," Mrs. Landers had said at once. "Men do tend to have such complicated minds, don't they? But I don't think it's harebrained at all, Phil—it won't do any harm to *look*, anyway."

Phil had spent last evening with Jean going over some rather modern family albums. Dr. and Mrs. Landers' wedding pictures, Jean and Tom as babies, children. A few older photographs. "That's my aunt Mary Brennan—Father's sister—and that's Father of course—and John's grandfather—"

They were all nice-looking people, but Phil frowned over the photographs. The only one that gave her pause was Mrs. Landers' aunt, Mary Brennan. There was just a look—

And later on, over a second album, "That's my grandfather, Robert Pitkin. A fine-looking man, wasn't he? We always said Tom— Oh!" Mrs. Landers stared at Phil excitedly. "He *does,* doesn't he?"

"He does indeed," said Phil. Robert Pitkin, photographed in sepia probably around the turn of the century, was a tall thin serious-looking young man in very proper Victorian dress, including a flowered silk waistcoat. He had a long droopy moustache, a long jaw, rather prominent cheekbones and brooding dark eyes.

"I never noticed it so clearly before," Jean had said, crowding close to peer at the print. "But I haven't looked at these for ages—Tom's the spitting image of him, Mother, if he had a handlebar moustache! That's extraordinary—"

"Not at all," said Mrs. Landers. "My own grandfather, after all. He married a Margaret Gorman, they had two children— And of course—"

"Yes," said Phil. "And that's your side of the family. Tom looks a little like you, you know."

"More like me—boys generally do take after mothers," nodded Mrs. Landers. "I used to call him—my goodness, I hadn't thought of that in years! But you think it might be on my side. Well, there are a couple of old albums, some tintypes in them—as old as that—I cleared out when Father died. I think they'd be up in the attic."

And now they were up in the attic of the old house, looking. The sewing chest came to light behind the coffinlike wardrobe trunk, and the albums were unearthed.

"They're filthy—don't you touch them till we take them down and wipe them off. These are both Father's, I'm pretty sure—but older things in them too. I should have said, of course Grandfather was a Junior. Robert Pitkin Junior, and his father—"

"Mother!" said Jean suddenly at the foot of the attic stairs. "*Great-aunt Serafina!*"

"Good heavens, yes! I expect she'd have the Lord knows what, back to Year One. But Jean, you know how she is. If she took a notion to Phil—but she'd just as likely not, you know how she feels about modern girls, and—"

"Great-aunt Serafina?" asked Phil.

"My dear Lord, that woman!" said Mrs. Landers in exasperation. "I expect most families have a difficult relation or two, but she is a cross to bear. She's eighty-five this year, and I swear I think she's too mean

121

to die. She won't go to a rest-home—heaven knows she's got the money, her father left her half the land and she owns four farms outside of town—and she won't admit she's not fit to live alone. All we can do is check on her every day or so to see she hasn't fallen and broken something— Well! You see, that's just what I was about to tell you—my great-grandfather, Robert Pitkin Senior, went beyond the pale, as I gather his family felt, and actually married an Italian Catholic girl—"

"Oh," said Phil. "That's where the dark eyes come from."

"I suppose so. A Maria Arnoldo, she was. We don't know anything about her family, I expect they cut her off entirely, and it'd have been back about eighteen-seventy-five anyway. I—"

"Where?" asked Phil interestedly.

"Oh, San Francisco. Great-grandfather came out from Iowa as a young man, for the gold I expect, but he ended up keeping a hotel in San Francisco. Anyway, they had three children—my grandfather Robert Junior, and Serafina, and Jean Ellen, but she died as a child. It was the reason—and I hadn't thought of it in years," said Mrs. Landers, "Tom being so dark as a baby, I used to call him my little *bambino,* just in fun. . . . Serafina never married, and she's been a cross to us for forty years—of course with all that farm income she never had to *do* anything—creeping about that musty old house over on Maple Street getting smaller and meaner and more suspicious of everybody by the day. *But*—"

"*And* more Italian," said Jean. "Her mother filled her with all these notions, you see, noble Italian heritage, and she goes on and on—"

"But," said Mrs. Landers, "if it's photographs of that side of the family we're after, she's got scads of old relics tucked away, I couldn't guess what all—things of her mother's and—"

"But you know how she is!" said Jean. "She's never let *us* see half of what she's got stashed away—"

"Well, we'd better figure out a way," said Phil. Suddenly Great-aunt Serafina's hoarded relics became a castle of treasures to be stormed by hook or crook.

The autopsy report on Anna Shaw came up at five-thirty Monday afternoon. For once Dr. Bainbridge, not besieged by too many corpses, had got on the ball. He sent a note along with the report, and Hackett handed it to Higgins with raised brows.

"Suggest you see lab report in re furniture at scene," Bainbridge had scrawled. "Bedside table right of bed. Also photographs of scene *in situ.*

Deceased's nightgown saturated with tea. Trust you or lab dusted teapot."

"Now what the hell?" said Higgins. They hadn't got a lab report on Shaw yet; those boys took their time. And this was such an open-and-shut thing—he and Hackett had already had a desultory look through Records for the similar M.O.'s, if you could say there was much M.O. about this.

Hackett got on the phone to the lab and was patient. "At least you can give us something, Duke. What about the bedside table on the right? . . . Oh? . . . Well, what does that say? Nothing. All right, all right, send up a report sometime. . . . There was blood on it," he relayed to Higgins.

"The bedside table? And so what?"

"Bainbridge," said Hackett, "is occasionally cryptic. Like our Luis."

After dinner, with the kids settled down to homework, Brucie the Scottie asleep at Mary's feet as she did some mending, Higgins said suddenly, looking up from the new *American Rifleman*, "You know, it's frightening. That's what I've been thinking—it just came to me, Mary. About Tom. A thing just—out of the blue. If a thing like that can happen to Tom, it could happen to any of us. It scares me, all of a sudden."

Mary's gray eyes smiled at him. "Not you, George. Nobody could ever mistake you for anybody else."

He laughed ruefully. "Maybe not. But—coming all of a sudden, like—*My God!*"

Mary jumped. "What?"

And after a long pause Higgins, on his feet, said abstractedly, "She was in bed, you see. All tidily tucked in. That was what—"

"Bringing work home," said Angel. "I know you're all fussed up about Landers, Art, and I can't blame you there, but it's no good worrying. And the rest of your puzzles will either get solved in time or end up in Pending."

"Easy to say," said Hackett. "I tell you, that Hatfield thing is haunting me. I have the definite feeling that this Jane Doe comes into it somewhere, but of course there's no possible way to go looking for her. . . . I only hope to God those I.A. men are as smart as they think they are. Luis saying—and damn it, he's only too right. And they don't know Tom. Personally. Damn impersonal, in fact, the damn lean-over-backwards *investigation*—"

"Hasn't he had any hunches?" asked Angel.

"I think," said Hackett slowly, "he's unsold on the idea of a frame. I don't see how it could be myself—and yet— It has got, you know, to have been a personal motive on Harriet Hatfield—the way you've got to read it. Hasn't it? Whatever was behind it. The way her face was battered in—a dozen blows at least, Bainbridge said—and it would be a wrought-iron hearth set, too rough to take prints. It looks like the sudden impulse, sudden loss of temper—but what the hell could have triggered it, on Harriet—" He stopped with his mouth open. He said, "My good God in heaven."

Angel looked up from her magazine. "Inspiration?"

"Ins—" said Hackett in a hollow tone. "My God. I thought we'd had our spate of offbeat ones for the year. The blood on the—the tea—and I saw the damn lab photographs of that—she was in bed, all the way in, the covers—and the teapot— Oh, my God!" He plunged for the phone. "I'd better call George—"

"The teapot?" said Angel blankly.

10

"WELL, I DID WONDER," said Mendoza, regarding the lab photograph of Anna Shaw's body and the bedroom it lay in.

"He wondered," said Hackett. "Two hundred years ago he'd have been burnt for a warlock."

"But, my God, that woman—" Higgins shook his head. "It looked so run of the mill—"

"Oh, you'd have noticed something wrong when you took a second look at the photographs," Mendoza consoled them.

"So what's it all about?" asked Grace interestedly. He'd been off yesterday and hadn't heard about the Shaw case at all. Palliser was off today. Hackett started to give Grace a break-down on it.

"Suppose you go and ask her to come in for a few questions, George," said Mendoza.

Higgins took Grace with him. They found Wanda Shaw at the shabby house; she told them Mr. Seward had said she could take a week off. She rode back to the headquarters building in listless silence, and it wasn't until they settled her in a chair beside Mendoza's desk and she noticed him there, slim dapper cynical-eyed Mendoza, watching her, that small fear came into her eyes.

"Miss Shaw," said Mendoza formally. "I'm afraid you didn't tell us quite all the truth about how your mother died, did you?" He offered her the box of cigarettes.

"Thank you, I don't smoke," she said. She looked up at him directly: the other men might not have been there. "You know, don't you? I always heard—the police here are—smart about things. But I thought— I suppose I was stupid, and so you know."

"We'd like to hear the truth, Miss Shaw."

"I expect you would," she said. She looked ghastly: no makeup on her sallow complexion, her graying brown hair lifeless and uncurled, clothes shabby and drab. She seemed to realize that suddenly, and flushed. "I'm sorry, I must look awful—I usually keep up, do my hair and all, the store, you know, you've got to—but I just haven't bothered, not going in. Since." She was silent, picking a piece of lint from her sleeve, and then she said without looking up, "If you've got to hear about it, you'd better hear the truth. It was just the last straw. The last. That was it. If I can explain it—if there could be any explaining it." Her voice was flat and tired. "The Bible says honor thy father and mother, and I did—I did try. Pa took a lot of the care of her before he passed on, that was more than ten years ago. But since, I tried—it was my duty and I did it. There's no other relatives, I was all—all there was. And you have to be patient and kind with old people, maybe you'll be like that some day. I *tried*. But—" she stuck there, making a hopeless gesture, and Mendoza urged her on with soothing murmurs. Higgins was taking notes.

"I don't like to say it but she was difficult. It was hard. I work all day, I have to, earn money to live on—for her too. And she knew that, but she always kept on, why couldn't I come home fix her dinner at noon. And why couldn't I be home to fix her supper at six, she liked it early. And half the time when I'd fixed it, she'd decide she wanted something else so I had it to do over. And massage her back, and I couldn't wash her things at the laundromat, the machines tear things to pieces, I had to do all those by hand, and be careful— And only get this brand or that of everything there was at the market, only she'd forget, and say I got the wrong one, have to change it. I don't suppose," said Wanda Shaw painfully, "that I'd ever have had a chance to marry anybody anyway, but she wouldn't have let me. She said so. Child of her own body, and all the terrible time she had *having* me, I had to take care of them. And her after Pa passed on. And get her in and out of the tub, and she had to have that Lilac Dawn talcum and it costs twice as much— And most nights she'd have me up, just after I'd got asleep, massage her back or make her a cup of tea. She never stirred out of the house, so of course she couldn't sleep. Oh, I sound complaining, and I shouldn't. It was my duty. But, you see, I was tired," said Wanda. "I was so tired. Just trying to keep up with—with the ordinary things, it was difficult. I'd be just starting to wash my hair, it'd be Wanda do this, do that. Or washing out my own things—trying to keep my nails nice, something like—she'd have to have the pillow turned over or— I was tired," she said to Mendoza. "It was my duty, but I was so tired."

"Yes, Miss Shaw," he said gently.

"And it isn't once a year I go to a movie, but it was the new Disney one, you see. I wanted to see it. It was a comedy, and I thought—it'd do me good to see it. And it was all *arranged*—for two weeks she knew I was going to see it, since I knew it was coming. And I felt good that night, when I got home. About going out, and the movie. I knew I'd have to hurry, the second show goes on at nine-ten, it's the Strand up on Alvarado, I'd have to take the bus, about a ten-minute ride. And I hurried, I fixed her supper and she said the egg wasn't done enough so I fixed another, and I had some toast and things while she was eating, and washed the dishes, and made her tea. She liked it by itself, a whole pot, after supper, and I was all ready to leave when I took it in—it was already after eight, I don't get home till about a quarter of seven. And when I put the tray down—she looked at it and she said—she said, Wanda, I think I'd rather have green tea tonight—and she *knew*— Have to boil another pot, I couldn't get the right bus—to make the second showing—"

"Yes, Miss Shaw?" said Mendoza.

"And all of a sudden, I guess I just lost my temper. Because she *knew* how I'd looked forward— And it was such—a—little thing," whispered Wanda Shaw miserably. "Just—a—movie—I wanted—I didn't realize what I'd done until—until I'd done it. I hit her with the teapot, she fell out of bed against the table and—"

They exchanged glances. "And when did you think of trying to cover up what you'd done?"

She shook her head. "I don't know. I sat there for a long while. I couldn't realize—what had happened. That she was dead. But she looked terrible there, it wasn't nice, her there on the floor. I was used to lifting her, I put her back in bed. And then I thought, suppose—suppose I had gone to that movie. Nobody'd know if I had or hadn't, we don't know the neighbors. And while I was gone—"

"Yes. What did you do with the portable TV, the other things you said were taken?"

"Oh, those. I put them behind Pa's trunk in the garage. We sold the car after Pa died," she said absently.

"We'll ask you to sign a statement," said Mendoza, and she nodded.

"It's funny, I'm not sorry you found out, and I had to tell you." Suddenly she looked at him with a timid smile. "I—I just thought of something. They'll put me in jail, won't they? In a cell?"

"Why, yes—until—"

"All by myself?" she said. "Alone? And I won't have to stand on my feet eight hours a day? Just alone in a cell, with *nothing to do*?"

"Well—"

"Oh," said Wanda Shaw, and her smile turned radiant. "I expect I'll go to hell for what I did, but you know, right now, that jail sounds just like heaven to me."

"I really thought we'd had enough of the offbeat ones," said Higgins. "I'll be damned. But you can feel sorry for the poor woman at that."

"People," said Grace. "They do come all sorts, boys. What makes life interesting." He had taken her down to the Alameda facility; the warrant was applied for. Subject to the D.A.'s approval, involuntary manslaughter. She might spend five years in; a jury might give her less, but it had been her own mother. As Higgins said, speaking purely physically.

"I'd still like to know," said Hackett to Mendoza, "what rang bells in your head, you just looking at her yesterday."

Mendoza grinned. "And listening. Experience gained from old sins, boy. The females who go throwing dears and darlings and poor sweets around are usually—to, mmh, use the vernacular—strictly from Siberia. And Wanda didn't strike me as usually given to overemphasis. That poor dear Mother just rang a small bell."

"Oh!" said Hackett. "Well, if you're at loose ends I wish to God you'd go out and have a hunch about Harriet Hatfield. That is still bugging me, with bells on."

Mendoza stood up and straightened his tie. Quite suddenly—they had both seen it happen to him before—he was all lit up, on top of the world. It always affected him like a stiff drink, a thing like this: Mendoza seeing right to the truth of some little puzzle, the X-ray vision. And he was still fussing about Landers, too, but he couldn't help the extra adrenalin shooting through him, the essential egotist Mendoza clearing up the little problem with a flick of his mind. He clapped Hackett on the shoulder.

"So you want the answer on Harriet, Arturo? Well, by God, I'll go and look—I might just pull it out of a hat for you." He took up the black Homburg and went out, clapping it on at a rakish angle.

"And, you know, he just might," said Higgins amusedly. "When he's in that mood—"

Hackett laughed. "Let's hope he does, George. Besides the Fantini girl —and I can't say I really care who shoved her over the balcony—Harriet's the only real mystery we've got on hand."

There was, however, plenty of the routine work to do. The court calendars were full, and only today was an inquest being held on Carolyn Katz; Piggott was covering that: the D.A.'s office had reports on Royce by now and would handle that as they pleased, full evidence or an open verdict. Business had stepped up a little for Homicide. The body yesterday was for pretty sure a natural death; just the paper work on it; but a new one had turned up overnight, looking like a suicide, out on Beverly; Grace had gone to cover that, after looking at the lab photographs and Schenke's overnight notes on it.

Just before lunch, there was a messy hit-run over on Third, and Hackett went out with Higgins on that. They had lunch before going back to type reports, and it was a quarter to three when Sergeant Lake looked in the door of the sergeants' office and said tersely, "Goldberg, wanting the boss."

Hackett picked up the inside phone. "What's up, Saul?"

Goldberg sneezed. "Just being neighborly. I thought Luis'd like to know they've picked up Durfee. I ran into Van Allen just now and he let it out and then tried to—er—pledge me to secrecy. He—"

"The hell you say. When and where?"

"Reno, this morning. He's just been fetched in and they're setting up a lineup with Landers now."

"Hell!" said Hackett, slammed down the phone, beckoned Higgins and ran. "Jimmy, you any idea where the boss is?"

"Nary a one. Don't you?"

"Damnation—he was going out on Hatfield but—" Hackett grabbed for his notebook. "Try the house, Jimmy," and he read off the number. But there was no answer there. He had Lake call Wilma Tanner's shop in Beverly Hills.

"Why, yes, the Lieutenant was here," said Miss Tanner's deep voice. "In fact he took Cathy away, but she's back now and—"

"Miss Tanner, did he happen to tell you or Miss Hatfield where he was going from—"

A hiatus while she consulted with Catherine. "No, he didn't, I'm sorry."

"Can't be helped—thanks," said Hackett. "Jimmy, if he comes in tell him where we are. We'd better get down there fast, George—you know he'll want to cover this."

When they came into the soundproofed room beneath the brilliantly lighted platform, and up to Southey and Macklin, the I.A. men nearly snarled at them.

"May I ask how you got wind of this?" asked Southey.

"A little bird, Lieutenant," said Higgins.

"A little bird with allergies named Saul Goldberg," said Van Allen grimly. "Which I'll remember."

"So that's Durfee," said Hackett. The man standing a little apart, with a uniformed man beside him, looked very much as he'd imagined Durfee might, from his mug-shot. He was big and burly, with an incipient paunch, and by his face he wouldn't have a very high I.Q. In fact, a stupid lout, thought Hackett in satisfaction. Either way Durfee should give the show away. If he didn't know about the other identifications, he'd deny Landers; if he did, he was too dumb to tell a plausible lie.

"All right," said Southey sourly. "You're here, you can stay. No talking to the witness."

"Offhand," said Hackett, "I can't think of anything I've got to say to him." He and Higgins took chairs to the right and behind the two I.A. men and Durfee.

"What's this all about, anyways?" asked Durfee. "Who'm I s'posed to look at?"

"Just tell us if you know any of the men up there, when they come in. If you've ever seen one of them before," said Southey.

"Well, O.K., but I don't get—"

Just as the room darkened further, somebody slid quietly into the chair beside Hackett. "Luis—thank God! I hoped you'd—"

"Wait for it," said Mendoza. The men began to file onto the platform up there, led by a uniformed man. Landers, in a gray suit and rather rumpled tie, was the fifth man in line.

There was silence from this little group in the dark; Al Durfee would have a slow mind. Then out of the dark his voice rose, holding complete and open astonishment, utter incredulity.

"I wouldn't 'a' *believed* it!—by God, I can't believe—anybody so Goddamn—can't take it in—"

Southey and Macklin jumped up; all at once there was confusion and noise. Mendoza made one lunge and pulled Southey away from Durfee and took Durfee's burly shoulder in an iron grip. "All right, what were you going to say next, Durfee?" he snapped. "*What?* Tell me! Anybody so close to looking like Speedy—was that it? Anybody so Goddamn like him? Tell me!"

Durfee pulled away, looking around wildly. Macklin yanked Mendoza off him. "Let go of that man, damn you! Goddamn it, you know the rules! By God, if you lay a hand on me I'll break you—"

And Hackett had seen Mendoza like that before too, and he dragged him back from Macklin by brute force. "*¡Bastante, amigo!* Suppose you ask Durfee the same question, Macklin! Just what did he mean and what was he going to say next?"

"None of you has any business here—" began Southey coldly, and Mendoza pulled away from Hackett and resettled his jacket.

"You haven't a hope of convincing me of that," he said hardly. "Ask the question, Lieutenant! You're supposed to be a smart cop. Ask Durfee the question!"

And all the while the line of men stood motionless up there on the lighted platform, staring straight ahead.

Southey and Macklin looked furious, but they were caught in front of the witnesses from Homicide. Southey turned to Durfee, who stood head down, sullen, a bewildered big bull confused by the red flag. "Well, Durfee? What did you mean? Do you know one of those men up there?"

After a moment Durfee seemed to make up his mind. He raised his head slowly, licking his lips, looking at each of them in turn. "I ain't sayin'," he muttered. "I ain't sayin' a thing. I got a bad memory for faces."

Southey cast a look of veiled triumph at Mendoza. "Come on, you're among friends," he said genially. "You know we've nailed you for this caper. Wouldn't you like to see your emp—"

"Careful, Lieutenant," said Mendoza. "You're leading the witness."

Southey compressed his lips. "You know those men up there can't see or hear you, Durfee. *Do you know one of them?*"

Durfee shook his head blindly, stubbornly abiding by the decision he'd made. "I ain't sayin'."

Mendoza let out a long breath that was half a sigh. For once in his life, Hackett had an urge to practice a little third degree. Durfee was a big bull, and bullheaded, but he knew something—maybe the whole answer here, and he might come apart if—

They went around on the merry-go-round a few more times before Macklin lost patience and told the sergeant to take him away.

"And don't we know what the famous imagination has put in your head now," said Southey.

Mendoza got out a cigarette. "Now look," he said in an unexpectedly mild tone. "We're supposed to be on the same team. We're both supposed to be interested in the truth, not winning points for our respective sides. You're not a fool, Southey, and you heard what Durfee said, looking at that line. He is a fool, which we both know. And I'd really like you to tell me just what else he might have meant by that. He couldn't believe anybody could look so much like—Speedy? Very probably. He—"

"For God's sake! You don't even know he was looking at Landers!" said Macklin.

"I really wish you wouldn't drag your heels so hard," said Mendoza very softly. "And don't try to tell me this is none of my business. *Por favor*, don't. I've got a little reputation around this place, friends, do I need to remind you?"

"Reputation for—"

"And if that man from my office has gone wrong, I really ought to have known it. He's my business, if you like. Will you tell me if you've identified Rosso?" Mendoza finally lit the cigarette.

"Yes, we have—" Southey consulted mutely with Macklin and shrugged. "We got some latents in the garage, the Feds made them for us. He's Gustavo Rosso, native of Brooklyn, time done back there for fencing, last picked up in San Francisco, twice, for auto theft. He's on P.A. from Quentin on another fencing charge."

"Well, well, well," drawled Mendoza, "isn't that interesting! Now, Mr. Bones, will you answer the sixty-four-dollar question and tell me just how a busy Homicide officer—we do get kept quite busy in the general way, you know—happened to get together with a pro crook last heard of in Quentin? A crook whose latest known beat was 'Frisco? That's quite a little trick Landers pulled there."

Southey said repressively, "We've turned up a little suggestive evidence in his home town. And that's all I'm going to tell you, Mendoza." He turned for the door; Macklin and Van Allen followed.

Mendoza stood rocking a little, heel to toe. "*Hagar sus apuntas*—stakes down and wait for the throw," he muttered. "Tell me what else he was going to say."

"Nothing else, obviously," said Hackett. "Somebody like Tom—the hell of a lot like him. Is that what he meant?"

"I took it that way," said Mendoza. "And damn it, that makes it all the more complicated. Coincidence? *¡Condenación!*"

"He wasn't acting," said Higgins. "Not that one. But I see what you mean."

"Rosso sounds just a little bit smarter," said Hackett.

"*De veras.*"

"And you got that point over—how the hell could Tom have met up with a character like that?"

"I hope," said Mendoza, "that Southey is as smart as he ought to be. Well, we wait and see. And we'd better get back to our own stamping ground." They started for the elevators down the hall.

"Did you have a hunch on Harriet?" asked Hackett, punching the button.

Mendoza contemplated his hat. "I don't know. I really don't know what I have got on Harriet, Art. Or if I've got anything. That's been a queer one all the way. It still looks queer. And as for what I have got— *Demonios,* I suppose there could be a dozen plausible explanations— the trouble is, I can't think of any. . . ."

He had not expected to find anyone at home in the house in Nichols Canyon; he had gone straight to Wilma Tanner's shop in Beverly Hills. He didn't think Hatfield, or the girl Linda, had much imagination. It was nearly twelve then, and he asked Catherine to have lunch with him. "You take the first hour, I remember. There's just a few things I'd like to talk to you about."

"Well—" She'd looked a little puzzled, a little wary; he put out some of his charm and she thawed. By the time he'd got her settled at a table at Frascati's, in the pleasantly dim dining room, and ordered her a martini, she was talking freely.

"I'm just trying to get a few new ideas, Miss Hatfield. We're finding this one a difficult case to sort out. You may think I'm asking you some funny things, but I'm supposed to be the detective, after all."

"Whatever I can tell you to help—"

"You all told us that your mother hadn't had—so far as you knew— any arguments or quarrels with anyone, any difficulty of any kind, oh, say in the month before she was killed. If she had had, the family would probably have heard about it?"

She nodded. "Of course. Mother wasn't—secretive. But she didn't quarrel—"

"No. Your father had been busy at his office. He told me that possibly she wouldn't have mentioned any little difficulty to him, knowing he was busy."

"Y-yes. That's true. But there couldn't have been—"

"Miss Hatfield," said Mendoza, finishing his rye, "I'd like you to think about this and take your time answering it. In the month or so before her death, do you remember your mother saying or doing anything—oh, unusual, or at least unusual for her? Something out of the ordinary?"

She didn't answer for a moment, and then asked, "Why?"

"Usually," he told her, "the motive for a murder isn't very important. That may sound strange to you, but it's so. Once in a while it is important. I think if we could find out what the motive for your mother's murder was, we'll be a lot further on."

She was an intelligent girl. "I see. Well, I can tell you something, only whatever it means—" She shrugged. "Daddy and I couldn't make head or tail of it, it was just—funny. It wasn't until after the second thing that I thought of the first one, and it might not mean any more to you than it does to us, Lieutenant. I'd just told Wilma about it this morning and she couldn't make it out either."

"What, Miss Hatfield?"

"Well, I'll tell you how it happened, Lieutenant. We've been starting to—to go through Mother's things—" She swallowed, blinked, and went on. "And I was looking through her dressing-table drawers, you know, sorting out things Linda or I might use, and I found my birth certificate in the top drawer. Right in the middle of her handkerchiefs, all folded up."

"Your—" Mendoza didn't know what he'd expected; it certainly wasn't that.

"It was funny. I showed it to Daddy and he was surprised too, he said he'd thought it was at the bank. In the vault, with the other things like—oh, their marriage certificate, and the deed to the house—the other birth certificates. Linda's and John's. He said Mother must have got it out for some reason, but why she would have—"

"She hadn't mentioned it to you?"

Catherine shook her head. "It was just—a funny little thing. It's just an ordinary birth certificate. And it was then I remembered the other thing, I'd thought that was funny at the time too, but it went right out of my head afterward—"

"And what was that?"

She finished her drink and turned the glass around on its little paper doily. "Well, it was about, oh, six weeks ago. I came home about the usual time—six-thirty—and Mother was in the kitchen. Johnny was at school of course, it was the middle of the week, and Linda was meeting Bob for dinner, so we'd be alone. Mother said Daddy'd called that he'd be late—she was drinking a cup of coffee at the table, and I sat down to have one too. You see, Lieutenant, Mother wasn't—I mean, she was always open, she said whatever she had to say right out. Which was why it was—funny. We were just sitting there and all of a sudden I realized she was staring at me, and I said—you know how you do—was my face dirty or what— And she looked at me so *queerly,* all I can describe how it was, and she said, 'Of course you're dark, dark eyes and all, but I always said you took after my father's side of the family.' And I said, what on earth did she mean, but she just shook her head and—and got up and went into the living room, and later on she just said she'd been looking at some family pictures. It was—queer," said Catherine.

Mendoza stared at her. And just what did that mean, if anything? He couldn't make head or tail of it either. But he'd asked for anything out of the ordinary.

"Miss Hatfield, do you mind letting me see that birth certificate?" he asked abruptly.

"Why, no, it's still at the house." He drove her up there after lunch, and she gave it to him.

And looking at it, he still hadn't a glimmer as to what that might mean. As she said, an ordinary birth certificate. Catherine Marian Hatfield, born 11 A.M., April 24, 1947. Lawrence Maternity Clinic, Western Avenue, Hollywood. Father Howard John Hatfield. Mother Harriet Anne Hatfield. Legitimate. Weight seven pounds six ounces.

Perplexed but automatically obeying training, he copied down the data and thanked her.

And no hunch came to him on Harriet Hatfield.

"Damn it," he said to Alison, finding her in the back yard as he drove in, "it just gets more muddled. Wait till you hear. They've picked up Durfee and—"

"Muddled you can say!" exclaimed Alison. Bast, ambling up to greet him, jumped and snarled as *el pájaro* swooped to peck her rear end. Cedric came galumphing from the back porch barking madly, and Sheba dabbed hastily at a new hole in the dahlias and ran for shelter on the porch with Nefertite and El Señor.

"*Yankee Doodle came to town!*" came the war cry from the alder tree. The twins erupted out the back door with Mrs. MacTaggart in vain pursuit.

"*¡Mil rayos!*" said Mendoza. "You'd think I'd be entitled to some peace and quiet when I come home—"

"And a man of your advancing years too," said Alison.

He smacked her accurately on the indicated spot. "You'll find out how advanced! *Caray*"—as the offspring landed on him—"let me get my breath! All right, all right, *los cuentos* after dinner, but get off me now, I've had a tough day, *niños—*"

Phil was feeling partly a fool and partly a traitor; she reminded herself that it was all for a good cause.

It had been Jean's idea. "Of course if she finds out she'll raise hell," she had said inelegantly, "but she might not. She probably doesn't go pawing over things every day. If all we want is to look at, well, whatever's there, I could smuggle it back before she knew. I've got a pretty good idea where to look. A few times when she was in a good mood she's brought out things to show me—I never paid much attention, but the family things, photographs and like that, she got out of this old chest in her bedroom. Now you collect antiques, Phil."

"I do?"

"Definitely. Great-aunt Serafina has a house full of antiques—marble-top commodes and whatnots and horrible little iron footstools and heaven knows what. I wouldn't give two dollars for the whole lot, but you," said Jean firmly, "are fascinated by antiques. You are a friend of mine from—from, well, the city—she won't ask which. And you want to see her antiques. But you can't do it in that dress, you'd better have one of mine, it'll hit you below the calf and Great-aunt Serafina will approve a nice modest girl. And I'm going to leave you there to admire the antiques while I do some shopping for Mother. Only I'll sneak back in while you hold her in the living room—excuse me, parlor. Double parlors," said Jean, "and a black marble mantel."

"Goodness," said Phil. "No antiques in her bedroom?"

"I devoutly hope not," said Jean. "You just hold her in the parlor. Admiring the fretwork on the plate-rail and the black marble. Oh, and she's got a stuffed bird under a glass dome, and her brother's collection of seashells."

And right now, Phil was saying admiringly, "And not a crack in the marble, Miss Pitkin—it's in beautiful condition," and feeling rather sorry for half-senile old Serafina, a little bent figure in black dusty ankle-length clothes, the cracked old voice, the snaggle-toothed smile. People could live too long. And at the same time, unwilling fascination kept returning her eyes to Serafina's wrinkled old face. Her brother, Robert Pitkin Junior, in that photograph—if Tom had a moustache, his spitting image, said Jean. And here was Serafina, age blurring what must have been at least a characterful face in youth—a long dark face, with high cheekbones and straight bars of brows, and dark eyes. It was her father who had married the Italian girl, and for some reason Latins didn't go gray very often; the brows were still black and the thinning hair in unfashionable pinned-up braids was black too.

"This was my dear mother's," said the broken old voice, "the only thing she brought from her old home when she married. The only thing. I can tell you like pretty things—"

"It's beautiful," said Phil gently. It was a hurricane lamp, an ornate thing typical of the period, clear glass with an etched design and prisms dangling from the candle-holder it fitted.

"It's old—old. She married my father in eighteen-eighty-two," mumbled Serafina. "I was named after her mother—"

Phil felt as if she'd been here for days, but it couldn't be over an hour since Jean had breezily banged the front door and called good-bye. She cast around for something else to say about the marbletops, the mantel, the stuffed bird, and Serafina said suddenly, clearly, "Of course she came of a very aristocratic Italian family. I remember—remember her telling me—often—her mother's family, all noble—"

Jean appeared suddenly in the front hall. "Here I am to take your visitor off, Great-aunt. Had a nice time? Lovely things Great-aunt has, don't you think?"

"Lovely," said Phil.

Serafina suddenly turned on both of them. "Come bothering at me, you young chits, making fun—I won't be bothered! You're young Jean, you and your short skirts and lipstick—I won't be bothered! Go away!"

"Yes, Great-aunt," said Jean soothingly.

"For heaven's sake," said Phil as they hurried down the front walk, "*did you find anything?* I never expected to have to play Little Theater when I had the harebrained idea—" They got into Jean's car and she started the engine hastily.

"She'll boil me in oil if she finds out—but I think I got something interesting." A block away she parked at the curb and opened her large straw bag. "Here you are."

Phil sorted out musty old papers, photographs. A very old, stiff sheet of paper, with onionskin sheets protecting it: *Contract of Marriage*— she spelled out the Latin slowly, dredging her memory. Robert A. Pitkin. Maria Anastasia Arnoldo. It wasn't a civil certificate; Phil laughed. "Look at this—Maria was a good churchwoman, she got him to be married by a priest. *Fr. Jesus Salvador Alvarez.* And—"

A large sepia photograph, names on the back in a fine spidery brown ink. Three folded sheets of delicate old paper, a hand barely legible now, the words not English, but she could make out the heading: *Rancho de la Vergine, Soledad, Cfrn., 18 octubre 1888.*

And a birth certificate. Or were there birth certificates that long ago? In the seventies and eighties, San Francisco a hamlet. Phil unfolded the brittle paper carefully. A baptismal record. Maria Arnoldo had, perhaps secretly, properly had her son baptized in the Church. The Church of the Good Shepherd, San Francisco, November 23, 1883, Fr. Patrick O'Hanlon Moriarty—

Phil let out a long sigh. "This might help a lot, Jean."

The trail leading to San Francisco now. Though there was also—

11

HACKETT GOT INTO THE OFFICE first on Wednesday morning, and found Sergeant Lake reading a teletype. "Relayed," he said, handing it to Hackett. "Sent up from Missing Persons just after six last night."

"Yes," said Hackett, reading it. "Carey was notified about the body, of course." It was a teletype from the sheriff of Santa Barbara County; an Antonio Camparo, local rancher, had reported his daughter missing, known to be in Los Angeles—Luisa Fantini. "So if she was married, how come the husband didn't report her?"

Lake shrugged. Mendoza came in, a little late, and looked at the teletype. "Well, well. She seems to have got missed a little late in the day." He went down to Communications and teletyped the news about Luisa up to the sheriff.

When he got back, everybody was in. It was supposed to be Piggott's day off but he had come in to be on hand if anything broke on Landers, and if business wasn't as hot and heavy as it sometimes was, they were still a man short. Hackett and Higgins had, for a wonder, got a pretty good description of that hit-run car yesterday afternoon, and all garages had been alerted to be on the lookout for it; it had probably sustained some front-end damage.

Grace, Palliser and Piggott heard the gist of what Al Durfee had come out with and agreed rather savagely as to what he'd meant. "Those damn watchdogs, just like you say, leaning over backwards—" said Palliser.

"They can't make a charge stick," said Piggott without conviction. But Piggott was always a pessimist.

But the business came along to be worked. The D.A.'s office issued a summons to Mendoza to present himself at once. Grace was saying he didn't like some funny things about this suicide, and went out on that again. The inquest on Anna Shaw was called for this afternoon; somebody would have to cover that.

A new call came in at ten-fifteen, one of those tiresome things making paper work for the Homicide office: accidental death on a construction site close in downtown. A scaffolding had slipped, or somebody been a little careless, and there was all the paper work to do, an inquest. Higgins went out to get the information on that, passing Mendoza just coming in. Mendoza was looking annoyed.

"What'd the D.A. want?"

"He doesn't like the idea of calling it involuntary manslaughter on Anna Shaw," said Mendoza. "He's making it murder second."

"And who argues with the D.A.?" said Hackett; and that was when the uproar commenced.

Confused loud voices out in the anteroom, shouts and angry sounds —Mendoza and Hackett went out to see what was up.

"Now quiet down, Mr. Camparo—just simmer down and let's—" And a little wiry dark man was shouting half in impassioned Italian at Carey and a third man who was just scowling back.

"Please be quiet, Mr. Camparo—just calm down and let's try to make sense of this—"

"He let my Luisa get killed—you show me my poor little Luisa there dead, flat, ice-cold—this *bastardo,* this son-a-bitch, why I marry my Luisa with him but I think he make good husband—I tell him—"

"*¡Silencio!*" said Mendoza sharply. "What the hell is this all about, Carey? You—quiet down—*¡Bastante ya! ¿Comprenden?*" The wiry man subsided, directing a fierce glance at them all. "All right, come in here."

"This is Mr. Camparo," said Carey in Mendoza's office. "As you gather. He—they landed on me half an hour ago. They've just identified your corpse. This is Joe Fantini, her husband. Lieutenant Mendoza—"

Camparo sketched a half bow. "How do. 'Scuse I am mad, say loud things—my little Luisa—" Fantini, who was a dark topheavy-looking young fellow about thirty with immense shoulders and short bowed legs, just grunted. "It seems that Mr. Camparo didn't know Luisa had left her husband until yesterday. His sister—"

"That Rita," Camparo interjected, "she don't never like Luisa, she likes make stink, bad gossip, scandal, however! She tells me—and Joe has a letter, she says, Luisa never comin' back—and I go to Joe—"

"Why they all got to mess in my business, Goddamn it," broke in

Fantini with a snarl. "So she's gone, and good riddance! I'm better off 'thout her, an' old man Camparo ain't goin' to—"

"Why else I marry Luisa with you?" shouted Camparo, in a sudden fury again. "She's bad, fast, naughty girl—in her thoughts only, I keep a good eye on, catch her sneak off with boys even in little children's school—better she's married young to good steady fellow, keep her safe! And you—you Joe! Better oughta you beat one like that, she talk back to you, won't work! How you act? How? You call her few names, is all —women don't understan' names! You use your fists, she wouldn't 'a' run off—"

"Damn it, I'm sorry she's dead, but what the hell could I do?" He appealed to the Homicide men, as unconsciously dramatic as Camparo. Both of them were in stiff city suits, obviously unaccustomed wear; they looked uncomfortable. "So she goes off, but I got work to do on my farm, I'm not about to—"

"Farm! Farm! Why else I marry her to you?" shouted Camparo. "Good land you got from your papa, good place—good steady husband, you keep the eye on this naughty girl—but what you do? You beat her good, scare her, she be nice girl, nice wife! You, you get her killed dead—some low-life down here kills her, you lettin' her run off—an' you say to me—"

"Now, look," said Mendoza, "let's get some order here. Jimmy! Mr. Camparo, if you'd just wait outside a few minutes, we'll talk to you presently." Camparo was still gesturing and shouting when Lake gently urged him out.

"Damn it," growled Fantini, "what the hell I let that ol' bastard drag me down here for—between him and Rita, nag, nag, nag— So all right, Luisa's dead, do I do any cryin'?" He glowered at them. "I was a damn fool let the old man talk me into marryin' with her—a damn pretty girl but no sense, an' a bad heart she had too."

"When did she leave you, Mr. Fantini?" asked Hackett.

"Who looks at calendars? Three weeks, a month. Listen, so it's over, finished, she run into trouble down here and got killed. So I pay for a funeral. I got work to do on my place—"

"Did you quarrel with her, was there some immediate cause for her leaving?" asked Mendoza.

"What? No, no, she just went off. Do I pay attention to what she says, complain, nag, I don't listen. Damn that Rita! I told you so, told you so, bad girl, bad wife—so she was, she didn't hafta rub it in day 'n' night! So I'm sorry for what happened, Goddamn it, what else do I say?

Goddamn Rita, has to go tattle to the old man an' he goes up like a rocket—you heard him." Fantini stood up.

"We heard him. Sit down, Mr. Fantini. Just a few more questions. You had a letter from your wife? What did she say?"

"Nothin'. Nothin', just she's gone for good, don't expect see her no more."

"And was there a return address on it?"

"What? No. No, I just seen it come from L.A. So what? I'm sick of her complain, complain, all the work, no fun—I'm not about to come looking, drag her back."

"You didn't report her missing?"

"Look, mister, she's grown-up, she can do what she wants. Why should I?"

"Did she have any money? Did she steal some from you when she ran away?" asked Hackett. "Like a thousand bucks?"

Fantini stiffened, his back to them. "How'd—now where'd I get a thousand bucks?"

"From the bank," said Mendoza, "with a little strip of paper around the roll with a note on it saying how much was there."

Fantini whirled on them, his face convulsed. "You— Nobody knew—"

"¡Ya está!" said Mendoza softly. "What a pity John isn't here—he did most of the spadework on it." Hackett looked amused and opened the door to glance out.

"He's just in," he said laconically, and beckoned, and Palliser came in looking curious. "We're just about to hear the whole story on Luisa."

Fantini was still staring at Mendoza. His muscular throat worked; suddenly he reached up and tore loose the stiff collar and tie. "You— you don't know," he muttered. "You try to trap me—I don't tell no lies, get in trouble—I never seen her again. She went off and I never seen her after. I don't know what money she—"

"The bank will tell us, you know," said Mendoza. "That you took out that thousand bucks in cash, Joe. What was it for?"

"I—I—you don't—"

"And why did you come back, Joe?" asked Hackett. "Walking into the trap?"

"That ol' devil!" spat Fantini suddenly, venomous. "Between him an' Rita— *It was all done with!* It was finished! I hadda be such a Goddamn fool, leave that letter around so's Rita seen it—I got work to do, I don't aim come back—but that stubborn ol' devil, he—"

Mendoza looked slightly amused now; the wiry little Camparo evidently the stronger character. "There was also," he said, "or I think there was, the pink slip on a car—"

"And that legal document," said Palliser, looking interested. "What was that thousand bucks for, Fantini?"

Fantini was glowering at the floor. "Land—land, that other field, 'n' Pancho he say cash—" His voice was absent; he looked up at them and suddenly his voice went high. "Goddamn that sneaky little bitch! Goddamn her! Nothin' but trouble, since the day I first laid eyes on her— an' that ol' bastard knowin' it, he pass her off on me! I shoulda *knowed* better! Me buyin' the little bitch a di'mond ring, her makin' eyes and me a damn fool as much as— But at least I got over it!" He had been on his feet pacing; now he wheeled and pounded an impotent fist on the wall, furious. "She runs off, I'm glad see her back, but that Goddamn little bitch, she takes my cash an' the certif'cate on my new truck I just paid for an' the *deed to my land*—an' she says, she writes, take another thousand bucks to give 'em back—that bitch, that bitch—"

"And so what did you do, Joe?"

"Goddamn, I got to get 'em back—I come to get 'em back! What the hell else would I do?" he asked chokingly, beyond any fear or discretion. "Sure there's an add-ress—she wanted more o' my money! She didn't get it, by God! I—"

"What she did get was a broken neck," said Hackett. "How, Joe?"

"You think you know so Goddamn much," said Fantini.

"We might guess," said Palliser. "She'd spent the thousand on clothes mostly, and a couple of weeks' room and meals. But she hadn't picked up a sucker with real money, so she took the piddling job, as little work as she could do, to pay her room rent awhile longer. She tried for some more money from you before she met the rich john. And I think you caught her just as she was leaving that night—leaving the house on Boyd Street—to keep her date. Didn't you? Maybe in the street, so nobody there ever saw you. I think—"

"Mmh, yes," said Mendoza, eyeing Fantini, "just enough superficial cunning to make the try for—er—your valuables, and cover up a little afterward. You told her you'd pay her the money. So she took you to the theater, didn't she? It'd make her late for her date, but the john was eager, and the prospect of another thousand bucks was worth it. She told you to wait five minutes and come up the fire escape—"

"My God, of course!" said Palliser. "Annie Sanchez never saw him—"

"And she pushed that door open and—"

"Just out there that dirty ol' place, inna box—*my proppity*! Anybody mighta picked it up—her laughin' at me—" Fantini smacked one big fist into his palm. "Oh, Holy God, I shoulda took that ol' devil's advice an' beat up on that one first week I married her! I shoulda—I was so God-damn mad I didn't know what I was—I went for her, just to get that box—*my proppity*—an' we sorta fell back through that door—"

"And not a soul in the balcony," said Palliser. "She was little and thin, and the handful of people in the dark down there wouldn't have heard or seen. You sent her over before you realized, didn't you? And then you remembered the diamond ring, and went down and took that back too."

Fantini stopped talking and turned to face the window. After a moment he said in helpless fury, "I hadda let that ol' bastard bully me, come down *look* for her—up like a rocket, he hears she's— It's all *his* fault, that ol' son of a bitch Camparo! It's all *his* fault!"

"My God," said Palliser, "and we haven't warned him about his rights —you know what the bench would—"

Mendoza laughed mirthlessly, eyes on Fantini's back. "It's a toss-up whether he'll give us that in a statement all over again after the warn-ing. But at least we know. Take him down to jail, John. We'll set up the machinery for a warrant."

And then they had a wild free-for-all out in the hall when it pene-trated Camparo's head that Joe was the one who'd killed Luisa. He was raving hysterically when a couple of officers from First Aid got there and gave him a shot and took him away.

They were all ready for lunch then, and Grace and Piggott came in as they were leaving. They heard about Luisa, and Grace said seriously it was an object lesson. They were all sitting round the big table at Federico's then, and the rest of them looked at him and asked what he meant by that.

"Not many people," said Grace, "get deliberately murdered, unless they've asked for it some way."

"Well, I won't say Joe did it deliberately," said Palliser. "Malice afore-thought."

"No, but she had sort of invited it, hadn't she?"

"The Katz girl didn't," put in Piggott.

"But if anyone ever did invite it," said Higgins, "it was Anna Shaw. That poor damned Wanda—"

"And that wasn't deliberate either," said Mendoza, "whatever the

D.A. thinks. And if Harriet Hatfield asked for it, I'm damned if I see how."

"No hunch?" asked Hackett.

"Nothing in the crystal ball." The waiter came up and Mendoza ordered a steak sandwich. They ordered all round, and Hackett looked martyred and gloomily said he'd have a salad.

"And at that, the calories even in oil dressing—Jimmy's found a new one. Low protein only. He says he's lost five pounds on it. But damn it, I'm out and around all day, I've got to keep up my strength—"

"I want to talk with you sometime about this suicide," said Grace. "I don't much like it. But meantime, I've been thinking about that Durfee." He brushed his moustache. "By what you said, that was—you might put it—straight from the heart. What he meant was, he couldn't believe anybody was so much like this Speedy. So I've got a simple mind."

They all knew that. "You've got an idea?" asked Hackett.

"Well, a smidgen of one. They've got computers downstairs. Suppose we add up everything about Tom that's—er—purely physical, and feed a computer with it. See if we've got anybody listed who conforms to the same description."

"Now that is an idea," said Hackett, unaware that it had already been attempted, before Phil had an even simpler idea.

"Is it?" Mendoza cast an ironic glance at Grace. "I don't suppose any of us upright American citizens are just too sure what ancestry might show in our pedigrees beyond a few generations back. Just on the— *disculpeme*—face of it, Jase, lighten your complexion three shades and darken mine ditto, we'd sound very damned similar on an official description."

Palliser looked from Grace to Mendoza. "By God, you would. That never struck me before, but—you're both about five-ten, one-sixty, medium, black hair, moustache—"

"And if you," added Mendoza, "were an inch shorter, John, you and Tom would sound alike. Five-eleven—you're six feet even, but what's an inch?—dark hair, long jaw, clean shaven—"

"I've got hazel eyes."

"And as for Art and George here—"

"No," said Higgins. "I have it on authority from my wife that nobody could ever mistake me for anybody else." They laughed and surveying his craggy face agreed. The twice-broken nose, prognathous jaw, and high forehead were landmarks that would hardly be duplicated in an-

145

other countenance. "I only hope the baby takes after Mary," added Higgins thoughtfully.

The waiter came up with a big tray and Mendoza put out his cigarette. "You never know how heredities will act. One of the twins taking after Alison and—genes are peculiar." And then suddenly he half-rose, upset his empty coffee cup, and said loudly, *"¡No puede ser! ¿Qué es esto? ¿Y pues qué?* But what the hell could—"

"I think," said Hackett, "he's having a hunch at last."

If it was a hunch, Mendoza didn't know what it might mean. All he knew was the direction it sent him.

At three o'clock he found the Lawrence Maternity Clinic and Emergency Hospital out on Western Avenue. What it might have been like twenty-four years ago was impossible to say; now it occupied nearly a square block, a rambling building of gray stucco evidently added on to from time to time. Inside the double front doors was a square lobby, a counter partitioned off to make a small office-area behind it. An efficient-looking uniformed nurse inquired how she could help him.

Mendoza produced the badge and introduced himself, which flustered the nurse considerably. "Oh! What—what do you want here? Did you say *Homicide?*"

"That's right. I don't quite know myself," said Mendoza. "I think for a start—" He was really groping in the dark— "I'd like to look at some of your records a while back—1947."

She repeated the date incredulously. "Why, that's years and years—I don't believe Dr. Lawrence—"

"You do keep records that far back?"

"Why, of course, sir, the doctors are most particular. We have records of every patient the clinic has ever— But I'm afraid I don't know— I'd better fetch Mrs. Headley." Mendoza had upset routines; she was annoyed but curious.

She brought him an authoritative older woman who asked him severely why he wanted to examine their records. "A little something came up in a case," said Mendoza vaguely. "Obstetric records. Nineteen forty-seven. If you could—"

"Really!" she said. "I think Dr. Lawrence had better hear of this—"

Dr. Lawrence couldn't have been over thirty, and he regarded Mendoza with more excited curiosity than annoyance. "Homicide!" he said. "What on earth are you after here, Lieutenant?"

146

"I'm not sure. If I could just see the records, Doctor? For nineteen forty-seven?"

"Well, I'll be damned," said Dr. Lawrence. "That's quite a long time back. And I don't know whether you'll find 'em just as orderly as they should be." He grinned at Mendoza cheerfully. "My uncle started this place in nineteen forty-five, it had hardly got going yet by nineteen forty-seven. His idea was to provide reasonable obstetric care at minimum costs, and he started on a shoestring—my God, nineteen forty-seven, there'd have been about fifteen beds and three nurses. Good doctor, you know, but rather a vague old boy—he still is. And where the hell records as old as that would be kept— Oh, well, Headley'd know. She always knows everything, she's been here since the year after that, come to think, nineteen forty-eight."

It took even Nurse Headley nearly half an hour to dredge up for Mendoza a dusty file-case full of alphabetized filing-cards: records of all the patients of that young, small clinic of all those years back. Strictly a maternity clinic then: evidently expanded since to offer other services. (Yes, the Hatfields young people then, without much money, saving as they could, this place licensed and operated by an M.D., so safe, but less expensive even then than a regular hospital.) These days there'd be more than one doctor on duty, a whole staff of nurses, office help.

There were not much more than a hundred and fifty patients on file for that year. The elder Lawrence still in private practice on the side then, while he tried to build up his clinic? Probably.

Mendoza shuffled through the cards, looking for dates.

He came up—groping in the dark, following the blind prompting at the back of his mind—with five names.

Ida Welcome (Mrs. Robert).
Ruth Hillyard (Mrs. Theodore).
Vera Kaufman (Mrs. William).
Jessica Manyon (Mrs. Kenneth).
Harriet Hatfield (Mrs. Howard).

All five of those women had had babies on the same day, April 24, 1947. The births ranged from 6 A.M. to 10:50 P.M.

All the babies had been legitimate: three boys and two girls.

Four of the births had been normal deliveries, one a breech.

And one of the babies had been stillborn, one of the girls.

Mendoza looked at his notes. Just what the hell did that say? Nothing at all.

But, annoyingly, he felt that it ought to say something to him.

Hackett, Higgins and Mendoza had all called Landers last night to offer him assurances that I.A. couldn't possibly make a charge. What Durfee had come out with—and what Rosso might come out with, if and when they picked him up—and in any case it was damn farfetched to suppose that Landers could have teamed up with one like Rosso or Durfee. Which I.A. could see.

But Landers was as much aware of some of the facts of life as they were, and he reflected glumly, on Wednesday night, just what the future might hold. Even if I.A. couldn't dredge up any solid evidence—which they couldn't, of course—the implication would be there, forever on his record. And so if he got any promotion at all, it would be slow and reluctant.

He sat there in the living room of the little apartment, on Thursday morning, and thought about it. With cold logic and a little knot of absurd fear at the pit of his stomach, he thought.

He'd never had another ambition. He'd gone to a junior college two years after high school, marking time; he'd taken a liberal arts course, and the one evening course offered in Police Science. After he'd come down here and joined the force he'd taken evening classes at Hollywood High, and passed the exams in Police Science II, III, and IV. He'd passed the detectives' exam and he was up to take the sergeants' exam again the next time round. He'd felt confident of passing that. But it would do him no good at all if this mark on his record would get him passed over for promotion.

He didn't know any other job. He'd never been much good with his hands, at anything manual; it had disappointed his father that he didn't want to follow his own profession, but Landers would have been no good at that. If he was going to be stuck in Detective rank until retirement age, he'd better resign now and get into something else. But what?

Of course there was only one answer to that: private-eye work. And he wouldn't like it. A man on the LAPD had something behind him, making him a little taller: pride, integrity, principle. A standard to live up to. A private eye was just a paid snooper.

And Landers was suddenly filled with a kind of furious and astonished anger, pushing away any other feeling. That the casual little lie could suddenly, like this, threaten to destroy him. Everything he had.

And Phil, he thought drearily. There'd been Phil. He'd started to think, the only girl he'd ever really feel like— But jobless, starting in somewhere else, how could he—? He'd thought maybe she'd felt—

But she hadn't, obviously, because she'd gone blithely off on vacation without even calling to say good-bye. Or good luck.

Phil got to the outskirts of San Francisco at noon on Thursday, having started out at dawn. The traffic slowed her down toward the city. And in San Francisco, of course, was Kitty: Mrs. James McCaffrey. Phil debated about it: easier to find a motel; but in spite of some differences, they were sisters. Phil drove west to Kitty's apartment and announced herself meekly.

And of course Kitty was all questions and speculations. Phil told her firmly she was on private business.

"I'll bet," said Kitty. "Whose?"

"Private LAPD business," said Phil, which was nearly true.

"Yah!" said Kitty. "A four-year junior officer the Chief sends on a delicate mission four hundred miles. And why you ever wanted such a job— What really attractive male would be interested in a lady cop?"

"You'd be surprised," said Phil, which was a mistake and started the questions all over again. "Now stop it, Kitty—I just want a bed and dinner and breakfast—and no interference! And I haven't asked about Jim."

"He's in Portland for the company. So I'm footloose and free—where are we going?"

"No place. I am going out," said Phil. "After I've had a shower and changed my clothes."

"Lady cops are no fun," said Kitty.

"I'm not here for fun," said Phil.

She looked in the phone books and as she'd hoped, found the Church of the Good Shepherd still there. If it was, of course, the same one. Not in the city, on the outskirts down the peninsula. Quite a way from the San Francisco of eighteen eighty-three—or earlier, she thought doubtfully. But she got back in the Gremlin and drove down there after lunch, and was slightly reassured by the main building: it was old, very old, with later additions tacked on.

She parked and went in; the suburb had grown around the old place, which must have once had more extensive grounds. The church, dim and cool, seemed to be deserted, but at length she came across a robed figure near the pulpit; her heels clattered on the tiles as she went down the aisle.

"May I help you, miss?" He turned to show her a gentle aquiline face, strongly Spanish in the liquid dark eyes and mobile mouth.

"I hope so." She smiled at him and introduced herself, explaining. If they could find church records that far back, trace the family—she showed him the ornate Latin marriage contract, the baptismal record.

"Dear me," he said, "that is some time ago, Miss O'Neill. But of course the church was keeping such records then when the civil authorities were not—San Francisco a very small town then, you know." Phil said yes and that was why she'd come to the church. "Yes, indeed. We should have records beyond that—we started, you see, as a small mission here in the years long before the gold was found. I beg your pardon, I should—I am Father Jaime Suarez. Now let us look and see what we can find. Of course we were very fortunate in the earthquake and fire—this far out of the city, we had some damage, I understand, but negligible. I think the records prior to nineteen hundred would be—perhaps we had better consult Father Rodolfo, he is more familiar—"

In the end, they found a few tantalizing items which helped Phil not at all, or very little. Among the earliest records of the church, they found a notation in a foreign-looking fine Latin script, the record of a marriage sanctified between Paolo Arnoldo, age thirty, and Serafina Maria Corpofretta, age twenty; that was dated 1851. Later on, 1861, there was a baptismal record for Maria Anastasia Arnoldo. And 1853, 1855, 1859, baptismal records of Luigi, Pietro, Matteo. Baptismal records of Maria's brothers, sisters? The Italian surname—so many people from all over flocking into northern California in the years after 1849— it might be no relation at all, but the dates would be about right, thought Phil. Serafina must have been born in 1831, then.

And then, nothing. Also at that period, people had drifted.

But it was disappointing. Phil asked about current records.

"Ah—looking for the same surnames? Well, we can look, but I'm afraid we have all too few parishioners these days."

In the current records appeared one Roberto Arnoldo, and Father Rodolfo could tell her something about him. A businessman, he said, living in Palo Alto. Two children—the record listed their baptisms. Phil didn't think Roberto was going to be any use to her, but she thanked the priest warmly.

She answered Kitty absently over a very good dinner—Kitty was domestic and a good cook—until Kitty said she'd shake her in a minute. "And don't tell me you're not mooning over some man! If ever I knew the signs—"

"I do not," said Phil in a dignified voice, "moon over men, and of all the vulgar phrases—"

"At least I got a rise out of you. Who is he? *What* are you doing here? I have the definite feeling you're up to something exciting and if you don't let me in on it—"

"It's *private*," said Phil; and relented. "Honestly it is, Kitty, but if it works out all right I'll tell you afterward. Because—oh, it's *got* to work out all right! His whole career—don't I know those boys at I.A.!" And she didn't know what had been going on down there—whether they'd picked up those other men, what they might have said about Tom. . . .

"Promise? God-strike-me-dead promise?" The remembered childish phrase set Phil laughing.

"Solemn. Only—it's got to be all right. I know it sounds perfectly harebrained—but Jean and Mrs. Landers didn't think so—"

She sat up in the guest bedroom after Kitty had gone to bed and studied the faded old sepia photograph . . . to be hoped Great-aunt Serafina hadn't discovered the rape of her dear mother's relics and caught Jean to boil her in oil. . . . But it had to be that side of the family, she thought. By all the evidence.

There were six people in the stiffly-posed photograph. Were they posed leaning on something, for the exposure of two or three minutes? But the faces, faded, were fairly clear.

The queer voluminous clothes of the middle eighteen-hundreds. Full skirts, high necks, tight sleeves: tight trousers, high collars, all very formal. They had the look, these people, of people uncomfortably dressed up in unaccustomed clothes to have their photograph taken. The photograph was mounted in a very worn, scuffed cardboard frame, and on the lower left of that appeared in ornate, once-gilt print the legend *Walton Studio, New York City*. On the back someone had written the names, the ink dried brown and faint. *Luigi Corpofretta, Maria, Pietro, Serafina, Leo, Tomaso*. (So Serafina had named three of her children for her brothers and sister.)

And Papa, dignified in his formal clothes, with the long sweep of moustache, had the high cheekbones, the straight bars of brows, the dark piercing eyes. The children, in these terrible clothes—Serafina looked most like him, but there was a look there in the boys, too—just babies, two or three at the most, but—

These would be—she worked it out—the parents of the Serafina who had married Paolo Arnoldo: and Serafina Arnoldo had been the mother of Maria who married Robert Pitkin Senior. This was the Serafina Great-aunt Serafina was named for. An influx of immigrants from everywhere, in the eighteen-thirties and -forties: this family, having its picture taken, could have been just off the boat.

And heading for California when? After the gold rush, of course. Like Robert Pitkin, who ended up keeping a hotel in San Francisco. But a few people got rich on the gold and then—

Other gold in California, thought Phil. She got out of bed and took out of her overnight case the brittle old letter. Rancho de la Vergine, Soledad, 1888. A long time ago. When that letter was written from the ranch of the Virgin, Soledad would have been three saloons, an assayer's office and a stage change, and all about it was the rich golden land, much of it virgin land, to be filled with the good crops—vineyards for the wine, grain and fruits—and for the cattle, the great herds of cattle—not then the white-faced meek Herefords of today, but tough range-cattle and some longhorns from the south. . . .

The letter was in Italian and she couldn't read it. It began *Mia cara Maria,* and ended, *con amore, tuo fratello Pietro.* She could work that out from Latin: with much love, your brother Pietro. Evidently if the rigidly orthodox parents had cast Maria off for marrying a Protestant, at least one brother had kept in touch with her.

Phil wondered, a successful brother? Owning his rancho? Passing it on to a son? Because people drifted, but sometimes they stayed put too.

It was such a very simple idea she'd had, she thought, that it sounded a little scatterbrained . . . only there had to be something in it, because—Tom's whole career—

Phil switched off the light. Tomorrow, she thought, crossing her fingers superstitiously, tomorrow. . . . Soledad wasn't far down the coast; and 1888 was a long time ago, but—

It had to come out all right, because Tom—

12

ON THURSDAY MORNING Grace and Palliser were waiting for Mendoza when he came in. "This suicide," said Grace plaintively. "We'd just like an opinion, Lieutenant."

"I saw your report on it. What's wrong with it?"

"Nothing exactly," said Palliser. "It's suicide all right, bathroom door locked inside, wrists slashed. But why? There just wasn't any reason—a young fellow, good health, good job, no debts to speak of, no girl trouble. It looks—"

"If you say funny," said Mendoza, "I'll turn around and go home. You've worked homicide detail long enough to know that people don't need reasons to do funny things. If you're sure it's a bona fide suicide, do the paper work and forget it."

"That'll be you," said Palliser to Grace. "I'm going down to the jail with Higgins to try to get a formal statement from Joe Fantini."

Higgins had come in, day off or not. I.A. was still hunting for Rosso, and might pick him up any time. Or, of course, not at all. Piggott came in just in time to meet Carey; Carey had a sobbing female in tow who'd just identified the latest corpse. He'd been, by the autopsy, a long-time user of the hard stuff, but evidently somebody would miss him. Resignedly, Piggott steered her to a chair and started to ask questions and take notes.

When Hackett came in late, having mowed the back and front lawns after breakfast, he found Mendoza sitting at his desk playing with the cards. He had run his fingers through his hair, and with a disarranged few locks over one eye, the rest untidily on end, a cigarette in the corner of his mouth, and the cards riffling through his hands, he looked—as Hackett told him—like a riverboat gambler of the old South.

"Sideburns," said Hackett. "All you need. What's bothering you besides Tom?"

"Damn it," said Mendoza to himself, "what the hell has that got to do with it? Hunch be damned—I'd have some inkling what a hunch was saying to me. I haven't. I've just got the irrational feeling that it's something to do with what happened to Harriet. And I don't know what. I can't imagine what it could have to do with it."

"What are you talking about?"

Mendoza squared the pack, shuffled, cut, and turned up the king of hearts. Shuffled and cut and turned the same card. Meditatively he said, "Ida Welcome. Ruth Hillyard. Vera Kaufman. Jessica Manyon. Talk about irrelevant." He shuffled and cut and looked at the king of hearts.

"And who are they and what have they got to do with Harriet? That one really—"

"I don't know. Nothing," said Mendoza, "nothing at all. They just happened to be in the same place with her at the same time, once."

"Well, I've known you to go off on some wild goose chases, but that—"

"I know," said Mendoza. He squared the deck and looked at it. "¡Condenación! And not a whisper out of I.A.—or the grapevine. They'll never get anything else on that at all, Art. And we know where that leaves Tom." He picked up the pack and began to stack it from left to right hand, methodically. He cut and put down the ace of spades. Shuffled, cut, laid down the ace of hearts. And again, ace of clubs, and again, ace of diamonds. Hackett said that was very pretty but it solved no puzzles. "Doesn't it?" said Mendoza. "The trouble with working puzzles from our end, Arturo, just as it is the trouble about sitting in a game with a stranger—which comes to the same thing—is that you never know when there might be an extra ace floating around." He laid down the pack and turned his palm to show Hackett a second ace of hearts.

"If I.A. should ever get any solid evidence on you," said Hackett, "you've got another trade to fall back on."

Mendoza laughed and got up. "Don't ask me where I'm going or why, boy. I'm groping in the dark. Harriet haunts me too. And this is such a damned irrational thing—but I think I'll sniff round the edges and see if anything faintly interesting shows up." He took up his hat and went out, leaving the cards scattered on his desk.

In the anteroom, Lake said, "Hold it," as Hackett came past. "The desk downstairs."

Hackett sat down at his desk and picked up the inside phone. The desk sergeant downstairs passed on a name and address. There had been an alert out to all garages in the county on that hit-run car: they had (they hoped) a fairly good description of it, either a Chrysler or Dodge or Pontiac, dark green, late model. By what the lab had come up with, it had a broken right headlight and possibly a dented right fender. A garage-owner in Chatsworth had just called in on that, said it was possible he had the car right there now.

Returning mild thanks that this wasn't three months later in the middle of a heat wave, Hackett drove out to Chatsworth, which was forty miles through traffic even on freeways, and introduced himself to Bill Godsden, the garage-owner.

"Look," said Godsden, "I don't like tellin' the tale on anybody, but I don't know this guy and it said in the news about that hit-run—a kid killed, wasn't there, and his ma hurt bad?"

"Six-year-old. The woman's still in intensive care," said Hackett.

"Yeah. Terrible thing. You gotta be careful in downtown traffic, can't make time. Anyway, this guy brings this heap in, just says fix it up, don't ask no estimate or nothing. Which I think is a little funny, and when I come to look—"

Hackett looked and saw what he meant. Smashed headlight, couple of dents in the right fender about child-height. He told Godsden to leave the car alone, the lab would be up to tow it in for examination. The car, a two-year-old Chrysler, was registered to Gary B. Raye at an address in Brentwood. Mr. Raye had probably figured that Chatsworth was far enough away that nobody out there might have heard of the hit-run. Mr. Raye had figured without the LAPD.

Hackett asked, "Did he say how he'd done the damage?"

"Told me his wife ran into the garage door."

Hackett got back into the scarlet Barracuda and started for Brentwood.

Mendoza didn't know what he was groping for in the dark at all. He just had a vague feeling that there was something there to grab if he could only catch hold of it.

Four completely irrelevant women. To each other, and certainly to Harriet Hatfield. In the same place, by chance, for a few days twenty-four years ago.

It was in the cards none of them lived here any more.

He had idled along Wilshire in the Ferrari, with no destination in mind; now he found a public lot, walked up to a drugstore on the corner, and proceeded to find out about that. They could all still be here: none of them might be. He looked in all five phone books, and found Kaufmans, Hillyards, a few Welcomes and more Manyons. That one was easier than the rest: the book listed a Jessica Manyon at a Santa Monica address. Of the others, going by initials he made six calls without answers and reached four Mrs. Kaufmans before finding the right Vera Kaufman in La Crescenta. Eventually he identified Mrs. Ida Welcome in Pasadena, Mrs. Hillyard in Tujunga. Suspiciously and curiously they confirmed their presence, those years ago, at that place.

Telling himself he was seven kinds of a fool for wasting time like this, Mendoza went out to the Ferrari again, poorer by several dollars in quarters and dimes, and got on the valley freeway for La Crescenta.

Mrs. Vera Kaufman had, in twenty-four years, turned into a grossly fat matron. She was slightly flattered by a visit from a police-officer, but utterly bewildered as to why he had come. So was Mendoza. She showed him a portrait of her son Paul, who had been born there that twenty-four years ago and was now in the Marines.

Being in the general area, Mendoza headed for Pasadena and Mrs. Ida Welcome. It was a neat white frame house with a green lawn in front. Mrs. Ida Welcome was glisteningly black and had a jolly smile. She offered Mendoza a cup of coffee—"I was just about to have one myself and I don't have any truck with instant, it's real coffee, sir"—and just as complete bewilderment as to what he wanted. Yes, her eldest boy had been born at that place, that was Jim, he'd just got married last year and Mrs. Welcome would be a grandmother pretty soon now.

Neither Mrs. Kaufman nor Mrs. Welcome had known Harriet Hatfield, since, or then, or lately. And of course there was no reason why they should have, every reason why they wouldn't have, and he really didn't know why the hell he was wasting time like this.

He drove back into the San Fernando Valley for Tujunga. Academically he thought what time had done to these five women, impersonal and careless time. The gross Mrs. Kaufman: jolly Mrs. Welcome probably not much changed, Harriet Hatfield risen a little, the husband making money, buying a house in a fashionable area.

Time had been unkinder to Ruth Hillyard. He found her in an ancient sagging house on the back of the lot, the front house nearly as dilapidated with a For Rent sign in the yard. There was no attempt at greenery; a half-full garbage can stood by the front step of the rear house, and children squabbled noisily in a yard nearby.

Ruth Hillyard, presently opening to his knock, was obviously suffering from a hangover. She looked at him blearily, once a nice-looking girl, now with raddled complexion and permanently bloodshot eyes. "Oh, you're the one called. What the hell police want of me—" She let him into a dusty, dirty living room, offered him a drink, without apology said she'd have one herself anyway. And why the hell he was here—

"Oh," she said, "that place. Yeah. Lessee, that was Charlie. Sure. The first one. I had three altogether, worse luck, though I wouldn't absolutely swear Charlie was Theo's, but that's water under the bridge and anyways I was married. No thanks from the kids. Charlie's off in the Navy and Doreen had t' get hitched last year and God knows where Lou's got to." She yawned. "Boy, I got a head. Sure you won't have a drink? You're kind of cute for a cop."

Feeling as annoyed at himself as he ever had, but still gripped by the vague conviction that there was something here to be groped after, Mendoza drove down to Santa Monica, stopping on the way for lunch at The Fox and Hounds. When he found the address listed for Jessica Manyon, it was the left rear unit of a dreary old court in the oldest section of town. His repeated ring at the bell finally brought response from the neighboring unit. The front door there opened and a cautious eye rolled at him; apparently reassured, she opened the door to reveal herself as an elderly thin woman in a gray ankle-length bathrobe and that article of Victorian respectability—Mendoza had never seen one before and was fascinated—a mobcap.

"Were you wanting Mis' Manyon? She's never at home this time o' day—she works. At Robinson's Beverly Hills, in handbags. . . . Oh, you're welcome, I'm sure." Her eyes were curious on him.

He drove back to Beverly Hills, parked the Ferrari in the huge lot of that huge store, and went into the ultra-smart sophisticated atmosphere of Robinson's. Consulting a directory, he found Handbags listed as on the First Level, and wandered up and down aisles until he found the right counters. A very Parisian-looking blonde was being waited on by the only clerk visible, a thin rather haggard-looking woman in correct department-store-clerk black and pearls; she just missed being smart. A check was being offered, there were murmured requests for identification. The blonde decided not to be offended.

Mendoza fingered a large emerald-green cobra bag with a brass buckle. If that was Jessica Manyon, she didn't look as if she had ever harbored any maternal emotions. Very much all on the surface: a facade, but the clerks in smart places like this usually were that type— And he was an absolute fool, running around looking at these women: these irrelevant women, nothing remotely to do with Harriet Hatfield or her sudden death.

"May I help you, sir?" She glistened at him, but impersonally, even absently.

"Miss Manyon?" said Mendoza.

She was surprised, thrown off stride. "Why, that's my name—how—"

"Never mind," said Mendoza, coming to a decision: talk about wild geese! "My wife just happened to mention you might help me—her birthday—I'll take this." He thrust the cobra bag at her; Alison could always use another handbag.

She looked confused. "It's sixty-five dollars, sir—would it be cash or charge?"

From the days before the old man died and all the loot came to light, Mendoza had a deep and ingrained horror of charge accounts. He pulled out a checkbook hastily.

Since yesterday, of course (Palliser had expected it) Joe Fantini had been provided with a lawyer, and he had shut up like a clam. To repeated coaxings from Palliser and the standard tough-cop talk from Higgins, he stayed dumb. They gave up on him finally and by then it was time for lunch. They found Grace and Piggott ahead of them at Federico's.

"So ten to one," said Palliser, "we'll never get Fantini nailed for it. He never said such a thing to us, well-known corrupt police just telling lies about him. Why the hell didn't somebody warn him when he started to talk? He was so surprised it probably wouldn't have fazed him then."

"From what you said, he came apart too quick," said Grace. "What bothers me, we shouldn't have been so surprised. Natural sort of thing, husband murdering a two-timing wife."

Piggott said, "That's the trouble with this job, we see so much of Satan's work we get used to it."

"Where's Art?" asked Higgins.

"No idea. Wherever he is, probably ordering cottage cheese or green salad right now."

"And he'd tell you it's not funny," said Palliser mildly.

"More to the point," said Grace, "where is Tom? I tried to call him just now—he's not home. I wonder if the I.A. boys—"

Palliser said, "Don't spoil our appetites, Jase."

The same taciturn sergeant had called for Landers and driven him downtown in silence. Up in the I.A. office, he was shown into an empty interrogation room with four chairs and a table in it, an ashtray on the table, and nothing else. Now what? thought Landers. He lit a cigarette and went over to the one window: there was a nice view out over the city, this clear day.

The door opened and he turned, but it wasn't Southey or Macklin who came in: it was Al Durfee. Clad in unpressed tan jail-issue pants and shirt, he stared at Landers and Landers stared back.

After a moment, then, Landers got mad. The oldest trick known to professional manhunters, and they tried it on him! Did they think he was an absolute fool? If they did, then they were fools themselves and the last officers to call themselves pros or be in a position to investigate fellow cops. Bug the room and let both suspects in here alone to hear what they might say to each other! Landers felt that helpless rage rising again. The casual little lie— And he wouldn't know this was Durfee, officially he wasn't supposed to know Durfee—unless he was guilty with him; but Mendoza had told him privately that they'd picked Durfee up, what he looked like and what he'd said at that lineup yesterday.

That part of it, Landers wasn't even speculating on: coincidence, resemblance, whatever. And Durfee was dumb but he wasn't that dumb: he'd know they had unseen listeners here too.

Landers said conversationally, "You're Durfee. And for Lieutenant Southey's benefit, I don't know you because we were in a racket together, but because I had you described to me, and I guess Lieutenant Southey can guess by whom." He went over and stood in front of him where Durfee had sat down. "Who is he, Durfee? This fellow who looks something like me?" he asked sharply. "You know him—you don't know me—and you know us apart, don't you?"

Durfee never said a word, just glowered at him. "Damn it, you know who he is!" said Landers. He had an insane impulse to seize those bull shoulders, try to shake it out of this lout, this dumb brute with just enough sense to try to save himself a little time in jail. Durfee just an employee in that racket, and if they never picked up the two principals Durfee would get a lighter charge. "Damn it, tell me! You know I'm not him—this Speedy! It won't do you any harm to tell them so—"

But it would, of course; and that was why Durfee was dumb. They could surmise (if they would, if they believed him that Landers wasn't Speedy) that he knew the other man's name.

Durfee growled at him and opened his mouth, only to say, "I ain't sayin' nothin'. Not nothin'."

Landers didn't try to talk to him again. Ten minutes later the sergeant came and led Landers out and told him he could go. Landers took a bus back to Hollywood, ate half a sandwich at a drugstore, and dropped into a movie-house showing old classics. When he came out three hours later and started home, he didn't remember anything about the movie at all except that just at the last the U.S. Cavalry had arrived to the rescue.

He wished he could think there'd be a last-minute rescue for Tom Landers.

Mendoza came home early, having forestalled Grace's effort to detail the funny suicide to him, and Hackett's to offer him a blow-by-blow account of how he'd picked up the hit-run driver. Mendoza came home to the house on Rayo Grande Avenue in the Hollywood Hills, and greeted his hostages to fortune very absently.

Mrs. MacTaggart told him he would have a dram to whet his appetite, and El Señor followed her kitchenward. Alison had been off on a day's painting trip and demanded opinion on the result, displayed on an easel beside the credenza. "I've missed the feel somehow—the light came out wrong—"

"I got you a new handbag," said Mendoza, handing over the package.

"Well, how very nice of you, amado—what prompted that?" She looked back at the little seascape. "Not at all what I intended, but this last batch of rose-madder I—Luis!" said Alison, having just come up with the sales-slip. "How dare you—sixty-five dollars—and it's real cobra—"

"Yes, and I thought it had cured me of an obsession," said Mendoza, "but it doesn't seem to have."

"It's beautiful—but sixty-five—" The cats appeared to be patted, and the shaggy dog Cedric; the twins were about to have their baths, and could be heard in noisy jollities down the hall. Mendoza swallowed the rye in three gulps, took off jacket and tie, went into the bedroom to hang both away, and came back to pace the living room. "What were you doing in Robinson's?" asked Alison.

"Chasing a wild, wild goose," said Mendoza. "An irrelevant wild goose. There is nothing in it at all—¡nada absolutamente!—and I thought I had put it out of my mind. Out. Irrelevant. Irrational. But I keep having the feeling—" He stopped short in the middle of the room and automatically caught Sheba as she leaped for him. She scrambled up to his shoulder. "Yeast," said Mendoza.

"Yeast?" Alison was investigating the handbag, and now said, "Well, of all things—talk about being modern—" The handbag was fitted out with, besides the usual mirror, a cobra-sheathed comb, compact, and handy pint-sized flask. She looked at him resignedly. "You didn't notice, I know. Yeast?"

"Working away," said Mendoza, "in the dark. My mind. Or mushrooms," he added vaguely. "I don't know what the hell is there in my mind—"

"You're fussing about Landers," said Alison. "I know. If they—"

"Oh, Tom," said Mendoza. He wandered out to the hall, up to his little-used den, and sat down at the desk and brought out a pack of cards. Sheba fled.

"¡Qué hombre!" said Alison. "¿Para qué?—what's the use?" She went to the kitchen to put the finishing touches on dinner.

Summoned three times, Mendoza finally sat down to dinner with her and absently consumed wild rice, pot roast, browned potatoes, asparagus in Hollandaise sauce, a slice of Mrs. MacTaggart's special chocolate cake, and four cups of coffee. When Alison asked him if he wanted more potatoes, he said, "¿Cómo? I could look forever at it, there is nothing there—how could there be anything there?"

"I don't know. If you'd like to tell me about it, amado—"

He held out his cup for more coffee. "What set me off in this direction? Oh— Ridículo. Nineteen forty-seven, I ask you . . . and the dog, of course—"

Alison steered him back toward the living room. "I don't think you're in a fit state to read Kipling aloud tonight. You'd better—"

The twins, of course, had other ideas. Powdered and pajamaed, they corralled him at the living-room door. "Los cuentos now! Máiri said," announced Johnny firmly. "All about El Gato all by himself—an'—an' —El Rinoceronte! Daddy—El Gato first—don' listen to Terry, niña tonta—"

"Daddy—Daddy—no Rinoceronte, La Ballena swallows el marinero! La Ballena, Daddy—"

"Really, you know—" began Alison.

Johnny planted himself insistently on Mendoza's shoes and tugged

161

at his trousers. *"El Gato!"* he shouted at the top of his lungs. *"El Gato*
all by himself—an' *la mujer* makes *el pacto* with—*la mujer* more smart
as *El Gato—"*

And Mendoza said, *"¡Diez millones de demonios desde el infierno!*
Jane Doe! By God, Jane Doe!"

Alison rescued Johnny as Mendoza ran for the phone. As he ran, he
brought up a few random thoughts from the yeast of his subconscious
mind.

"Tired-looking—she was—and why not? But why—why the hell? Jane
Doe—Santa Monica? But that store— Art? Meet you at the office in
half an hour . . . I don't know. Something. Nothing. It's ridiculous,
damn it, but— I'll see you."

Hackett had stopped telling him he was going senile by the time
they came to the door of the shabby old duplex unit of the court in
Santa Monica. They waited, Hackett shifting his bulk restlessly, and
the door opened. There wasn't any screen door, and the little living
room behind the woman in the doorway was lighted brightly. Mendoza, with his long sight, saw over her shoulder in there the large
framed photograph on the table, and he let out a sudden deep breath.

"¡Ya está!" he said very quietly. "It was a hunch after all—only we
didn't hold the extra ace."

"What is it?" Her voice sounded tired too. She snapped on the porch
light, saw Mendoza first. "Oh, you were in the store— Yes?" His eyes
led hers to his outstretched hand, with the badge in it. For a moment
she didn't move. Then she turned and walked into the room, tacit
invitation. They went in.

Hackett had just discovered the photograph. "But, my God," he said
in naked astonishment, "that's—but it can't—"

Mendoza picked it up: a glossy eight-by-ten photograph in a silver
frame. Holding it, he looked at Jessica Manyon. She had once been a
pretty woman: fair complexion, brown hair, hazel eyes. Habit and necessity had kept her groomed, clean, neat, but her face was too thin and
she looked older than she probably was.

She turned away from them, and then reached to the coffee table,
took a cigarette from the box there. Mendoza flicked his lighter. "I
think," he said, "you have something to tell us, Mrs. Manyon."

"I don't know your name."

"Lieutenant Mendoza—Sergeant Hackett. Central Homicide."

"Yes," she said. "And I can't imagine how you found me. But it really doesn't matter. It was just—the last thing of all the bad things, and I wasn't going to live with it any longer. I was going to the police tomorrow. So it really doesn't matter at all."

"Sit down, Mrs. Manyon. I have to inform you that you needn't talk to us if you'd rather not, and you are entitled to—"

"An attorney, yes. Don't be stupid. I'd decided to tell the police, and so it doesn't matter at all. You know, I never was superstitious, but I wonder now if there are—jinx people. If I'm a jinx to—everybody I touch." She looked at him reflectively. "The worst of this is, it's not only going to affect me. Innocent people too. But I suppose it's—impossible that it—shouldn't have to come out. All of it. Would you do me a favor, Lieutenant? You'll find a bottle of bourbon in the kitchen, if you'd make me a drink? I think it might help. Do have one—yourselves—if you'd like."

When he brought her the glass, she took a long swallow and put the glass down beside her. "A jinx," she said. "I wonder. I'll tell you just how it happened, and maybe you'll wonder too." And she found a small smile for Hackett, who was still studying the photograph. "That," she told him, "was my husband. Kenneth Charles Manyon. He was killed in a silly little accident on Christmas Eve, nineteen forty-six. He'd been all through the fighting in Europe, and then he came home—to be killed like that. He was twenty-six and I was twenty-five. We were expecting our first baby in April."

"Oh, yes," said Mendoza. "Yes, I see."

"Do you? After Ken was killed—I wonder if you can understand how much I wanted that baby. Something of Ken's. Of ours. We—we'd decided on names, Martha for a girl, Charles for a boy. Of course I got his insurance—he was still in the Army—and I came back here, I'd grown up here. It was home even though I was alone—my father died when I was twelve, and Mother the year before Ken was killed. There weren't any relatives at all. I came back here—and I went to Dr. Lawrence. I liked him, he was a good doctor, I'm sure of that. He'd just started his clinic—and—I went there—to have the baby. He—"

"Oh, yes." And Mendoza heard the echo of young Dr. Lawrence: *about fifteen beds and only three nurses.* Could you say, hurried and overworked nurses?

"And then—and then they told me—the baby was dead. Stillborn. I wanted to die—it wasn't fair. But you don't die, you go on because you have to. It seemed as if Ken had died all over again. But I—picked up the pieces, and I went on." She took another swallow of her drink.

"I don't want to bore you, I needn't go into details. I got married again four years after that, but he was—no good. A drinker, a drifter. I divorced him, and I took Ken's name again. It—well, never mind. And I've had to work, of course, but it didn't seem worth the effort to—take courses, get a better job. It didn't matter. There wasn't anyone to care. And time went on—until about—six weeks ago. Funny. A day like any other day. When—she—came—to—my counter—to look at handbags." Her eyes were wide, blind now. "When I saw her—the first time—"

Mendoza reached over and took the photograph from Hackett. "When you saw Catherine Hatfield," he said, "and realized—" The photograph showed a good-looking young man in uniform; and uncannily, Catherine Hatfield was a latter edition of him. The same olive skin, straight nose with flared tip, dark eyes, wide smiling mouth, pointed chin, dark smooth hair.

"She was Ken's daughter!" said Jessica Manyon, and she still sounded astonished at that little fact. Her mouth was trembling. "*Our* daughter. I couldn't mistake—it was like seeing Ken young again—even his smile, one-sided—and—I knew—then I knew—"

The hurried, harried nurses, perhaps a couple of deliveries coming along at once, the doctor busy—or summoned and not yet there—and the little unforgivable mistake about the name. "It was Harriet Hatfield's baby who was stillborn," said Mendoza.

"Oh, my God," said Hackett.

She nodded tiredly. She swallowed more of the drink. "I knew. I—I could have been fired, but I couldn't help it—I had to know who—who she—who she *thought* she was . . . I just walked off—followed her. *My* girl—my daughter, that I'd never known, never known about—Ken's daughter. She went—to that shop." Only a couple of blocks from the big department store. "I went in, she was waiting on the customers. I pretended—I don't know how I did, I'd realized it but it was like being in a dream—I got her talking, I found out her name, where she—" She raised her head and there was stark misery in her eyes. "A *mistake*— just a mistake—all that time ago. And if it wasn't my fault—it wasn't theirs either—those people—all those years, she'd been their girl, they thought—I couldn't be so cruel as to tell her, right then—"

"So you went to see Mrs. Hatfield," said Mendoza gently.

"What else would I do? What else *could* I—" She looked a little wild; she took a deep breath, controlled her voice. "I called her—to be sure she was alone, and I tried to be—calm and sensible about it. I took Ken's picture—so she could see for herself— She didn't believe me, of course

she didn't want to believe me, and at first I couldn't blame her—but—
It's not as if I wanted *much*," said Jessica Manyon desperately. "They'd had her—my daughter—all those years, and I'm alone, I haven't anyone. I said if I could just see her sometimes—if she could just know, and understand how I felt— But she—Mrs. Hatfield—she wouldn't agree to that. She was—I could tell—trying not to believe it, even after she saw Ken's picture, after— She wanted to go to that clinic and ask, but I knew there'd be nothing to find there—the mistake made—all that time ago, the doctor'd have found out then—if there was any record."

"Yes. You went to see her several times," said Mendoza, leaning to light her new cigarette. So the dog had seen her there before, and hadn't barked, next door. "You were seen walking up the hill."

She put a hand to her head. "The car went out on me last year—it wasn't worth getting repaired. I can take the bus to work. Yes. I kept— at the last I was pleading with her—I didn't care what I had to do—but somehow, I had to get her—to say—it was only right, you can see that. All that time she'd thought—her own daughter, and I couldn't—" She was a woman of integrity; maybe this wouldn't have happened otherwise.

"That last day," she said, "if I can explain it to you—I was feeling— desperate. She didn't want to believe me, and by then she'd just shut her mind to it. She was—hard, because—I know now—she was frightened. That was it, of course she was frightened." And of course the normally open Harriet Hatfield hadn't told her family, her nice close-knit family, anything at all about this. "She said—it just wasn't possible, and I wasn't to bother her anymore—and I was just a—a fanatic with a queer idea and she wasn't going to have me—upsetting her family." Jessica finished her drink. "I'd been so sorry for her at first, you know. Any woman would be. But I—when she said that, I—I tried not to be sorry for myself, but sometimes—it's hard. And all I could think, right that minute, was how she had—so much, so much, and things I'd never had—and it wasn't right that she should have *my daughter* too, just because—

"I don't remember hitting her, you know. I'd tell you about it if I did, but I don't. I remember—it was funny, I could only get out a whisper at her, wasn't I ever to have anything, when she had—and then—and then, she was lying there—"

There was a little silence, and she looked up with a tired smile. "A jinx," she said. "It wasn't her fault at all—Mrs. Hatfield's. But I suppose I wasn't—seeing that very clearly at the time."

And then she asked, "Do you want me to come with you now?"

・ ・ ・

"I think he's got one of those things Socrates called his daemon," said Hackett to Angel. "He didn't really know there was anything there, he just felt it. But, my God, those two poor women—and the girl— Couldn't Hatfield or somebody sue that clinic for—"

"What good would that do now?" asked Angel soberly. "But I know how she must have felt. And in a way, the worst still to come—"

"The press uproar, God knows. And I'm damn glad, my Angel, that we can—identify ours so easy. Mark like me and Sheila with my mother's hair and—" Even that didn't make her laugh. "I think I'll call George," said Hackett.

Higgins came back from the phone and said seriously to Mary, "It's a kind of relief. The kids. Stevie's going to look a lot like Bert, and Laurie with your eyes and all. I hope the baby takes after you too—if it's a girl, I mean. But at least let's hope it looks like one of us."

"Why?" asked Mary, amused. "I'm keeping fingers crossed it isn't a girl. The worst spoiled brat in the state, between you and Steve. But why the sudden anxiety, George?"

"That Hatfield thing," said Higgins. "What a thing. That was Art on the phone. The damnedest thing you ever heard—"

"But, Luis!" said Alison, horrified. She sat up in bed, looking very fetching in a blue nylon gown, her red hair curling crisply, burnt flame in the bedside light. "What an awful thing—and with the press falling on it, new sensation, as they will—you don't know who to feel sorriest for. The girl, or—"

"My bet would go there." Mendoza stripped off his trousers, deposited his watch on the bureau tray. "To have that sprung on her all of a sudden—mmh, yes, you can sympathize with everybody concerned in this one."

"But I'll say something else." Alison hugged her knees, looking thoughtful. "If that girl's got any good stuff in her—or the Hatfield husband any common sense and kindness—they'll stay by the Manyon woman. The girl, anyway. Any woman would know how she'd feel."

"Pues sí. And I'm relieved to reflect," said Mendoza, buttoning his pajamas, "how much Johnny looks like you and how much Terry looks like my grandmother. Enough to give any parent a qualm or two—"

"¡Bastante!" said Alison. "Don't be silly. They're really terribly careful about that kind of thing, there's not a chance that—"

166

"Are you reassuring me for the past or the future?" Mendoza switched off the light.

"Now really, Luis— Well," murmured Alison, "of course they do say that children born to elderly parents are apt to be more intelligent—"

"Elderly!" said Mendoza. "*¡Gatita roja, mujer malvada,* miscalling me—"

13

PHIL WAS FEELING FRUSTRATED when she headed out of Soledad north on Thursday evening. The trouble was, she thought, she'd got her mind so firmly fixed on historical records that she'd forgotten a few contemporary facts.

She'd got to Soledad at ten that morning, and thinking of those possible records down in black and white, had made for the courthouse. A motherly clerk had fallen easily for her tale of doing genealogical research for a history of the early state, and helped her look: and nothing had turned up at all. No records of wills, marriages, deaths, births, or anything with either of the surnames she was looking for. By two o'clock there wasn't anywhere else to look, and she sat in the car wondering where else to try, and thought of the local newspaper.

There was a public library; it had back files of the local paper, and she pored over them for some time, without success. What she was looking for, of course, was some evidence of one of those families being still around; but in all the years, she thought, even if there were any descendants here, the name might have changed.

And then it came to her what an idiot she'd been. Two ways. First, of course the important records would be at the county seat, which was Salinas. The second thought opened up wider vistas. When that letter from the Rancho de la Vergine was written, the fact that it was headed *Soledad* didn't mean a thing. In 1888, Soledad would have been the stage-junction, the place the letter was handed on for eventual delivery; and very possibly the only junction in a hundred miles or more. That rancho could have been anywhere in two or three big counties; she didn't think they'd got round to drawing county boundaries then.

Impatient at herself, she started north again for Salinas, not a long drive. She got there too late to do anything that day, checked into a motel and was up early on Friday only to find that the courthouse didn't open its doors until nine-thirty. She fumed over breakfast and was waiting when the custodian arrived.

Again she was lucky in finding a friendly clerk; in fact, she reflected later, it was luck that had sustained her all the way, not good sense. He was a little perky man named Oakes who reminded her of a robin. He suggested property transfers as the most likely fertile source— "Because of the surname of course, but that we can't be sure of, I can see—" but when nothing turned up, he said apologetically that before 1900 people had been very lax about such legalities—little enforced county authority. At any rate, there was no mention of the property known as the Rancho de la Vergine.

"Well, we needn't be so easily discouraged," said Mr. Oakes brightly. "Suppose we look at a little later period—"

Nothing turned up. Even until rather recently, Phil thought, with all the new rules and regulations, not every will got formally offered for probate. Property deed-transfers would be on record somewhere; not necessarily here. For all she could be sure of, that property could now, with boundaries drawn, be over in Merced County or up in Stanislaus County.

"Death certificates," said Mr. Oakes. "Marriage licenses—" But they were a rather recent requirement too, and Phil said absently that if the property had stayed more or less in the family, they had probably been Catholic. And thought about church records, not hopefully.

But it was another place to go, and also, church records (so divorced from state regulations) might go back a long way, if there were any. The only thing was, the church harboring them might be anywhere a good long way from Salinas.

Or would it? Phil thought about that. Back all those years ago, there probably wouldn't have been a church in Soledad, or for miles around there. What would there have been? A few Indian missions, priests traveling about? And Salinas was an old town too.

She debated about trying the old mission, but that was over toward Monterey and she wasn't sure it was open, or harbored any records. In the end she drove around and chose the oldest-looking Catholic church she found, which didn't look so ancient at that, and went in.

Here she found a brisk young redhaired priest who was instantly fired with interest in her search. "Fascinating, history," he told her enthusiastically. "People. Eighteen eighty-eight, you said, that'll be a while back, but let's think about it. No church here then, of course. The mission, the big one, that is, but St. Artemus had a small mission hereabouts, I seem to recall—that's us. Every Christian place then—few and far between, you know, Miss O'Neill—would send priests out on regular tours, a week or two weeks' journey around—marrying people, burying 'em, baptizing—that sort of thing. Necessary, with only a few men of the cloth in hundreds of miles, you see. Let's have a look at some of the early church journals." He unearthed these from a chest in a bright little room at the side of the church, and looked interestedly. And it was in that old journal, near the front of the tall old tome, that they came across two lines of Latin script recording the ceremony of marriage between Elena Ranulfo and Matteo Corpofretta of the "ranchero on the fork of the River San Joaquin near El Pináculo."

"Well!" said Father Murphy, interested. He translated that for her. "That gives you the location, anyway, Miss O'Neill. Of course in the last seventy-eight years"—the marriage was dated 1893—"the property may have changed hands a dozen times, or been broken up—and even if it hasn't, and any descendants are still around and still good church-members"—he chuckled—"they'll still hardly be dependent on traveling priests these days, any later records would—"

"But where was it, what do you mean?"

"Show you a map." He found a map of the state in a drawer, unrolled it. "Right here—here's where we are, and here's the San Benito Mountains, east and north of Soledad—and the Pinnacles National Monument. Your rancho'll be somewhere in that territory, or it was. There's a number of tributaries of the San Joaquin through there."

"Well." Phil looked at the map. And again she thought she'd been an idiot, wasting time. Not very big populations around there, Soledad or east of it. But of course she hadn't known a more precise location for the property. Now she thought that there should be a few old-timers who might, hopefully, remember old names and people and places.

It was only a little after two o'clock. She snatched a sandwich at a drugstore, got the gas-tank filled, and headed back for Soledad. She didn't stop there but found a secondary road leading east away from town.

Six hours later she was admitting she was lost. The road had led up into hills and more hills, empty and wild; presently a sign directed her to the National Monument. It occurred to her, discouragingly, that the original rancho might have been purchased by the government for the National Monument. Another road led her north through completely wild land, and when she came to one looking slightly newer and more promising, going east again, she took it, but it led her through more emptiness.

She drove on; she must come to some evidence of civilization sometime. It was full dark and she was nearly starving to death and watching the gas-gauge anxiously when around a curve of the hilly road she came suddenly on human habitation. A gas-station: a lighted café: four parked cars: across from the café a row of four houses.

"Thank heaven!" said Phil.

The woman in the café fed her on waffles and maple syrup and very good coffee, and said she guessed Phil could use her extra bedroom, no motels around there. To further questions she added that Captain Adam Watkins knew pretty well everything about these parts, his grand-dad had come here back in the seventies. Captain Watkins of the Highway Patrol—station just up the road, him and Corporal Fosdick was all there was but about all the law needed around here.

"Thank you very much," said Phil. "And I could eat another waffle, please."

Friday had been a somewhat hectic day for Central Homicide.

Mendoza had called Howard Hatfield at eight o'clock, asked him please to keep the family home. He had broken the story to them as gently and tactfully as possible, but of course it wasn't a story they could listen to calmly. He'd brought a policewoman with him, and that was just as well: the girl broke down and Hatfield was incredulous, bitter, angry, and breathing vengeance in turn.

The Hatfields were in for an unpleasant time. Unfortunately truth was not always pleasant. The press, casting around for new sensations, was going to fall on Harriet Hatfield, Jessica Manyon and the Lawrence Clinic as manna from heaven.

It would be, Mendoza reflected, only neighborly to warn young Dr. Lawrence—but before he got round to it, he was summoned to the D.A.'s office for a conference.

The D.A., having read the first reports on the Hatfield case, couldn't decide whether to call it murder first or second. Mendoza couldn't help him there. The warrant would be processed sometime today.

The inquest on Grace's suicide was scheduled for Friday afternoon, and Grace and Palliser were still wondering what was behind that one. "Waste of time," said Mendoza over a hurried lunch. "As long as you're sure it was suicide."

"Oh, that it was . . . I'm just curious," said Grace. "This Hatfield thing is making headlines. Those poor damned people."

But there wasn't anything Homicide could do to make it easier for the Hatfields. Homicide's business was getting at the truth, and sometimes the chips flew far and wide.

William Royce was up for arraignment today; Piggott could cover that, offering the brief evidence. The Hatfield thing, now entirely out of Homicide's hands, was annoying because every time a Homicide officer appeared in the main lobby the press was around him clamoring for more details.

They had still to get a formal statement from that Raye, the hit-run driver, and get that warrant through.

At six o'clock on Friday evening, just as Mendoza was thinking of going home, the D.A.'s office called and one of the prosecutors informed him that they were making it murder first on Jessica Manyon. "Always providing the psychiatric examination shows her to be competent."

Mendoza, hat in hand, went out to the anteroom talking to himself about psychiatrists and passed that on to Grace and Higgins, just leaving as Sergeant Thoms took over the switchboard. "Competent!" said Mendoza. "Would you take a bet that if they say she's neurotic they'll call it temporary insanity?"

Grace laughed. "Which has always struck me as about the silliest charge there is. Temporary insanity kind of like saying temporarily dead."

"*Exacto*. Silly is the word." And inevitably they were waylaid by reporters on their way out.

On the way home Mendoza thought about the silly phrase and muttered to himself. Jessica Manyon was sane, he thought; but everyone had a breaking point, and to some it came easier—or quicker—than others. If Jessica had had anything else—a live husband, another child, even an aged aunt—it could be that the little unforgivable mistake wouldn't have sent her to the breaking point.

But the thing in him, the part of Luis Mendoza that worried around and about any little puzzle like a dog with a bone, had settled down and was satisfied about the Hatfield thing, now. And as a result of that, it had started to worry and wrestle again with the puzzle about Landers.

On the one hand it was nothing, the casual lie or mistake built up into more than it warranted by the perennially suspicious I.A. men— or make that watchful. And on the other, of course—

Mendoza swore aloud, turning into the driveway. It wasn't quite dark yet, and as he came out of the garage a vigilant whistle greeted him from the alder tree: *Yankee Doodle came to town!*

"If that—creature—stays around here permanently," he said to Alison, "I wish to God one of you would teach him the rest of that tune."

"I know," said Alison. "Like waiting for the other shoe to drop."

Saturday started out even more hectic than Friday. At least no court-rooms demanded attendance, on a weekend, but business at Homicide had stepped up. June would be fading into July in a couple of weeks, and July with the first of the summer heat always brought a rise in the crime-rate. It hadn't gone over eighty last week; today it was edging up past eighty-five.

Another body had turned up in MacArthur Park, but not a mys-terious one. Hackett, coming back to type a first report on it, said tersely, "Kid about eighteen. Typical description. At a guess, the over-dose, let the surgeon say if it's acid or H or speed. No I.D. on him." Before starting the report he sent a description down to Missing Persons.

Grace and Palliser had gone out to look at another corpse, but both of those were run-of-the-mill business, no problem for Homicide except creating the everlasting paper work. The second corpse was that of an elderly man horridly, but naturally, dead in a cheap room on Temple Street. He had hemorrhaged his life away on the thin flowered rug there; among other things in the room were papers identifying him as an outpatient at the General Hospital, so Grace and Palliser went around there to find out more about him.

Just before noon on Saturday a shocked and incoherent young Dr. Lawrence invaded Mendoza's office. "My God," he said, "what *is* this? I was away overnight—my sister's birthday—the press falling on—and Uncle nearly had a coronary—my God, but these things don't *happen!* It's just impossible—I tell you, these things don't—"

All Mendoza could offer him was sympathy.

And he was wrestling again with the problem of Landers, the im-possible, handle-less answerless thing. Ordinarily he managed to con-trol his temper with the brashest pressmen, but today a couple of them annoyed him considerably with some crude questions about Jessica Manyon. He came into Federico's feeling dangerous, and unprece-dentedly put down a double rye.

It was just nicely warming his empty stomach when Lieutenant Southey came up to the table.

"Well, now," said Captain Adam Watkins comfortably, "not that I've laid eyes on many policewomen, you're about the fetchingest one I ever saw, Miss O'Neill. So you're just expecting me to answer questions without knowing why?"

"It's a complicated sort of story," said Phil apologetically, "and besides I don't want you to—get any preconceived ideas. I can only tell you it's about something terribly important and—and it involves a man's whole career."

"Well, I don't mind obliging you," said Captain Watkins. This little rural barracks of the California Highway Patrol had one room up and one down. The corporal slept upstairs when he was on duty; Captain Watkins had a comfortable ranch home of his own back in the hills, and a wife who worried about his meals when he was on shift away from home. Phil thought it was wasted effort; the captain had a little round paunch, a round rosy face, and shrewd blue eyes.

"You said you'd like to hear some gossip about local folks? Well, that's a thing old-timers like me do real good, Miss O'Neill—"

"Maybe there are families around who've been here for a long time," suggested Phil. "Since the seventies and eighties?"

"Some of 'em, sure," he said. There was a desk in this little office but the captain seemed to prefer his old rocker by the window to the swivel desk-chair. "You interested in any particular families? My grand-dad came here back in eighteen sixty-four, time he got out of uniform. First Virginia Rifles. I guess I know most of what there is to know about most local folks—besides bein' an old-timer I'm the law around here."

Phil didn't want to lead him directly. "There was a ranch," she said. "I don't know how big, or exactly where, but somewhere around here, and it was—" she started to say the name, and substituted, "owned by an Italian named Corpofretta. Pietro Corpofretta."

"Oh, them," said Watkins. "That old Fir Green ranch. I always did wonder how it came by the name, there aren't any firs on it as far as I remember." Eighty-three years, thought Phil, and the foreign-sounding name getting garbled; perhaps the descendants of Pietro not even knowing the language, American now, and not knowing what the name meant. "That place," said Watkins. He brought out his pipe and started methodically to fill it from an old pouch. "Old man Cris Corpofretta owns it now. It was a good workin' ranch when he inherited it from his dad. Around four thousand acres, call it. He's let it run down some. Doesn't run more than a couple of hundred head of cattle, and

174

raises just about enough to grain 'em decent. That was one o' the biggest and best properties round here once. There was a tale—I recall my grand-dad telling that—that the first Corpofretta won the land on a horse-race. I don't know if that's so, but it's the kind of thing that used to happen when this country was young—Americans just coming in, you know." He puffed energetically, at last got the pipe lit. "Anyway, Cris came by it by marriage you could say. His great-uncle—he had the same name too—all he had was a daughter, and she couldn't take title to the land, acourse, so by all accounts—I heard that through hearsay, little before my time it was—he married her to her first cousin, that'd be Cris's grand-dad. This the kind of thing you want to hear, Miss O'Neill?"

"Just the kind of thing, please." But— "Does this one, the man who owns the ranch now, have any children for it to go to?"

"Well, I guess you could say that's the reason he's let the place go downhill," said Captain Watkins. "There isn't properly speaking any-body except the grand-kids, and no telling if either of 'em 'd want to work it. I expect Cris'll leave it to John Trebizond in the end. He's married to Cris's granddaughter Julia. Sure, Cris had a boy, just the one child, Matthew. He wasn't interested in the place, he turned out a city man—went away to college, and then the war came and Matthew joined up. He was killed at Anzio in the Second World War."

"Oh," said Phil. "Then he had children?"

"Yes, he did," said Captain Watkins. "He got married while he was in college, and he had two—a boy and a girl. Their mother used to bring them to Cris's ranch, summers. Till she got married again. Julia, she's the older of the two, she loves the place, a nice girl Julia is, she came back here to live with Cris and finish high school. The boy—Ran-dal his name is, they call him Randy—well, he's a city man too."

"You said this Julia lives here—"

"Yep. Married to Johnny Trebizond, got two good boys, Johnny's in real estate over in King City. Could be the boys'll show some interest in the ranch, they get older, and Cris maybe'll leave it to them. Couldn't say. I don't figure he'd think about Randy at all."

"What about him?" Phil thought, he would be about thirty-three, thirty-four?

"City man like I say." Watkins contemplated his pipe. "We never saw much of him, since he used to come here summers when he was a kid, up to the time he was twenty-one, twenty-two. Since, he comes back to visit Cris every once in a while. Not so often, and no special time. Be here a week, a month, off he goes again. Very pleasant-spoken feller, and he gives out that it's when he's out of a job he turns up here—" Watkins cocked his head at Phil. "I been wondering about that, just lately. No real reason to. He's supposed to be a salesman of some kind. I can't say I've seen much of him—I'll just hear he's stayin' with Cris again, awhile, and then he's gone. I do know that Julia nor Cris never hear from him, one year's end to the other, till he turns up here—once in a long while."

"Oh," said Phil. Suddenly her heart started beating a little faster. "Did you say he's there now—at the ranch?"

"Didn't say, but he is. Sure enough. I heard it from Fred Whitehead just the other day, he's the rural-delivery driver. Old Cris never says much when he does come to town, but I got it figured he doesn't so much cotton to Randy landin' on him, even as often as he does which isn't often. City man," repeated Captain Watkins. "Doesn't turn a hand when he is there."

Phil stood up. "Captain Watkins, could you—could we drive out to this place and—maybe I could get a look at this Randy? That's all I want to do. It might—it just might be—terribly important, and help a lot."

"Well, I don't know why not," said Watkins easily. "I haven't been over that way in a spell, and the corporal can hold down the station. Isn't often I get the chance to take a pretty girl for a ride in my cruiser."

As they went out, Phil found she had, absurdly, crossed the fingers on both hands tightly.

Hackett came into the dining room with Higgins just in time to hear the loud raised voices down at the front of the room, and they both ran. Mendoza was swearing violently in Spanish; Hackett got there just in time to grab him as he swung on Southey.

"Insubordinate—" said Southey, white and furious. "You know I'll report this, Mendoza! You've no business inter—"

Mendoza told him what he could do with his report. "Goddamn it, Southey, you watchdogs have built this thing up out of nothing and you know it! You've got no damned reason to keep my man suspended and by God I'll expect you to—"

"On the contrary," said Southey, "we've turned up some evidence from his home town that he was once known by that nickname. We have the identi—"

"That's impossible," said Hackett and Higgins together.

"On the contrary," and Southey's voice was pure ice, "it is perfectly sound evidence. From a former school acquaintance of Landers', Fred Barker, and the more we turn up on this the more I—"

"For God's sake simmer down, Luis!" said Hackett. "Go away, Southey. Take your Goddamned meaningless little evidence on a man you don't know at all and get out of our sight—I'm not going to hold him forever."

Southey stalked off. "You needn't ruin the press of this jacket," said Mendoza, and Hackett let him go. "What the hell, Art? They can't have evidence—on *Tom?*"

"It's some damned nonsense they've built out of nothing, it's got to be. What set you off at him?"

Mendoza laughed shortly. "A double rye and something he said about Tom. Never mind. But what the hell they think they've got—"

For once Hackett ate his low-calorie plate without martyred comment. They cut lunch short; afterward they got into the Ferrari and Mendoza drove up to Fountain Avenue.

They found Landers, in sports-shirt and slacks, gloomily watching an old movie on TV. He greeted them with apprehension. "What now?"

"That's what we'd like to know," said Mendoza. "The I.A. boys now tell us they've got evidence that you were once called Speedy. Back in school, up in Fresno."

"Oh, don't be ridiculous," said Landers. "I never picked up a nickname in my life, let alone a silly one like— Where'd they get that from?"

"One Fred Barker," said Hackett, sitting down. "Who is he?"

"Who? *Barker*," said Landers, staring. "Oh, *him.* Oh, for God's sake! I just hope all their evidence is as worthless as that! Barker's a little fellow who never made friends at school—hanger-on, didn't know anybody very well. Or vice versa. Where he dreamed that up for I.A. God only knows, but anybody in town who knows me could tell you that's a lie."

"*¡Condenación!*" said Mendoza. "And by God, what I wouldn't give to turn up some real evidence to show them they've been chasing a mirage—and rub their noses in it well and good!"

"Amen to that," said Hackett. "And that'd be quite a trick, Luis."

"At any rate, that little piece of their so-called evidence we can scotch —and I really thought they were supposed to be better trained than that, taking hearsay for— But how to get you off the hook altogether—" Mendoza swore again.

And Hackett said rather heavily, "When the chips are all down, boy, I think somehow the deck gets stacked on the side of the good people."

"Go say that to Mrs. Manyon, Art," said Higgins quietly, "or Catherine Hatfield. Or Wanda Shaw."

"Oh, hell and damnation!" said Hackett angrily. "What else can we do about this, Luis?"

"Hold the good thought," said Mendoza dryly, "that what you just said holds true at least fifty percent of the time, Arturo."

And if any official prayers were put up on it, it was probably by Piggott, or possibly by Mrs. MacTaggart, who in her sojourn with the Mendozas had come to take a proprietary interest in the LAPD.

In any case, whether it was official prayers or Mendoza's flights of profanity, the answer walked into the Homicide office at seven-forty Saturday night.

Mendoza and Hackett were still there because just as they'd been leaving at six o'clock, a sergeant from Missing Persons had brought in a distraught middle-aged woman in tears. She had just, said the sergeant, identified the teen-age kid full of dope as her son. She sat in Mendoza's office and wept, and as she wept she talked.

"It was all the boys he went with—real bad boys—but he wouldn't listen, he wouldn't listen—they know it all, that age, they never believe anything bad can happen to them—it was the boys like that Chavez, and Harry Rodriguez, and Alfonso Real—they got him to taking the dope—he wouldn't listen, I tried to get him to listen to me, but—"

They wanted the names of any other users, pushers, sellers, and the night men weren't in yet. Sergeant Thoms called Alison and Angel; police wives get used to that sort of thing. They got the woman's name, which was Juanita Enriquez, and asked patient questions. By seven-thirty they'd got all she could tell them, which was quite a lot, including some addresses and the names of a few adults possibly selling the stuff. They called a squad car to take her home.

"I'd better pass this up to Callaghan's office," said Mendoza.

"I suppose," said Hackett. "Damn, I wish I could think of something constructive to do about Tom. Everything they've got—or think they have—is all up in the air, and don't tell me they don't know it! Those damn bloodhounds leaning over backward—"

Mendoza got up, frowning, and stretched. "¡No es verdad! The point is—incompatibility. If that's the word."

"Come again?"

"Incompatibility. They don't know Tom. We do."

"Oh. Yes," said Hackett. "But that's past praying for."

Mendoza picked up his hat, and Sergeant Thoms appeared in the doorway looking surprised. "Lieutenant—" He stood back, and a little pert-looking blonde came into the office. She wasn't exactly pretty, and she wasn't cute either because she had a pair of very steady sensible dark-blue eyes to offset the freckles on her nose and a new sunburn. She looked tired, and her green silk-jersey dress was wrinkled. "Lieutenant Mendoza?"

"That's me. What can we do for you?"

"I'm Phil O'Neill. Oh, I mean—" She fumbled in her bag and produced a badge. They looked at it, surprised. "I thought I'd better come to you. Because I.A. probably wouldn't listen to me at all. I'm just a clerk down in Records. I work the computer."

"Oh, you work the computer," said Hackett. "But what—"

"I'm doing it all wrong," she said. She shook her head, feeling one temple. "I'm still muzzy from driving—sorry. I'm a friend of Tom's, you see. And when this funny thing happened—well, of course it's awful, but to anybody who knows Tom it *is* funny—in a sort of way—and I just had an idea. I'm sorry, I just didn't think you'd listen to me, Lieutenant—of course Tom's told me this and that about you, the other men—but it wasn't even as if it was a hunch. It was just a simple little idea."

"About Tom and this funny thing?" asked Hackett.

"Well, yes. And my vacation was coming up, so I—"

"*Phil* O'Neill?" said Mendoza.

She blushed through the new sunburn. "Well, Phillipa Rosemary—only not for a junior officer LAPD. You can see that. And so I went looking—it sounded fairly crazy, but Mrs. Landers and Jean didn't think so, of course—"

"What," asked Mendoza, "was the idea about, Miss O'Neill?"

"Genes. I came as soon as I could. It was just about ten when— And it's nearly five hundred miles, but I made it in just over eight hours. And considering some of the roads before I got back on the coast highway— But we mustn't waste any time, Lieutenant," she said earnestly. "You're the one to take it up to I.A. and—and shove their noses in it. They still wouldn't listen to me."

"Take what? To I.A.? What do you—"

"Why, I've found him," she said. "I knew *in my bones* he had to be somewhere—but just as Mrs. Landers said, it was such a simple idea the men wouldn't even think about it—probably laugh your heads off. But I found him. And Captain Watkins is keeping an eye on him for us, and you'd better send him a teletype to arrest him—material witness will do to start—"

"Found who?" asked Hackett blankly.

"Oh, for goodness' sake, *men!*" said the pert blonde impatiently. "The one these idiotic witnesses thought they were identifying—the dead ringer for Tom—the real Speedy. His name is—"

14

MENDOZA STARED AT HER for a moment and then let out a yell of exultant mirth. "*¿Parece mentira? ¡No me diga!* My God, do you mean— Oh, by God, but what a facer for those—" He leaned on the desk, laughing helplessly.

"And I think you ought to teletype Captain Watkins," said Phil urgently. "He couldn't arrest him just on my say-so, of course, but you— Not that I think he's likely to run, he hasn't an idea he's been spotted, I was very careful, but—"

"My God!" said Hackett. "My God—a ringer for Tom? But what— how'd you find—"

"Well, he'll startle you," said Phil. "I thought it *was* Tom ten feet away—of course they're fourth or fifth cousins, I haven't worked that out, but—we really had better get him nailed, you know—"

Mendoza pulled himself together. "Oh, by God, what a—by God, *how* I'm going to enjoy— Yes, Miss O'Neill. Yes, we had." He leaned down and planted a kiss on her freckled nose. "If I'd known there was a real detective working on it— Come and tell me where to teletype."

When they came back Hackett was talking excitedly with Galeano and Schenke. "No, that's all I—Luis took her to— Did you get him?"

"Captain Watkins is going out into the wilds to nail him right now," said Mendoza. "I've got the C.H.P. to say they'll fly him down tomorrow. Material witness. But what a—*Dios*, and wasn't it just the sudden scatterbrained idea a female would have, and then get it to work out just as— Oh, I can *hear* Southey and—" He collapsed again.

"I called Tom," said Hackett. He had also tried to get everybody else; but Higgins had taken the family out to see the new Disney, and Palliser was at a discount house with Roberta haggling for a new re-

frigerator. Everybody he had got had asked excited questions and casti-
gated him for not knowing the answers. They demanded details from
Phil now. "Tom said he'd be right down—"

Phil, overtaken by yawns after the long drive, told them about it
sleepily. "It was just logical," she said. "Genes. And he takes after his
mother's side and by the photographs quite a few of them looked a lot
like Grandfather—no, it'd be Great-grandfather—and so I just went and
looked. I knew *in my bones* that Speedy had to show up somewhere
along the line. And—"

"Women," said Schenke. "Women! She knew! She just went looking—"

"*What* did you say his name is?" asked Galeano.

"Corpofretta. Randal—Randy. And when I heard from Captain Watkins—"

"I'll be damned," said Galeano. "In very rough translation, that's what
that means."

"What?" said Schenke and Hackett.

"Speedy," said Galeano. "You could say. A rapid body. That's the
damnedest funny one I've heard, but I bet that's how he came by that
nickname."

They were still asking questions when a breathless Landers arrived
to hear about it all from the start. "—Fifth cousins, I think," said Phil
through a yawn. "And you might be twins. Well, brothers. Uncanny.
Taking after Great-grandfather."

"What?" said Landers blankly. "What—you don't mean—I'll be eter-
nally damned! All the while you've been chasing around looking—
why, *Phil*—"

"On the scatterbrained idea," said Schenke. "I can't get *over* it. She
just knew, so she went and looked and boom, there he was."

"And I'm starving, if anybody's interested," said Phil.

"I'll buy you the biggest steak available, Miss O'Neill," promised
Mendoza.

"I don't want a steak," said Phil. "I want bacon and eggs. I've been
thinking about bacon and eggs ever since I passed through Guadalupe
at five o'clock."

"*¡Mi pobre niña!*" said Mendoza. "We'll find you bacon and eggs—"
The phone buzzed on Sergeant Thoms' desk.

"Hassle over at the U.S.C. Medical Center," he relayed a moment
later. "Sounds sort of confused—you'd both better go." Swearing,

Schenke and Galeano went out. The rest of them took Phil up to a bar and grill on Wilshire and fed her bacon and eggs.

"Heavenly!" she said, buttering toast. "—And then there was Father Murphy, he helped too, and of course Captain Watkins—I wonder if Randy's got a pedigree somewhere. It rather sounded like that—and I think Captain Watkins had started to wonder too. If he thought he was a little hot, he'd make tracks for Grandpa's isolated ranch in the hills—"

"I'd take a bet on that," said Mendoza. He and Hackett had been starving too, and for once Hackett hadn't counted calories, but absorbed a large T-bone and a pile of french fries, listening to the story of the hunt.

"That Italian girl way back there—it was just a kind of family joke!" said Landers. "Oh, I don't mean joke exactly, but you know what I—my God, my great-grandfather—it never crossed my mind there'd be relatives, but—"

"Italians," said Phil, "usually reasonably prolific. I knew— Oh, we've got to call Fresno! My heavens, if Great-aunt Serafina found out about—"

"What do you know about—" Landers stared.

"Goodness," said Phil, crumpling her paper napkin and standing up, "if Jean hadn't burglarized Great-aunt Serafina I'd *never* have found Speedy! And they'll be dying to know—Jean was so furious at that I.A. man, and he was rather Prussian—have you got any change? Go get some. There's a pay phone in the lobby—" She trotted off briskly and Landers went to get some change.

"Of all the damned far-out things!" said Hackett. "I'm going to be curious to see this Speedy. And—"

"You and Tom."

"And you know something, Luis? I think—"

"Oh, yes," said Mendoza, laughing. "Yes, indeed, Art. Tom's got quite a girl there, hasn't he?"

"—Fifth cousins," said Phil. "I think. Maybe even sixth. But it's just the way I guessed—genes. It's really no wonder—so many of the family seemed to take after that old man in the photograph. Oh, Jean, I'll send those back right away—if Great-aunt Serafina—"

"No!" said Jean excitedly. "Honestly? No, that's all right, Phil—she thinks she's mislaid them somewhere, I can just slip them back— Does he really look like Tom? I know you said it must be like that, but how queer—"

Landers thrust his head into the booth. "*I* want to talk to them."

"Yes, in a minute . . . Well, every family's bound to have one black sheep. The rest of the family sounded quite respectable. We think this Speedy may have a record somewhere—"

"I wouldn't be surprised," said Jean. "Phil, are you and Tom—"

"He's right here," said Phil hastily, "he wants to talk to you—"

"Yes, just a minute, here's Mother."

Phil handed the phone to Landers. When he hung up ten minutes later she was propping up the side of the booth, and he said he'd drive her home, she was dead on her feet.

"Don't think I could drive 'nother ten feet," she agreed. When he stopped in front of her apartment on Kingsley she was sound asleep and he had to shake her awake.

"Well, of all the queer things!" Alison sat up in bed, hearing all about it with fascination. "Not but what I don't see exactly how she reasoned. A thing any woman would think, and don't say scatterbrained, Luis. It's just as you were saying about the twins—perfectly logical that they should look like both of us, only different sides of the family—"

"Occasionally," said Mendoza, buttoning his pajamas, "women still astonish me."

"And really not surprising," said Alison, "that they should turn out so much alike—Landers and this Speedy, I mean—even in the fourth or fifth generation. The genes still there. Dormant or whatever."

"But to jump to such a conclusion right off the—"

"Not at all," said Alison. "She sounds like a very bright girl, Luis. Simply postulating a probable possibility."

"*¡Ay de mí!* But scatterbrained or not, the conclusion seems to have justified the—mmh—jumping. I'm going to be damned interested to see this fellow. And—*¡Santa María y José!*—how I'm going to enjoy shoving I.A.'s nose into this one!" He started to laugh again.

"It's just another illustration," said Alison with satisfaction, "of the old adage."

"*¿Cómo?*"

"Never," said Alison sedately, "underestimate the power of a woman."

She called Angel the next morning as soon as Mendoza had left and the twins, full of breakfast, were tearing around the back yard with Cedric in pursuit, the cats hiding under bushes, and *el pájaro* swearing at all of them from the now completed nest.

184

"Isn't this the most—"

"I was *fascinated* when Art told me. Of all the queer things—Mark, leave the pussy alone!—and yet you know, Alison, it was a perfectly logical sort of thing to think of—"

"Which I said to Luis. But they don't like things to be so simple. Not just Luis—of course he's got that complex mind to start with—but any of them, Angel. Men. A fairly complicated result, like Landers getting identified that way, they think it has to have a complicated reason. But this girl sounds very bright. She—"

"She sounds a dear. I want to meet her. Do you suppose she and Landers—"

"I haven't an idea. But when she went to so much trouble—"

"Mmh," said Angel. "I think so. And he certainly couldn't do any better, by what Art said. Oh, dear, they *are* looking forward to telling off those I.A. men! Art was up two pounds and he never even swore . . . Well, depending on when they *do* get married, I thought a shower— with everybody—"

"By all means," said Alison, and then began to laugh. "Really, Angel —speaking about jumping to conclusions—"

The hassle at the U.S.C. Medical Center had turned into quite a thing; Schenke hung around to outline it to Mendoza. A trio of juveniles riding very high on something had been brought in by an irate parent; as the parent happened to be very much a V.I.P., an internationally known entertainer—"In quotes," said Schenke rather disgustedly, and mentioned his name—he had not been turned away to the General. In the process of admitting the juveniles one of them had turned out to have a gun. One intern had been shot dead, a male nurse was in serious condition, and one of the uniformed men in the first car to get there had been shot in one hip. After the Homicide men got there—"He'd got up on the roof of one wing then, and he had a dozen boxes of ammo on him," said Schenke, "he'd just run wild" —he'd got Galeano in the shoulder and leg. Schenke would be sitting on night shift alone for a while; when he left Nick in the hospital, he said, they weren't sure if any bones were broken.

"These Goddamn idiots of kids," said Schenke further, angrily. Yes, they had got him; Schenke had put a bullet in his leg. "I'd rather have made it his head." The well-known entertainer was the sniper's father, and it turned out that the other two juveniles were the offspring of another V.I.P. from the same sophisticated milieu.

"And how very convenient," said Mendoza, sounding pleased.

"*Convenient?*" said Schenke. "With Nick in the hospital—"

"Maybe Art's right and the cards get stacked in our favor. *De veras.* The press has still got the Hatfield thing, but this will—mmh—fill them with joy all over again. It should be very easy to squelch any stray rumors about suspicion of a ranking officer—especially when we've got Speedy to hand over to Van Allen. The bird in hand." Mendoza grinned; Hackett was excitedly relaying the story to the rest of them, out in the anteroom. "George, I'll let you and Art share the exquisite pleasure of telling the tale to I.A. John, you and Jase might find out whether Speedy has a pedigree with us." They had queried San Francisco on that overnight.

"—And," said Mendoza, sitting back at his dapper ease in the chair beside Captain Macklin's desk, "I think that sums up the explanation for your benefit, gentlemen. We all do make mistakes, and while it was entirely understandable that you should—given the initial rather outlandish reason—want to look into the matter, I should have thought," and he smiled slowly at them, "that you would know just a little more than is apparently the case about rules of evidence. In any case—"

"Be damned to that," said Macklin. He sounded suspicious. "I'll believe this rigmarole when I see it proved out myself! All you've got is this fool girl's word—what the hell was a Records clerk doing at—"

"On her own time," Hackett pointed out enjoyably. "And she rang the bell loud and clear, didn't she?"

"I'm not taking that without any more than you've given us!" said Southey sharply. "You were exceeding your responsibility in authorizing the arrest of this man—it's all extremely irregular, bringing in the Highway Patrol, for God's— You haven't an iota of evidence, and—"

Mendoza dropped a little of his suavity, crushing out his cigarette. He stood up. "Put up or shut up, Lieutenant. You can soon judge for yourself. The C.H.P. will be landing him at International this afternoon—"

"And Captain Macklin and I will meet the plane," said Southey.

Mendoza looked at him in silence for a moment. "Afraid I'd try to coach the witness? I might trust you to meet the prisoner, Lieutenant," he said gently, "if you promise to take along a couple of uniformed men from Traffic to make sure he doesn't get away from you between there and here."

"He'll be brought in," said Southey grimly, "and we'll see for ourselves if there's anything to this—tale—or not."

"And you'll arrange it all nicely according to Hoyle," pursued Mendoza, "with a lineup and the three witnesses. Detective Landers is quite ready to cooperate—just one more time, Lieutenant. Say four o'clock?"

"There'll be enough of us there to see fair play," added Higgins to that, and gave them his craggy grin.

The I.A. men didn't bother to say that they knew that. The men from Homicide came out, and Mendoza leaned on the wall and started to laugh again.

"By God, but it was worth—all the worry and fuss!" he gasped. "Their faces—and all because—all because a little blonde Records clerk—had an idea! *Dios*, the more you think of it—"

"I'll say one thing," said Higgins, grinning in sympathy. "By what you tell me, Tom's got something going for him in that girl. I'm damn curious to see this Speedy, but also that blonde. Pretty?"

Hackett considered. "Little," he said, "and dangerous."

"Dangerous?"

"Have any male wrapped around her little finger," said Hackett, "with him convinced it's just opposite." Higgins grinned again and said, That kind.

Phil didn't remember falling into bed. She woke up at one o'clock, hungry again, and made herself a healthy ham sandwich after a long shower. She was just finishing the sandwich when Mendoza called.

"We thought you were entitled to be present at the lineup I.A.'s arranging. Four o'clock."

"I'd love to," said Phil. "Did they say some terribly unkind things about me, Lieutenant?"

"Well, they claim to be gentlemen. They were annoyed, shall we say, by your unsolicited interference. And I hope, Miss O'Neill—you realize we've taken you on faith—that you weren't influenced by wishful thinking when you described Speedy."

"Oh, my," said Phil. "You just wait, Lieutenant." Her car was still parked down in the headquarters lot, she'd have to take the bus. . . .

When she came into the dimmed room with the bright-lighted platform at its front, a little crowd of men was already there. Even before Mendoza came up to introduce her, she recognized them from what Tom had said, various times. The men from Homicide he worked with. The two big ones, sandy Art Hackett, dark George Higgins with his ugly but somehow attractive face. The middle-sized dark fellow would be Matt Piggott, seeing the devil's hand everywhere, and maybe he was right. Dapper brown Grace, tall dark Palliser with his grave mouth.

Off to one side was Captain Van Allen of Auto Theft: it was queer to realize that this had all started as one of his run-of-the-mill cases. The witnesses Byron and Dunne sat with a uniformed man beside them; Al Durfee sat between Macklin and Southey.

The two I.A. men had already seen the ringer, thought Phil; Mendoza had told her they had fetched him in from the airport; but their faces were wooden. Then the platform brightened up there, and they all watched as the line of men filed onto the platform in silence.

Landers was second in line this time. Three more men of the same general type, and then—

"*Jesus!*" exploded Byron and Dunne simultaneously. There was a little hushed murmur of incredulous profanity from some of the Homicide men.

Durfee stared up there and then slumped in his chair. Southey nudged him sharply. "What about it?"

"What do I say?" asked Durfee in a surly tone. "I didn't *believe* it—naw, it wasn't him, but it mighta been his twin—but I'm gonna say it ain't? Just to get a guy I don't know from Adam off the hook? And me further on the hook? I ain't no flat wheel."

"All right, so which one is the fellow you know as Speedy?"

"Well, that one, acourse," said Durfee reluctantly. "Now you got him, it's no skin off my nose. The one at the end of the line. But, jeez, you can see why I—"

It was queer seeing them together, thought Phil. She remembered the moment she'd first seen him—Captain Watkins casually hailing the old man, just cruising around, showing the pretty tourist the country, how's tricks, Cris—and the tall city-dressed man slouching up. It could have *been* Tom—and then she had seen the differences.

But up there, in line separated by three men, the likeness was uncanny—and yet they were unlike.

Corpofretta was the older by two or three years, but he had the same quality (was it freshness of complexion, the way the eyes were set, the mouth?) of looking young—younger than he was. There were the same features, harking so strangely back to that strong-featured man in the faded old photograph—high cheekbones, wide mouth, dark eyes, dark hair growing straight off the forehead, the straight bars of brows—

"God," said Dunne in the darkness, loud and incredulous, "you couldn't hardly tell which was which—but—"

But, with the other one, with Speedy, there was a weak cast to the mouth, an indefinable air of cheap arrogance. Seeing them together, anyone who knew either would know them apart, she thought; and that was queer too.

"Satisfied, Southey?" asked Mendoza. "Would you like to thank Miss O'Neill for finding the missing jigsaw piece? Well, perhaps Captain Van Allen will."

And Southey said stiffly to the uniformed sergeant, "Will you go and ask—Detective Landers—to join us, please?"

Van Allen somewhat grudgingly let the Homicide men sit in on an initial questioning. By then they had Speedy's pedigree: a rather lengthy, if minor, pedigree all around the Bay area, and two counts from L.A. County with the sheriff's boys. B.-and-E., burglary, auto theft and fencing.

He shrugged at them: it was how the dice fell, he said. Almost worth getting dropped on to find out he had a double. He laughed at Landers and said that was a real hot one, all right—he'd got a big kick out of finding he could double for a cop. But close to, they were all seeing that they weren't really doubles: only at first sight, apart from each other.

"Rosso?" he said. "How should I know where he's lit out to? We come back and find the place lousy with fuzz—we took off. That's all I know. Whole operation shot to hell, and we musta had a dozen real sweethearts in ready to go—call it six, seven grand profit. Way the ball bounces. I figure I'm hot, I make tracks for the old man's place—good place to cool off, nobody knows about me up there." Or did know, he'd be adding to himself; he looked angry.

And later, "Sure, some guys call me Speedy. I don't know the lingo, all the Italiano to me's the name, but I remember Grandpa sayin' that —it's kind of what it means, see."

He was small-time, Randy Corpofretta; they left him to Van Allen.

"So, welcome back to the team," said Mendoza to Landers in the hall.

"And, my God, you don't know what a relief— But, damn it, you know what I've got to worry about now?" Landers laughed. "That damn pro lout is going to be passing himself off as me—now he knows about it—"

"Don't borrow trouble," said Mendoza amusedly.

"At least," Hackett reminded him philosophically, "I.A. knows about it too."

"There is that," admitted Landers. He'd looked around for Phil, but she had disappeared.

"Miss O'Neill," said Mendoza, "is a very understanding girl, Tom. She said she thought we'd rather have an all-male reunion, but you can take her out to dinner."

"Oh," said Landers. "Oh, yes, thanks."

"You know, Tom," said Hackett, "if you want my advice, you'll take out a permanent lien on that girl before somebody else does. If I wasn't an upright married man—"

"I had the same thought," said Palliser. "Not that I ever went much for blondes, but she's quite a blonde, isn't she?"

"And a smart one," said Piggott, "which they aren't always. Now you take redheads—" Maybe some day Piggott would get around to proposing to his redhead.

"You buy her a good dinner," Grace told him seriously. "She's earned it."

Mendoza clapped Landers on the shoulder. "Come on, boys—I'll buy drinks around."

They got waylaid by the press, but—even as Mendoza had predicted—the press hadn't an inkling about an upright detective getting confused with a pro; the press was agog with interest in the celebrities' offspring.

"We ought to go see Nick," said Mendoza as he and Hackett got into the Ferrari. "Do you know what he likes to read?"

"*Es muy extraño,*" said Hackett. "Detective novels."

They had Jessica Manyon's arraignment coming up, and Wanda Shaw's; the paper work on the other current cases to get through, and from now on as the heat built up business at Homicide would increase as it always did in summer. But the latest crisis was past, and Mendoza's daemon was for the moment at rest.

As he switched on the engine and the Ferrari roared to life, he muttered absently, "Eggs . . . So Alison said. A new batch. And if they turn out like their father— That damned bird deviling the cats—¡Caray! A man wants a little peace and quiet when he comes home—"

"If you really did," said Hackett, "you wouldn't have."

"Wouldn't have what?"

"Married the redheaded Scots-Irish girl."

"I mean, there's no way to say thanks," said Landers. "When I think of all the trouble you—"

"It was interesting," said Phil. "I'd sort of got my teeth in it by then."

"And where you got such a crazy idea to start with— Well, it was, Phil! My father said—"

"Oh, men. Your mother and Jean saw it right away. Naturally."

"And when I think of you tackling that awful old woman— Great-aunt Serafina," said Landers, "replaced the bogeyman for Jean and me as kids. Phoo! She is a terror—"

"No, she's not," said Phil. "She's just a lonely old woman who—who never had much, Tom, and she's jealous of the little she does have."

Landers looked down at her in silence. He'd brought her to Frascati's on Sunset Boulevard, the nice quiet place where you could be private and leisurely, and he'd enjoyed a meal for the first time in days. Phil looked very neat and cool and self-possessed in a blue cotton-lace dress and the high-heeled white sandals that still only brought her blonde curls to his chest.

"Well, I can't get over Jean," he said. "She used to be terrified of the old lady. You seem to have hit it off with Jean and Mother just fine."

Phil smiled and then canceled the smile primly. "Oh, well," she said vaguely, "your mother's just fine. I expect Jean can be a little—um, you know—bossy, if you're around her much."

"That's absolutely right," said Landers, gratified by her perspicacity. "I've often thought Bob's too soft with her—a very nice guy, but too easygoing, if you know what I mean. But what I wanted to say was, well, it was damn good of you, Phil—go to all that trouble, just on a hunch—that is, it was *my* trouble, and you needn't have—"

"It was interesting," said Phil again. "When I joined the force, I hoped eventually I'd be doing some real police work—but this was the first chance I had, really. If it wasn't exactly official."

"Yes, but—well, I'm grateful," said Landers. "For your having the crazy idea at all."

"Men," said Phil, and smiled at him.

"And you know something?" said Landers. He reached down and told hold of her left hand with his right, and put her cigarette out. "You smell nice—something like lilies—"

"Spring Jonquil, and I'm glad you appreciate it, it's four dollars an—"

191

"And I guess the boys gave me some good advice."

"Oh? Lieutenant—"

"And Art Hackett and Higgins and Palliser and— Come to think, they've all got wives, except Matt, and ought to know. I think maybe I ought to take the advice."

"What did they—"

"Come on," said Landers, dropping bills on the table and getting up, pulling her up with him. "Let's get out of here. I'll explain it to you in private."